Frances Brody left schoo.. as a
secretary age nineteen, taki.. able
years and a short-story wr.., she
returned home to Leeds an.. After
winning a place at Ruskin.. glish
and History at York Unive............

Frances has published.. urder
mysteries featuring Kate Shackleton, three historical novels and two
Brackerley Prison mysteries. She has been nominated for many prizes,
including the CWA Historical Dagger. She won the HarperCollins
Elizabeth Elgin award and was a finalist for the Mary Higgins Clark
Award. Frances's stage plays have been produced by Bradford's Theatre
in the Mill, Manchester Library Theatre and Theatr Clwyd. Her play at
The Gate, Notting Hill, was nominated for a Time Out award. She was
Writer in Residence with Nottingham Youth Theatre and with the touring
Roundabout Theatre Company.

Visit Frances Brody online:
www.francesbrody.com
www.facebook.com/FrancesBrody
www.twitter.com/FrancesBrody

Praise for Frances Brody:

'Frances Brody has the indefinable talent of the born storyteller'

Daily Mail

'Brody's writing is like her central character, Kate Shackleton: witty,
acerbic and very, very perceptive'

Ann Cleeves

'In Yorkshire we are proud to have such a first-rate crime novelist in our county'
Yorkshire Gazette & Herald

'Brody's winning tale of textile industry shenanigans is shot through with
local colour'

The Independent

'A superb series that gets better all the time . . . a page turner which I
thoroughly recommend'

Carol Westron, Promoting Crime Blogspot

'Brilliant'

Peterborough Daily Telegraph

By Frances Brody:

BRACKERLEY PRISON MYSTERIES

A Murder Inside
Six Motives for Murder

KATE SHACKLETON MYSTERIES

Dying in the Wool
A Medal for Murder
Murder in the Afternoon
A Woman Unknown
Murder on a Summer's Day
Death of an Avid Reader
A Death in the Dales
Death at the Seaside
Death in the Stars
A Snapshot of Murder
The Body on the Train
Death and the Brewery Queen
A Mansion for Murder

HISTORICAL NOVELS

Sisters on Bread Street
Sixpence in Her Shoe
Halfpenny Dreams

FRANCES BRODY

Six Motives for Murder

A BRACKERLEY PRISON MYSTERY

PIATKUS

PIATKUS

First published in Great Britain in 2024 by Piatkus

1 3 5 7 9 10 8 6 4 2

A CIP catalogue record for this book
is available from the British Library.

ISBN 978-0-349-43199-4

Typeset in Perpetua by M Rules

Printed and bound in Great Britain by
Clays Ltd, Elcograf S.p.A.

Papers used by Piatkus are from well-managed forests
and other responsible sources.

Piatkus
An imprint of
Little, Brown Book Group
Carmelite House
50 Victoria Embankment
London EC4Y 0DZ

An Hachette UK Company
www.hachette.co.uk

www.littlebrown.co.uk

Remembering F Tennyson Jesse

whose notable books include

Murder & its Motives *(1924)*

and

A Pin to See the Peepshow *(1934)*

The law condemns the man or woman
Who steals the goose from off the common
But leaves the greater villain loose
Who steals the common from the goose.

ANON

When

August and September 1969

Where

HMP Brackerley, Yorkshire
An open prison for women
Brackerley Manor House and grounds
Brackerley village

Who's Who

Nell Lewis, Prison Governor
Roxana, Nell's daughter

Prison Officers

Chief Officer Jean Markham
Training Officer (Catering) Barbara Kitteringham (Kit)
Nurse Florence

HMP Brackerley Catering Team, aka Prisoners or Residents

Cherry Davenport
Diane Redmond
Linda Rogers

Tenant Farmers

Oliver and Christine Ramsden

The Wedding

Bride Amanda Chapin

*Bridegroom Frederick Rudyard Harding,
leader of the Northern Knights band*

Band members: Bob (Best Man). Tim

Father of the bride Lancelot Chapin

Stepmother of the bride Penny Chapin

Family friends Norman and Gloria Thwaite and son Paul

Visiting guests Lesley and Peter Kufluk

*Dr Block, Proprietor of the Maternity
Home and Home for the Elderly*

Dr Matthew Hampshire, GP

Retired Nurse Susan Taylor and friends

Police

DCI Julian McHale

DI Ian Dennis

Sergeant Angela Ambrose

Constables and Special Constables

The Wedding Day

Linda was nearest the marquee flap that opened onto the path. Officer Kitteringham had told her to look for Diane, who had not returned from her afternoon break.

Linda kept her head down. She hated being in public. She feared being seen and pointed out. Schoolgirl killer. But the easy way, the only way, was for a prisoner to do as she was told.

She crossed the path to the Portakabin toilet block and called Diane's name, her own voice sounding strange to her. She pushed the doors marked vacant, and waited for occupants to come out of the doors marked engaged. Even checked the Gents.

From the Portakabin, she walked the path to the bench behind the marquee, she'd seen it when they were shown round this morning. A good place to have a smoke.

That's when she saw the body, the man on the bench with a knife in him and blood on his shirt.

She backed away, wanted to call for help but could make no sound. And then he seemed to move, to slide. A dead man, a corpse, too big for his bench. Linda turned back down the path, all the while feeling someone was behind her, reaching out to grab her. And then she was back at the edge of the Portakabin, being sick, and could still feel someone on her back.

One

Six Weeks Earlier

Saturday, 9 August 1969
HMP Brackerley

Nell Lewis woke as the birds began their dawn chorus. She liked her flat on the top floor of Her Majesty's Prison Brackerley. After two years in the police force and eighteen years in the prison service, this post as prison governor might well be the pinnacle of her career. Looking out across the grounds still gave her pleasure.

Brackerley House was saved from demolition, the fate of many country houses, when bought by the prison service, first for use as a borstal and now as an open prison for women.

Nell intended to make her mark. She would make a difference to the lives of the women in her care. If all went according to plan, with good intentions and hard work, prisoners would leave here with skills and a chance of a better life in the world beyond the gates.

Overseeing HMP Brackerley still felt new. Taking a walk each morning helped her start the day. Before the walk, Nell would search the grounds, a task she alternated with her chief officer.

Always immaculately dressed in public, Nell smiled as she donned the khaki trousers, left behind when the borstal boys had vacated the building in the spring. Her bunch of keys in her pocket, she pulled on the old sweater that she didn't mind snagging. Carrying her boots, she walked quietly down the stairs, so as not to disturb the residents' slumbers.

On the first landing, she avoided the floorboard that squeaked. The stained-glass window made a pattern of the sun's rays. Nell carried her torch, ready to shed light in hedges, nooks and crannies. Since Nell had improved security, most contraband came in over the high wall, late on a Friday or Saturday night, or in the early hours.

Previously, the pond had provided a hiding place for weighted bottles and containers that might conceal cigarettes or drugs. Improved fencing and patrolling reduced intrusions, though in what was once a country house, with gardens and a prison farm, there would always be some risk of intrusion.

Nell slid back the bolts and turned her key to unlock the front door. Locking it again behind her, she set off on her rounds.

From Nell's point of view, the greatest security would come from the residents' knowledge that being imprisoned here was a far cry, and a better bet than the secure units they had come from.

Eyes peeled, Nell walked the broad footpath, stepped along the garden borders, the stretch between gardens and high wall. She trod carefully, directing the torch's beam between flowers and hedges. She stopped when she saw a piece of rope that formed a snake shape near the wall. The other end of the rope was wound four times around a cardboard carton. One hand on the top, another supporting the bottom of the carton, she carried it to the gardener's hut and placed it in a wheelbarrow. The knot was neatly tied and easy to undo. The contents were well packed in layers of newspaper and cardboard, separated by strips of plywood: a bottle of gin, a bottle of vermouth, fifty Woodbines. The message on the birthday card read, 'From your old chums'. Nell knew the birthdays of the prisoners who had been here some little while. Today was Diane's birthday. Diane had worked as a barmaid at her local pub. There had probably been a whip-round.

Diane had lived in Hull, the perfect place for contraband goods to be smuggled into the country by sea. She was a minnow, caught – and not for the first time – storing alcohol and tobacco in her cellar. A widow with two children, she had expected a fine. The judge decided differently.

Nell wheeled the barrow of contraband alcohol and cigarettes to the front door, placing the bottles and cigarettes on the doorstep as if they were milk bottles and a carton of eggs.

Once inside, Nell took her booty to the contraband cupboard. Cigarettes would be sold to the women, with proceeds going into the general fund. The alcohol would make excellent raffle prizes for charitable village efforts.

Nell returned the wheelbarrow to the gardener's hut.

There were worse starts to a day, and there was still time for her early morning walk.

Nell exchanged a few words with the gateman as she signed out at the prison gates. Passing the church, she crossed the road and walked up Willow Lane. Through these walks, Nell had learned to know the place, developed a feeling for the villagers' lives. Two parades of shops on either side of the lane provided whatever the villagers might want, including a bank and the post office. Beyond the shops, the lane widened. In well-kept grounds half a mile apart from each other were two brick buildings, Brackerley Maternity Home and Brackerley Home for the Elderly. Between these two, and set back, was an older stone-built infant school. A person might remain in Brackerley from cradle to grave, with brief interruptions for schooling beyond eleven and travelling into towns for work. There was no police station, but no need for one. The local special constable, Mr McKenzie, kept the post office, along with Mrs McKenzie. Mr and Mrs McKenzie were the founts of information on all official matters.

As far as Nell could see, the only amenity Brackerley lacked was an undertaker.

Beyond the home for the elderly was open countryside, paths to meadowland, and woodland. As Nell stepped across a puddle, she spotted a familiar figure ahead of her. Susan wore her usual hand-knitted green hat with matching scarf.

Nell called to her.

Susan turned. She was a sprightly woman, resident in the Brackerley Home for the Elderly.

'Nell! Good morning. Walk me back to the institution, will you?'

'Glad to.'

'And I'm glad of a touch of sanity. You won't guess what the main topic of conversation has been in the madhouse.'

'Tell me.'

'The withdrawal of the halfpenny as legal tender. Should we gather them up to hand over at the post office, where the McKenzies will kindly exchange them, or ought they to be kept as souvenirs in case of future rarity value? To which I answer, "We should live that long."'

Nell laughed. 'Halfpennies were always handy for children who wanted to play at shops.'

'So was the farthing but we don't hear about that any more, so I'll stick to the present. I had another letter from Florence.'

'How is she?'

'I'm sure that being by the sea for these few months since the major's death has done her good. Now, there'll be holiday-makers tripping over each other. August is the busiest month. Florence won't like the crowds. She doesn't say it in so many words, but I get the impression she misses us all, misses her friends, and misses her work.'

Nell thought that understandable. Florence and Major Harding, the retiring governor of the borstal that became HMP Brackerley, had planned to marry. Nell had taken up her post here on the 28th of April. She and Major Harding had arranged to have supper in the Hare and Hounds. Nell had looked forward to hearing about his many years of service, and background information he might have to pass on to her. When she'd called for the major, she'd found his body in the back garden.

It was a great shock for everyone. Florence had been dis-traught at her fiancé's death. She left the area, deciding never to return.

Florence was much missed. The arrangement had been that the prison nurse would share her time between work with women prisoners at HMP Brackerley and at the Brackerley

General Practice, run by Dr Hampshire. Both Nell and Dr Hampshire were sorry to see Florence go.

Florence had confided in Nell that she almost did not take the job. She had been warned off coming to work in Brackerley. The person who warned her would not say why, just told Florence to steer clear of the place.

Nell and Susan paused in their walk as a squirrel dashed across their path.

'Have you a replacement for Florence yet?' Susan asked.

'Not yet.' Nell did not say that she hoped Florence might come back when she tired of walking with the major's sister and dog along the beach, and filling in at the nearest hospital when needed.

Still on the subject of Florence, Susan said, 'The major was far too old for Florence. He wanted a nurse and a purse. I saw through him.'

Nell was still finding her way in Brackerley. She liked that Susan was outspoken, giving out the sort of information that gave Nell more of an understanding of Brackerley and its inhabitants.

As Nell was walking back to what she liked to call 'the house' rather than 'the prison', she took the road that ran past the manor house. A small group of people holding a home-made banner caught her eye. It was a nicely done banner. Someone had painted wildflowers.

As Nell drew closer, an elderly man with bushy white hair and beard thrust a flyer at her. 'Will you sign the petition?'

Before Nell had time to reply, a woman in a tweed costume whom Nell recognised from church said, 'Miss Lewis won't be allowed to sign petitions. She's prison governor.'

Nell held up the flyer. 'I'll read it.'

Nell strode on and turned the bend before glancing at the sheet of paper.

There was nothing fancy about the flyer. It had been printed on a spirit duplicator.

SAVE OUR ANCIENT MEADOWS

FLOWERS NOT FLATS

BLUEBELLS NOT BRICKS

SIGN THE PETITION –
STOP THE CHAPIN SALE

This was news to Nell. She had walked by one of the meadows. It would be a shame to lose it. But if the land belonged to Lancelot Chapin, he was probably entitled to sell it.

Two

Prisoners heard the rumour first. Mr and Mrs Chapin of the manor house intended to ask Governor Lewis if the prison would cater for their daughter's wedding, to be held in the manor house grounds.

On this fine Saturday of blue sky and still clouds, Linda was at the prison farm, mucking out the pigs. Of all the prison jobs, she liked this best. Linda and the pigs were on good terms, regarding each other with interest and, she thought, affection.

Linda could quash thoughts of how life might have been different, of how one reflex action changed her life. In what could not have been more than five minutes, she lost all she had worked for. Good exam results counted as nothing if the person who gained those results was branded 'murderer' before she could even meet her roommate, attend a single lecture, or walk once around the campus.

She had gone to the student room that she would be sharing

with another girl. Proud to be carrying the key, she put down her small case and thought how lucky she was.

As she turned the key, she heard footsteps. She stepped into the room, and he was behind her, a hand on her shoulder.

She had turned. He was there, the oldest of the three abusers, smirking down at her, filling the space, leaning towards her. She backed into the room she was to have shared, bumped against a desk, turned and reached for something to fend him off. Had he followed her? Did he work here? Did the three want her to know there was no escape? The something she grasped was her roommate's paperknife.

Later, the man appointed as Linda's solicitor explained that he and her barrister could not help her if she would not help herself. Linda had nothing to say.

What defence could she voice for stabbing a stranger in the eye, apparently in just the right place to bring his life to an end?

Except that the 'stranger' was a friend of her father. He, and two of his friends, had abused her since childhood.

Linda could not speak it. She did not have the words. She could only feel the hurt, the humiliation, the throb of her own silence. She pleaded guilty to murder.

Looking back, after counselling sessions with other prisoners, Linda now would have found the words to speak in her defence; but still, she could not imagine uttering them. She was safe in Holloway Prison and now safe here, at Brackerley Prison. She had been uneasy at first, until she learned that gates and doors were locked not to keep 'residents' in but to keep intruders out, and that no unauthorised person was allowed entry.

*

Linda was still mucking out, being diverted by the pigs, when Officer Kitteringham arrived with Diane. 'Hello, Linda,' said Miss Kit. 'Diane's come to give you a hand today.'

'Right,' said Linda, immediately suspicious. Diane had no fondness for muck and farm animals.

'What's going on?' asked Linda when Miss Kit left.

'You'll see. What do you want me to do?'

'Nothing. It's all in hand.'

'I have to do summat,' said Diane.

'Look out for Brendan. He brings slops for the pigs. Just give me a shout when he comes.'

Diane followed Linda to the pigsty. 'Thank you for the birthday card.'

'That's all right.'

'Nothing came over the wall for me this morning. I was expecting some cigs and a bottle of something.'

'The governor or chief officer get there first, before they unlock us for the day.'

Diane turned her back on the pigs. She was looking past Linda towards the gates. 'Linda, can you keep a secret?'

'No. I'd break under interrogation.'

'My sister's boyfriend is bringing the kids to the farm gate. Is there somewhere I can take them to play where we won't be seen?'

Linda pointed. 'That barn can't be seen from the house. There's a ladder. Send the kids up to the hayloft.' Always wary of reporters and cameramen raking up her past, Linda knew the boltholes.

Diane asked, 'What about that lad who brings the slops?'

'Brendan?'

'Will he give me away?'

'He won't care. It's no skin off his nose.'

Diane suddenly gave a huge sigh. 'The kids might not come. My sister is terrified I'll do summat that gets me a longer sentence.'

'Just look busy, Diane. Sweep the yard. You'll have a better view of the gate.'

Brendan, the gardener's grandson, his freckles multiplied by sunshine, arrived with the slops. He was a regular helper at the prison farm which was managed by the Ramsdens. Brendan earned his pocket money here on weekends and after school. Mrs Ramsden had a soft spot for Brendan because he did not have a great home life and was willing to turn his hand to whatever was asked of him. He liked to think of himself as being in the thick of things. Today, he brought news. 'Amanda Chapin is coming home from London to be married.'

'Never heard of her,' said Linda. Linda disliked the way Brendan wanted to know everyone's business. She could not bear the thought that just as he came here talking about Amanda Chapin, he would be going somewhere else talking about 'that prisoner, Linda who does Saturdays at the farm'.

'You've heard of the Chapins, at the manor house?'

'Yes,' Linda said wearily, knowing silence would only fuel his determination to tell, tell, tell.

'Well, Amanda is their one and only daughter. The Chapins want your lot to do the catering. They thought you did all right at the fête, and they're too mean to pay a proper price. They're going to ask your governor if she'll let you lot take over.'

'How do you know they're going to ask for us?' asked Linda. Her curiosity was aroused not through interest in the

13

wedding, but out of a dread that she might be dragged into some public event.

'A few of us went to the pictures,' said Brendan. 'One of the lasses does a bit of cleaning at the Chapins. She overhead them talking about it.'

Linda had been sentenced to life imprisonment.

From Holloway, where she had worked in the library and helped prisoners who could not read or write, Linda was eventually sent to Brackerley. The model prisoner, Linda did not want to be back in the world outside. She took correspondence courses, advised other prisoners, and kept her own counsel. Only once had she broken down and in confidence told Miss Lewis part of her story. That was on the day of her father's funeral, when Miss Lewis took Linda to Undercliffe Cemetery.

Photographs of Linda and her crime had filled the press. She dreaded being pursued again by reporters and photographers.

Linda pretended not to be interested in what Brendan had to say but she was glad to have this alert.

One way or another, she intended to avoid the wedding. There would be people with cameras, people with memories of old newspaper articles. She felt that familiar shudder at the thought of being recognised, at the thought of notoriety.

She also thought of Mr Chapin.

He was in church every Sunday, blundering in, sucking up all the air, swaggering, just like her father, just like her father's friends. The resemblance scared her.

He and Mrs Chapin would sit in the front pew, right in front of the women prisoners. A stained-glass window proclaimed the Chapins' eminence. A marble effigy of a supine pair of Chapin ancestors took up a great space at the side of the altar.

Brendan emptied his bucket of slops into the trough. 'Tell you what,' he said, 'if you do get the serving food job, give a thought to poisoning Lancelot Chapin.'

'What has he done to you?' Linda usually tried to ignore Brendan. He was annoying. Did he know something about Chapin that Linda didn't?

Brendan went to where he had propped a square piece of wood nailed to a batten. He turned it around, revealing a banner painted with wildflowers. A slogan below the flowers read: BULLDOZE THE MANOR HOUSE NOT THE MEADOWS

Brendan raised the placard. 'Chapin is stinking rich and plans to get richer. When he's sold off half the village so builders can throw up a housing estate, he'll sell the other half. Rents will double.'

The flowers were beautifully painted. 'Who made the banner?' asked Linda. She did not want to become involved, but she wondered whether Brendan the Annoying had artistic talents.

'The lass I went to the pictures with, she did it. Her granddad and mine are in the protest. So are we. Chapin won't get away with it. He'll listen to reason, or else.' Brendan had brought his air rifle. Picking it up, he aimed at a crow perched on a branch. The shot rang out and the crow flew away.

'Brendan, don't do that!' said Linda.

'I just wanted to scare it,' he said. 'Thing is, that land isn't rightfully Chapin's land to sell, see? It's ours. It belongs to the village. Chapin and his ancestors took the land by force.'

Linda had heard this before. She went to talk to the pigs.

Diane came back from the gate. 'A watched pot never boils. A watched road never brings the car you want.'

'Whose car?' Brendan asked.

'Her Majesty's, with a royal pardon and compensation for wrongful imprisonment. Wasn't me carried stuff down to my cellar.'

Brendan laughed. 'It's the old, old, story, Missis. It's the rich what gets the money and the poor what gets shafted.'

Diane said, 'Spot on, lad, only it's not funny.' She took hold of the brush again and started to sweep the yard.

'Tell you what,' said Brendan, 'if you lot cater for the wedding, I bet you'd poison Lancelot Chapin.'

'Why?' asked Diane, 'And why me?'

Brendan began to retell his tale of Chapin's plan to sell the meadows.

'Not on your nelly, lad,' Diane said, shaking her head. 'Leave me out of it. I've two kids waiting for me at home. I want to be out of here, not doing a lifer.'

Brendan walked across to the yard, took the brush from her. 'I'll sweep up for you while you wait for that car.' Diane went to wait by the gate.

Diane's common-sense sister prevailed. The car bringing Diane's children did not come.

Three

Nell and Dr Block, director of Brackerley Home for the Elderly and the Brackerley Maternity Home, usually exchanged a few words on Sunday mornings. As Nell led her residents into St Michael and All Angel's Church for the service, Dr Block would arrive with a nurse, and a couple of volunteers, escorting his elderly residents. He struck Nell as a man of infinite patience. They would chat after the service.

The doctor was in his early fifties and his hair was already turning grey. He was impeccably turned-out, with a certain old-world charm; the sort of man people noticed. He was quick to smile and had a friendly manner.

As well as accompanying his residents to church, he had also brought several to the summer fête in the prison grounds. Those not so able arrived in wheelchairs.

Dr Block had bought raffle tickets for them and ensured all were supplied with refreshments. Nell was impressed by his

17

unflappability and good humour as much as by his impeccably tailored suit and hand-made shoes.

At the church door, the doctor caught Nell's eye and made a beeline for her. 'Miss Lewis!'

'Dr Block.'

In hushed tones, he invited Nell to visit his Home for the Elderly. Today was the ninetieth birthday of the home's oldest resident, and there was to be a tea party.

Nell accepted. She guessed that the invitation had come thanks to Susan, as she had never met the man who would be ninety.

Brackerley Home for the Elderly was set back from the well-made road that wound through the wooded area of land, where Nell sometimes walked in the early morning. The building was four storeys high, so there must be a lift. It was stone-built and fitted in well with its rural surroundings. Nell walked up the path and rang the bell. She had wanted to see this place for some time, thinking it might be a good idea for her residents to visit and talk to this older generation, who had lived through interesting times. They would have tales to tell. Perhaps there could be some project, a memory book, or some shared social activity.

A minute or so after Nell rang the bell, there was a tap on the window to Nell's right. She turned to see an elderly man with a handlebar moustache, standing by the curtain and nodding at her. Nell guessed this must be the man celebrating his ninetieth birthday. He gave a salute and then turned from the window and appeared to make an announcement.

Moments later, Dr Block came to the door.

'Miss Lewis, welcome!'

18

Dr Block wore an expensive grey suit, white shirt, and a sunset-red tie. He smiled as he straightened the tie. 'This is for high days and holidays. Residents like a bit of colour.' He glanced at Nell's dark red suit. 'We complement each other, Gov— May I call you Gov?'

'No, you may not!'

He smiled. 'Worth a try, ma'am.'

He led her into a large, opulently furnished room where, despite the warmth of the day, a low fire burned. Nell had not expected such luxury. Residents sat at several round tables. There were plates of sandwiches, pastries, and dishes of trifle.

The gentleman with the handlebar moustache approached. He was dressed in an elegant suit and what Nell guessed were handmade shoes.

'Here's Victor Hawthorn, the birthday boy,' said the doctor.

Victor bowed. 'How do you do, ma'am. Thank you for coming to my party.' He held himself erect, tilted his head slightly to the right. He narrowed his eyes, as if trying to get the measure of his latest guest.

Nell handed over a boxed cake and two cards, one from Nell and her staff and one from prison residents. This was a card made in the prison under contract to Woolworths, where a decorative patch of satin was added to the front. This may have appeared a slightly odd choice for a ninety-year-old gentleman who, according to local information, had spent his life in the upper echelons of the Civil Service. Nell explained that the cake and the card were made specially at HMP Brackerley. Victor smiled and appeared delighted.

Nell had checked that there was no rude message on the back of the card. 'Thank you very much. I love having something lavish that is also semi-official. It comes remotely from

Her Majesty, since it is made by those who dwell in Her Majesty's prison.'

'It's our pleasure,' said Nell, producing her own card.

He opened the box and admired the cake and its impeccable icing. He placed the cards on the crowded mantelpiece. The centrepiece was an official-looking card, bearing a coat of arms.

'Please join me at the top table, ma'am,' said Victor.

Dr Block looked on benignly. 'And which table is that?'

'By the window, Doctor, and today I am inviting ladies only.'

'Good for you!' said the doctor. 'I'll be champagne waiter.'

Victor offered Nell his arm and escorted her towards the table by the bay window where two women were already seated. Victor whispered, 'We are in an alcove here, Miss Lewis. The chattering residents will not hear us.'

In his precise, upper-class accent, Victor made the introductions. 'You have already met Susan Taylor, and this is our good friend Emma Whitaker, an honoured member of the entertainment profession. A magnificent Ophelia and charming in *Charley's Aunt*.'

'A revival of *Charley's Aunt*,' said Emma, 'not the original production.'

'Of course not, my dear,' said Victor. 'You are far too young.'

Emma acknowledged his comment with a gracious nod.

Victor explained his name. 'I am Cedric Victor Hawthorn. Cedric, after a grandfather and Victor in honour of Queen Victoria. It was the intention to call me Victor. Because of a slip up, Victor is my middle name.'

'Well then, you are a Victor,' said Nell, 'and you use that name because you choose to. People do.'

Noticing how impressed Nell was by the luxury, Susan whispered, 'We are not all loaded. Some of us are what you might call "grace and favour" residents. This grand room is largely used to impress relatives who wish to know that their elderly nuisances will end their days in a pleasant manner.'

Dr Block brought champagne. He toasted Cedric Victor Hawthorn and glasses were raised.

After the toast, the good doctor excused himself. He had to gather his papers and pack for a journey tomorrow.

Nell went to look at the mantelpiece where Victor's cards were displayed. There appeared to be no relatives, nor many friends. The large card with the coat of arms simply said, Happy Birthday, and the message, 'Greetings from we few left standing, and the new boys and girls who salute you.'

There was not a single name on the card, and nothing personal, none of the jokey remembrances that a former workmate might choose to remind Victor about.

Later, Nell's three companions took her out to see the garden.

Susan brought a pair of secateurs and began dead-heading roses.

'This is such a lovely place,' said Nell.

'Ouch!' Susan had pricked her finger. 'It would be a lovely place,' she said, 'but with a drawback.'

'What drawback?' Nell asked.

'The grim reaper.'

This surprised Nell. But perhaps it ought not to have. After all, octogenarians and those reaching ninety and beyond must give some thought to the end of their allotted span. 'It comes to us all,' was the best comment Nell could muster, and one she immediately regretted.

Susan deadheaded another rose, saying, as petals scattered and fell, 'Ah but here, Miss Lewis, death strides in too soon.'

Nell considered a philosophical reply, such as a reference to the toll of bells. She was still pondering when Emma chipped in. 'Susan is referring to untimeliness.'

Victor shook out a large white handkerchief and blew his nose. 'Endured but rarely inured.'

The front door opened.

Susan cleared her throat. 'Victor ought to know. He was in intelligence. He knows things.'

'We all know things, Susan,' said Emma, 'but not everything is a suitable topic, depending on the company.'

Nell felt she must be missing something. These three knew each other so well that they talked in shorthand.

Dr Block came out, carrying an overnight bag and a brief-case. He put the luggage in the boot of his car and then came towards them.

Miss Whitaker said, 'Ah, Doctor, you're off. You have missed my care-of-roses demonstration to Miss Lewis.'

Nell smiled. 'It was a delightful party. I'm glad to have been invited. Thank you, Doctor, and thank you, Victor.'

'Do come again, Miss Lewis. See you in a day or so, Victor. Ladies. One or two more things for the car.' He went back inside.

Emma sighed. 'One should always say goodbye. Sometimes, a person goes to bed apparently well, and does not wake again.'

Nell thought it natural that they should think about death, and she ought to be able to say something sensible. 'That's so sad. It's hard to lose someone suddenly, and always a shock, but isn't dying in one's sleep a peaceful way to go?'

Victor bowed an acknowledgement.

'It's been delightful,' said Nell. 'Thank you!'

'Do come again,' said Victor.

'Perhaps I might bring a couple of my residents?' said Nell. 'I should have asked Dr Block.'

'Oh, he'd love that,' said Emma, 'but, please, no piano thumping and singsongs, unless you have trained singers.'

'And no memory books,' said Victor. 'We cannot all divulge our pasts.'

'What then?' asked Nell.

'Do you have anyone who plays chess?' asked Victor.

'Not that I know of, but one of the residents is trying to teach herself.'

'Perfect!' said Victor. 'Send her along if she'd like.'

The three waved Nell off at the gate.

Nell had walked a few yards when Dr Block drove up and stopped alongside her. He wound down the window. 'I'll be passing your gates. May I drop you off? I'm set for London, a meeting one is obliged to attend.'

'Thank you but on such a lovely day, I want to walk.'

'Quite right. I'd prefer that myself to racing down the M1.'

'Makes it a quicker journey,' said Nell.

'Ah, you're obliged to do the same?'

'Occasionally.'

'If ever our London meetings coincide, we might share the drive.' It was a harmless offer, on the face of it. Nell was careful regarding the line between acquaintanceship and friendship. In her position, she had to be.

'Safe journey, Doctor.'

'Thank you, Miss Lewis.'

Nell was glad to have got to know Dr Block.

Four

Monday, 11 August

After her early morning search of the grounds, Nell was checking with the gateman that he had a note of an expected visitor, when she caught a fleeting glance of her new acquaintances from the home for the elderly.

As Nell and the gateman were talking, a car horn honked. They turned to see the motor. An old London taxi that had drawn up by the gates, driven by a smiling man who wore a chauffeur's cap. Cedric Victor Hawthorn, Susan Taylor and Emma Whitaker waved, royal style, from inside. A fourth elderly female passenger raised her hand in greeting as the car moved on.

'Friends of yours?' said the gateman.

'Yes, well, three of them are. I don't know the lady in the blue hat.'

Nell idly wondered where they might be going. This was the day Dr Block would be in London.

*

It was association time. The women were in the sitting room. *Coronation Street* would be coming on soon. Meanwhile, Cherry was the centre of attention. She was sitting on the floor with a sketch pad, designing a waitress outfit for the wedding. Cherry had class. She could wear a work overall and look stylish. She had won awards while still a student and made a name for herself in the world of London fashion. A range of clothing bore her trademark. She was featured in magazines as the 'young woman to watch'.

The other prisoners liked her. She was a friend who had needles and thread. She would sew on a button or turn up a hem. She would give advice on what would suit them. When they were roped into catering for the Brackerley Summer Fête, Cherry had designed and made their outfits from blackout material left over from the war. She created and raffled a dress, with the proceeds going to charity. The other prisoners basked in the glory of her actions.

Cherry's downfall, her trial and imprisonment, had come suddenly, on the cusp of her success. She was set to move into premises in partnership with her boyfriend, a graphic designer. They had met at art school. This business venture would be the perfect set-up, in a good location, with a shop on the ground floor, a workroom and flat above. They just needed a little more capital. Cherry thought she could talk the bank manager into extending a loan but, disappointingly, the application was rejected.

The boyfriend had an idea. It would take one trip to bring in top grade marijuana. No one would stop Cherry. The boyfriend couldn't do it. He had been stopped when bringing more than the allotted amount of alcohol into the country after a short trip to France. He had asked the customs officer, 'Why did you pick me?'

'Because you have a beard,' came the answer.

'No one will stop you at customs, Cherry,' said the boy-friend with great confidence. 'Just one trip. That's all it will take.'

The *Coronation Street* theme tune filled the sitting room. The prisoners relaxed. For half an hour they would be transported to another world. No one would dare mock this drama, because northerners in the room outnumbered the southerners. Any criticism of Weatherfield's much-loved characters might start a fight.

Diane wondered whether Elsie Tanner would ever find the right man. Linda, who had experienced so little of places beyond a few miles from her house and her father, wondered if there were places like Weatherfield, and like Elizabeth Gaskell's Cranford. Cherry paid attention to the costumes. She wondered whether soap operas would have much effect on the fashion taste of people who bought their clothing at British Home Stores and Marks & Spencer.

As the theme tune played again and credits rolled, Cherry thought of her return to Heathrow, carrying her suitcase with its top layer of clothes and a concealed bottom layer of contraband. She was stopped by a customs officer with a beard.

Cherry's knowledge had expanded since her court appearance. She now knew that there was often a great disparity in sentencing. She later thought the judge who came down on her like a ton of bricks must have regretted his sentence, because, a week later, presiding over a similar case, he sent a woman down for a quarter of the time he'd given Cherry. He told that woman she was lucky. The week before, he had felt obliged to make an example of a young woman.

The boyfriend and his sister made off with Cherry's portfolio, her sewing machine, her sketchbook and pencils, as well as her stock.

When Cherry had slightly recovered from the shock of finding herself in a shared cell in Holloway, she scraped herself up from the cell floor and approached an older woman, a Holloway inmate who was regarded as royalty in the prison and in the criminal world. Her Royal Highness of Holloway listened sympathetically to Cherry. Messages were passed to the world outside. The boyfriend was persuaded to give up his ill-gotten gains. All was safe for when Cherry would be released. What's more, Cherry would have a backer for her new business.

Bowed but not defeated, Cherry was transferred from Holloway to HMP Brackerley. Here, she flourished.

People who had never heard of Cherry, the fashion designer with a once-great future, had heard of her now.

The owner and manager of Harrogate's fashionable Bon Boutique could not believe their luck when, as part of her rehabilitation, Cherry came to work in the boutique as a Saturday girl.

The boutique's manager wrote to her friend Amanda Chapin to tell her the news.

Amanda Chapin had just written to her boutique manager friend asking did she know any reliable person who could be trusted to make alterations to a vintage wedding dress.

The letters crossed in the post.

When the *Coronation Street* theme tune ended, the chat returned to the subject of a wedding.

The main speaker was Cherry.

'Some news,' said Cherry. 'I've been asked to make slight alterations to a vintage wedding dress. Amanda Chapin will wear it at her wedding on Saturday the twentieth of September, here at the local church. Afterwards there'll be a reception in the manor house grounds and apparently there's a whisper that "the prisoners" – our good selves – will be asked to cater.'

'Who's she marrying?' asked Diane.

'A local chap, Fred Harding. He has a band. I met him ages ago, in London.'

Diane had a sudden attack of the shivers. 'Do you mean the old borstal governor's son?'

Cherry put her hand to her mouth. 'Oh, you know what? I didn't even ask. We just talked about Amanda's dress.'

'If he has a band, and he's called Fred, it's got to be him,' said Diane. 'Maybe I'm old-fashioned but I'd be disappointed if anyone of mine married before a year was out. Me and Linda cleaned the old fellow's cottage, not long before he was murdered. He had a photo of Fred with his guitar.'

'Major Harding was all right,' said Linda. 'He made me a cup of tea and reminded Miss Kit that I was still in the cellar, freezing.'

Five

Nell sat at her desk going through the paperwork for women who would be arriving from three different prisons. She was part of the way through this task when the telephone rang. Nell answered.

'Nell, Penny Chapin here. So glad I've caught you. Favour to ask.'

'Hello, Penny. What can I do for you?'

Being good neighbours with local people was part of Nell's job as prison governor. The Chapins of the manor house were the nearest personages to local squire and lady.

'You may have heard that Amanda will be marrying at St Michael's next month.'

'Yes, I heard on Sunday.' The vicar of St Michael and All Angels was also prison chaplain. He and his wife kept Nell informed of village news. 'How lovely to be having a wedding. Congratulations!'

'Thank you! St Michael and All Angels is such a wonderful setting, Lance and I married in a register office, him being a widower and Amanda being so little, and of course his first wedding was at St Michael's.'

'It is a beautiful church, with so much history.'

Penny Chapin paused. Her next words came across the telephone line in a somewhat breathless fashion that made Nell think she was nervous. 'I'll come straight to the point. We've been let down by the caterers. Your prisoners did such a superb job catering for the fête that I am hoping they may cater for the wedding. I know they're allowed out, and we're practically on the doorstep.'

'What a good idea. Give me some details and I'll check whether it's possible. Some of our residents are making good headway in their cooking and catering work. Tell me when and where.'

'It will be Saturday, the twentieth of September, at eleven. The reception will be here, in the manor house grounds. We have had some lovely Septembers and will be praying for fine weather. There'll be a marquee, a podium, and a Portakabin with toilet facilities. The vicar will read the banns from a week next Sunday.'

'What about alcohol?' asked Nell. She must guard against residents nicking bottles of champagne. 'We wouldn't be able to provide bar facilities.'

'Oh, that would be taken care of. The landlady at the Hare and Hounds would see to all that. It's a large marquee. I'm imagining that food would be at one end and the Hare and Hounds bar at the other.'

Nell could hear the anxiety in Penny's voice and thought, we must be last on the list. Nell wondered about the short notice. A prominent family would normally plan months ahead for such an event. As if she heard the unspoken question, Mrs Chapin repeated her explanation. 'We were let down by the caterers.'

Nell glanced at her diary. This afternoon was free. The paperwork would wait. In her most reassuring voice, as if catering for weddings was something she undertook on a regular basis, she said, 'We ought to talk in person. If we can help, we will. How does three o'clock this afternoon suit you?'

Three o'clock suited Penny Chapin very well.

Nell hung up. She looked at the day's timetable. She would ask the admin officer to take over from Catering Officer Kitteringham.

The one omission in the conversation was a mention of the bridegroom. Nell knew from the vicar that Amanda's fiancé was Fred Harding, Major Harding's son. It gave Nell a shiver as she thought of that dreadful day when she found Major Harding's body. He had been shot through the head while sitting in his garden.

Nell knew a little of the history of the Chapins. They were landowners, going back a long way. Mr Chapin, an amiable man, was master of the hunt. His ownership of land and property stopped short of the former mansion that was now Her Majesty's Prison Brackerley, and the farm that went with it. A son who lived in the Caribbean had died in a boating accident. That would make a future son-in-law an important choice for Amanda's father.

Both the Chapin and the Harding families had a tragic past. She hoped the next generation might enjoy a fresh start, with perhaps a touch of magic to make up for previous misfortunes.

Six

At half past two, there was a tap on Nell's office door. 'Come in,' she called.

Officer Kitteringham appeared. 'Ready, ma'am.' Kit certainly looked ready in her pristine uniform, dazzling white blouse and well-polished shoes. She had subjected her gently waving light brown hair to the scissors and a tight perm, a bubble-cut. The new style made young Kit look more definite somehow. Perhaps the intention of the change was to give herself a harder edge.

'Then let's go,' said Nell, leading the way into the hall and out of the front door to where her car was parked. Kit opened the door to the front passenger seat. She hesitated and then slid onto the seat. Nell had spotted the old magazine someone had left on the round table in the library, opened at a page with an article headed, 'Enter His Motor Car with Elegance'. Perhaps Kit was practising.

Kit was good at her job but new to the prison service and lacking in confidence. Nell needed Kit's expertise; she was well qualified and had worked in the catering trade. She would know what menu prison residents were up to tackling as they developed their skills.

Nell started the car and drove the short distance to the gatehouse, where they each signed out. Kit took out her notebook, wrote the date and 'Manor House Wedding'. Looking satisfied that her biro had cooperated, Kit returned the notebook to her bag. The gateman opened the gates and waved them off. Nell began the drive along the leafy winding lane towards the village.

Nell had rented a house in the village but not yet moved in. There was work to be done, but she was permanently busy, and still finding her way. She had intended to buy a house, but the lease on the land was owned by Mr Chapin and the lease was not for sale. Nell decided not to buy the house without owning the land on which it stood.

The Chapins' manor house was beyond the turn off to Brackerley Village. The family owned the village as well as land on the other side of the manor – hunting land, farmland, meadows, and fields hired out for camping.

The land on which the prison stood had escaped the grasp of several generations of Chapins.

It seemed unlikely that Kit, new to the area, would have much to say about the Chapins, but Nell thought it worth a try. 'I'm glad we'll be seeing Mrs Chapin again. We've chatted after church a couple of times, and I was pleased that she came to the fête. Did you meet her?'

'I said hello. She won't remember me.'

Nell knew all too well that feeling of not being noticed. 'She will remember you, Kit. That's why she has asked that we cater for her stepdaughter's wedding.'

Kit smiled. 'I hadn't thought about that. I also happen to

know their weekly bakery order,' said Kit. 'A large white, a Turog and half a dozen teacakes. Mrs Chapin orders a meringue for herself, a jam roly-poly for Mrs Thwaite, the housekeeper who comes in every day, and a cream bun for Mr Chapin. He's master of the hounds.'

'Yes, I'd heard that he hunts.'

Kit gave a grunt, which could have been disapproval. 'I don't think Mrs Chapin will chase foxes again, not after what happened.'

'Oh, what happened?'

'She came off her horse. Last year, hunt saboteurs stretched a trip wire across the track. Mrs Chapin took a serious tumble. Now she walks with a limp.'

Nell had noticed the limp and that Mrs Chapin sometimes carried a walking stick. When without the stick, she leaned on her husband's arm. 'Poor woman,' said Nell.

'And poor fox. I hope it got away.'

Kit and most of the staff, including Nell, were townies, with no reverence for country pursuits. 'Well, Mrs Chapin won't want to talk about her accident, or foxes. Today will be all about the wedding.'

Nell drove between a pair of ivy-clad gateposts, topped with orbs big enough to squash a small car. The tree-lined approach to the house was overgrown. Nell slowed, manoeuvring her way around a blue van emblazoned in green with the words, 'Green Fingers for your gardening needs', and below that, in black, a Brackerley telephone number. Despite the size of the place, Lancelot Chapin did not run to keeping a gardener.

The stone-built manor house came into view. It had a modern extension in the same local stone, creating an

L-shape. In the original part of the house, the heavy oak door stood dead centre with a wide entryway of steps leading up. There were three windows on either side of the front door. The floor above mirrored the ground floor. On the far side of the roof, beyond the big chimney, were attic windows, built up to give more height to the upper rooms.

Nell and Kit stepped out of the car. Beyond the path were neat flowerbeds and a rockery. Nell turned to Kit. 'Have you been here before?'

'No, ma'am, not in the grounds. I went for a walk, following the footpath that's on the Ordnance Survey map. The right of way from the church goes by here and through the back field, but Mr Chapin keeps a bull there, to deter hikers – oh and a sign saying, Trespassers will be shot once, or twice if still standing.'

A man, perched on a ladder short of a rung, was painstakingly attempting to remove graffiti from the wall.

HANDS OFF OUR MEADOWS

The graffiti looked as if it had been spray-painted.

Nell could not remember where she first heard the phrase that now popped into her head: 'land rich, cash poor'. Might that be true of the Chapins? If so, perhaps the lease of her recently rented cottage might, eventually, be included with a sale. Her own rent was at a market rate, but she had heard that villagers were on an economic rent that had been fixed by Lancelot Chapin's grandfather.

Concentrate on the wedding breakfast, Nell told herself.

Kit stared at the message on the wall. 'Good heavens! What a nasty thing to do. I should have mentioned that there's ill-feeling in the village about Mr Chapin's plan to sell portions of his land to builders.'

Nell said, 'Kit, the Chapins were let down by the caterers at short notice. Is that a common thing to happen?'

'No, ma'am, and not if it was a reputable company. The customer would have paid a deposit to cover the cost of the food. The Chapins will be entitled to a refund.'

If they paid, Nell thought. Or perhaps the caterer valued meadows above money and decided against taking the job.

'I hope Mr Chapin moves the bull from the field before the wedding,' said Kit.

Nell rang the doorbell.

A few moments later, they heard footsteps in the hall.

At the fête, tall and slender Penny Chapin had worn white sandals, a calf-length floral skirt, a maroon blouse with balloon sleeves and square cut neckline, more Laura Ashley than Mary Quant.

The door opened.

Penny, barefoot, wore a kaftan in shades of ochre, from pale yellow to rust. Her fair shoulder-length hair hung loose, brushed into shining submission. Nell glanced at the ornate grandmother clock which struck three as Penny uttered words of welcome and ushered Nell and Kit towards the drawing room. Nell caught the slightest whiff of marijuana.

Penny will have me down as a stickler, thought Nell; someone who arrives on the dot, keeps to the times and the rules. She will see herself as the free spirit. Free spirits and a free ride sometimes go hand in hand.

Penny's opening gambit was an apology for not having visited the prison properly.

'But you came to the fête,' Nell reminded her. 'I hope you'll come again next summer.' Nell did not encourage visitors. They took up too much time, and residents did not like to be gawped at.

Penny tilted her head and gave an endearing smile.

Nell returned the smile. 'Mrs Chapin, I believe you met Miss Kitteringham at the fête.'

There was no flicker of recognition as Penny answered, 'Yes of course,' and then, 'Oh, yes! Your hair was longer.'

'It was.' Kit nodded. She looked uncomfortable. 'I wanted a change.'

'It suits you,' Penny said, unconvincingly, 'and it will grow out soon enough.' She glided them into the shabby but cosy drawing room, waving towards a plush sofa.

As they were sitting down, a plump middle-aged woman, her hair captured under a turban, entered with a tray, and began a ceremony of tea pouring. Nell had seen her in church, sitting with her husband, Norman Thwaite, the man from the local garage who always wore a worried look.

As Penny excused herself and went to find a folder, Kit said, 'Ma'am, I don't believe you've met Mrs Thwaite. Mrs Thwaite, this is Miss Lewis, prison governor.'

Nell offered her hand. 'We said hello at the fête, but it's good to meet you properly, Mrs Thwaite.'

After tea pouring and niceties, Penny and her visitors got down to business.

Nell learned that Amanda Chapin, bride to be, worked as a receptionist at the Royal Academy. She would come home three days before the wedding, having booked two weeks off work.

Nell placed her cup back on the low table. 'And I believe

that Amanda is marrying a local boy, Fred Harding?' Nell asked.

Penny smiled. 'Yes. He's the late Major and Mrs Harding's son, Frederick. He never spent much time in Brackerley. He was sent away to school, stayed with a London aunt during school holidays. He works in the City, in what they call the Square Mile, where it's all banking and finance.'

'Oh,' said Nell in her most interested tone of voice.

This was not Nell's image of the late governor's son. When Major Harding was murdered, a colleague at prison service HQ had difficulty tracking down the deceased governor's next of kin, Frederick. Frederick Harding and his friends had moved from a squat in Hampstead to a squat in Holland Park. An enterprising young prison service clerk finally caught up with Mr Harding the younger in Trafalgar Square, his favourite busking spot when not working theatre queues. As far as Nell knew, the major had only one son – Frederick the one-man band.

Nell said, 'I believe young Mr Harding has musical talents?'

'He does indeed.' Penny beamed. 'I can't imagine how he finds the time with such a high-powered job in the city. Barclays Bank, I think. Fred leads a band called the Northern Knights. Knights, with a K. According to Amanda they could become as big as the Beatles.'

'I wish them well,' said Nell.

This was not a wedding where money marries money, but a squatter marrying into a family who were busy selling off assets.

Nell steered the conversation to the job in hand. 'It's unfortunate that you were let down by the caterers for Amanda's wedding. Did you get as far as creating a menu?'

'We did.'

Kit took out her notebook, saying, 'May we have a copy? That would save time.'

During the next half hour, a menu was decided, adding here, cutting there. Kit was thorough. She had good ideas, she sized up the kitchen and inspected the area where the marquee would be erected. She took the guest list, promising to return it after making a copy, and asked for details of who would supply trestle tables, chairs and cutlery.

Nell rounded off the conversation. 'We'll let you have the costings. There'll be a deposit for food and preparation, and a cost for labour.'

The voice from the doorway came out like the low hiss of a gas poker waiting for its lit match. 'Labour costs? I don't expect to pay prisoners.'

Penny combined an adoring smile with a scolding tut-tut, saying, 'Darling you are a wag. Don't tease.'

Lancelot Chapin wore a Harris Tweed jacket that did not meet across his belly. He brought a whiff of smoked cigars and the outdoors, strode across the room, giving a courteous nod, and a murmured, 'Good afternoon, Miss Lewis and erm . . .'

'Miss Kitteringham,' Nell supplied.

Chapin glanced briefly at Kit before giving a greedy nod of recognition. At the village fête, Chapin ate well, supped well, and eyed up the younger women. A large red-faced man with white hair and matching eyebrows and lashes, he boasted fat lips and cheeks that would easily hold two gobstoppers at once. At sixty, he was about a quarter of a century older than his wife.

When they had shaken hands at the fête, Chapin made a

pressure pump action with his thumb on Nell's wrist, which had felt odd enough to have been a secret and sinister sign.

Penny Chapin said, 'Lance, we're in excellent hands for the catering. That's a relief, eh?'

Lance Chapin cleared his throat and frowned. 'But what's this about paying prisoners. I'm a taxpayer, I'd be paying twice.'

Nell had one of those instinctive flashes of warning that ought to be taken notice of but are sometimes brushed aside. This job would be the perfect follow-on to HMP Brackerley's successful hosting of the village fête. It would be a diversion for her residents and look good in the annual report.

She spoke pleasantly, calmly. 'Mr Chapin, Brackerley residents receive a modest payment for their work, as do all prisoners. Our emphasis is on rehabilitation and encouragement. That includes a small wage.'

In a low, persuasive, totally reasonable voice, Chapin explained to Nell why paying prisoners, who owed a great debt to society, not least for free board and lodging in a country house, courtesy of Her Majesty's Government, courtesy of the taxpayer, was not a good idea.

Nell thought that his almost-whisper ensured that the person he talked to must pay great attention to catch his words.

He said, 'I had lads here doing the garden when the borstal was open and Major Harding was in charge. There was no question of paying the borstal boys.'

Penny was about to speak, but paused and took a breath, saying, 'Lance, darling, don't tease the governor.'

Nell did not need an enemy, especially the most influential neighbour in the area. Perhaps Major Harding had been given a bottle of whisky, or Mrs Chapin paid the borstal boys and kept it quiet.

Nell spoke to both Mr and Mrs Chapin. 'At Brackerley, we do undertake a certain amount of charity work. Our maintenance officer helps the elderly in the village. Unfortunately, catering for Amanda's wedding would not come into that category. We aim to be as self-sufficient as possible.'

Nell might have made an enemy had she not spoken so sincerely and kindly.

Penny absent-mindedly took a joint from her skirt pocket, along with a small silver lighter. 'You were right to think of the Brackerley residents, darling. It's up to people like us to support our neighbours. Miss Kitteringham and her girls will do us proud, I'm sure.' Mrs Chapin was about to light up but thought better of it. She put the joint back in her pocket. 'Lance, darling, I'll get your cheque book.'

'Please don't,' said Nell. 'We'll send you a formal quotation. On acceptance of our quotation will be soon enough for the deposit. The deposit would cover the amount spent on food and the work undertaken to date.'

'When should we decide by?' Mrs Chapin asked.

'Given the short notice, within two days of receiving our quotation,' said Nell, 'which we'll supply as soon as possible after your requirements are clear. It helps that you have a list of food ready.'

The four walked through the house. Apart from plumbing, electricity and the modest extension, the place appeared to have suffered no serious alterations or improvements in over four hundred years. As well as this sitting room, it consisted of two ground floor chambers, one with a dangerous-looking minstrel gallery, and a kitchen.

Chapin took them outside. 'You could buy a small house for what they charge for the hire of a marquee,' he said, pointing out where the marquee would be erected. 'Not to mention the hire of Portakabins, so we don't have sixty people traipsing through the house. It would be cheaper to hire Harrogate Town Hall.'

As they walked the grounds, Penny's limp seemed to worsen. Kit slowed her pace and fell into step with Penny.

Nell carried on walking with Lancelot, who clearly had something to say to her. He invited Nell to sit on a bench by the wall, saying,

'My wife has her head in the clouds. We don't know enough about young Harding. I met him two months ago, on his best behaviour at my London Club, but my daughter's set on him and I suppose his credentials add up. A City chap, musically inclined, which Penny takes as a recommendation. Amanda has visited his people and gives the family a good report.'

All Nell knew about the extended Harding family was that the major's sister lived in Filey with a view of the sea and had taken custody of her late brother's dog.

'But you've both met Frederick?'

'Oh yes. Fred took Penny to tea at the Ritz.' Mr Chapin said this as if there were something rather sleazy and underhand about such a treat. 'Do you know anything of young Fred Harding, Miss Lewis? His father was proud of him. Said how well he did at school. We'd have reports from the major about Fred singing in the choir and coming out top in exams.'

'I'm sorry but no, I don't know about Fred.' Nell covered her lie by looking at her watch. 'Thank you for the tour. We must be getting back.'

'Indeed! Don't let the prisoners escape and run riot.'

'We call the women "residents", Mr Chapin. They have served a good deal of their sentence and are preparing to return to society, with skills, and with dignity.'

Suddenly, a voice called, 'Penny! Lance! I've found just the spot.'

A young man, barefoot, wearing jeans and T-shirt, came bouncing across the lawn. He made a beeline for Penny and took her arm. They were both smiling broadly.

Lance made reluctant introductions. 'Miss Lewis, Miss Kitteringham, this is Bob, Fred's best man and a member of the band. He is trying to talk us into building a stage. The band intends to play and sing two of their tunes at the wedding and then have a disc jockey! Bob, these ladies – Miss Lewis and Miss Kitteringham – are here to talk about the wedding breakfast.'

Bob seemed close in age to Penny. They looked more like a happy couple than best man and mother of the bride. After a few pleasantries, Nell brought their chat to a close. She waved, 'Bye Penny! We'll be in touch soon. Bye Mr Chapin. Good luck.'

Kit needed no signal. She was beside Nell and ready to leave.

As Nell drove out of the manor house gates, Kit said, 'The trip wire that caused Mrs Chapin to fall off her horse and left her with a limp – I heard it said that the wire was meant for Mr Chapin.'

'How unfortunate. Do you know why?'

'I heard that it might have been because he was illegally closing down the rights of way.'

It was useful to Nell to have information, even if it was at second or third hand, but it didn't do to have staff thinking that the governor snapped up gossip.

They caught up with Mrs Thwaite the housekeeper at the turn onto the road. Nell stopped the car and offered her a lift. Despite the warm weather, Mrs Thwaite wore a heavy coat. Nell guessed she had set out early that morning. Now her forehead was dotted with perspiration.

'Thank you, madam.' She looked tired. 'Just take me to the signpost for the village, near the bus stop. I'll walk up the lane.'

Nell said, 'How far up are you?'

'I'm just at number thirty-three.'

'We can take you to your door.'

'Thanks, but it's all right. Norman looks out for me. It might give him a bad turn if he sees me being brought home in a car.'

Nell drew up by the grass verge. Kit got out and opened the door for Mrs Thwaite, who paused long enough to say, 'Mr Chapin might seem a bit gruff, but his heart is in the right place. He says how much they appreciate me.'

'I'm glad to hear it,' said Nell.

'There is no side to him. He's always been straight with us.'

Mrs Thwaite set off walking, Nell watched her go. Pushing her fingers under her turban to give her head a good scratch, and then striding out along the lane.

Seven

As she turned from the road onto Willow Lane, Gloria Thwaite's clear view gave her sight of Norman standing at their gate. They waved to one another and he went inside. She walked up the hill, stopping to talk to Mrs Robson who was sweeping her path, which she did whenever she wanted a natter. Mrs Robson asked after Gloria's sons Paul and Steven, and for news of Amanda Chapin. It was always Gloria who was asked about Amanda's doings. After the first Chapin died, it was Gloria who had taken care of Amanda as if she were her own.

Gloria thought she would never get away. She would walk up the other side of the street next time Mrs Robson was sweeping her path. Gloria was sweltering by the time she reached her gate. Norman had been tidying the garden. Having a fierce, angry dislike of dandelions, he watched for their appearance and dispatched them, roots and all. No dandelion clock was allowed to fluff its weedy way around number 33.

Paul used to ask why Dad was always so mad about weeds.

Gloria put Norman's anxiety down to the war: he had been in the Royal Army Service Corps, and then had dodged fire while riding a motorbike carrying despatches. He'd come back with nightmares, couldn't sleep, couldn't go back to his work at the foundry. She took him to the doctor. Norman explained that there was nothing wrong with him. He had come to the surgery only because his wife insisted.

Then there was the mishap that they did not talk about, during the winter of snow. Lancelot Chapin came to Norman's aid, setting Norman up with his own garage. But now the anxiety was back, settling on him like a second skin.

At least the boys weren't here to see the change come over their dad again. Steven worked in Manchester and Paul in Leeds. There was nothing for them round here. But if the boys were home, Norman wouldn't be so anxious. Gloria felt sure of that.

She knew about anxiety. For instance, she knew there was too much traffic in the cities. It was in the paper. A man got off the bus, crossed the road behind the bus. In an instant, a motorist knocked him down.

Paul worked with pen and paper, but Steven worked with greetings card machinery which he insisted was not dangerous. All machinery is dangerous. City streets at night can be full of drunks. Gloria pictured rolled shirt sleeves and fists, men who reckoned a night out was a waste of time without a fight to round it off. Her boys were peaceable. That's how she brought them up. What's more, they knew how to look after themselves, as Norman did when she first knew him.

Paul was the first of her boys to go; went off with his bag packed, two shirts and a good second-hand tweed jacket.

46

Amanda had gone to work in London. Gloria had never seen Paul look so desolate as he did when he came back from seeing her off on the train. Norman said, 'Paul's taking it hard that she's gone.'

'Of course he is. She went first, and left him behind.'

When Amanda was little, and scared of the stairs that creaked at the manor house, Paul was the one who got her jumping on each step and chasing away the ghosts.

At her gate, Gloria wondered why she'd kept her coat on. She began to unbutton it.

She opened the door and the smell hit her. Gas. She left the door wide open, took a great gulp of air, snatched off her turban and held it to her nose and mouth as she ran through the front room into the kitchen. He had done it again.

There he was, kneeling on the green velvet cushion, his head resting on the other green cushion in the gas oven. The mad thought came to her – Norman needs matching cushions to take leave of life! He'd taken out the top shelf and stood it on end. Gloria turned off the gas and heard a scream come out of herself as she ran to open the back door, and then back to him. The oven wasn't wide enough for her to hook her arms under his armpits. He'd kept his jacket on. She tugged his collar and his trouser waistband and pulled.

Because of the cushion there wasn't space enough between his head and the top of the oven to shift him. When his head bashed the top of the oven, he cried out in pain.

Like some kid in a fight, Norman said, 'I give in, I give in.'

'If you can't stand a bit of pain, why try topping yourself?'

The game was up.

He was out, on all fours, coughing and yapping that she ought to have let him be. She didn't have the breath to speak but went round opening windows. Picking up a newspaper, wafting the air with it, she went back to him. Dragging at him, saying, 'Come on! Help me to help you. God helps them that help themselves.'

He said. 'Who's here?' And then he couldn't speak for coughing.

She manoeuvred him to the back door. 'Breathe! Breathe some sense into thyself, man.'

She began to thump him on the back with her clenched fists to get the gas out of him. If they were in a town, he'd have to give up this nonsense. They'd be finished with coal gas and have safe gas by now. What would he do then?

'You're off to the doctor,' she said, 'and no saying nay. You want your head examining properly this time.'

He was spluttering. 'You'll be better off without me.'

'Let me be the judge of that, you great galumper.'

She shuffled him across to the kitchen sink and moved to get the bucket but was too late. He leaned over, throwing up bread and chewed cheese, dyed dark with strong tea.

'Get it all up,' said Gloria, 'and think on what would happen if I came through that door smoking a cigarette.'

'You don't smoke.'

'You've addled your brain.' She filled a glass with water, saying, 'Just keep breathing.'

The hens came clucking, to see what was going on. Gloria made Norman sit himself on the bench under the window. Luckily, neighbours on either side weren't in their gardens. She gave him the glass of water and then went back inside and began fanning the kitchen with the *Daily Mirror*. A wasp came in on the instant, giving off an air of having been kept waiting. What was the matter with Norman? Did he want attention?

Did he want to die? One of these days she'd let him. It was an insult to her, that's what it was.

Later, they sat at the table. She had made a salad with hard-boiled eggs and cold new potatoes. He looked at it, hoping for chips, she thought.

'You were a long time coming home,' he said.

'Mrs Chapin had company,' Gloria told him. 'The prison governor was there. The girls from the prison will be doing the catering at the wedding.'

'Fair bit of spit in the food then.'

'They're supervised, and from what I saw of them at the fête, they're likely lasses that you'd see at the shops or the school gates.'

'I meant you was a long time coming from the bottom of the street.'

'So if I'd tripped and fallen on the way up, broke my ankle, you wouldn't have come to the rescue. I would've been too late.'

Last time, Dr Hampshire had not let her go in with Norman. Let him try and stop her this time. When she'd pressed the doctor, he said it may be a cry for attention, a cry for help. Well, she had given Norman attention. She had asked what ailed him. He couldn't say or wouldn't say.

They sat for a long time, until he ate the hard-boiled egg and a lettuce leaf, saying, 'You could have done us a baked potato.'

She glared at him. 'We only keep heads in that oven.'

'I could bake it on the fire.'

'Baking a potato isn't your job except on Bonfire Night.'

'You weren't here,' he said peevishly.

'I'm here now. And while we're on about whose job's what,

49

your job is to stay alive until the Lord takes you. If you did go first, I'd be in the dark. From now on, I want your earnings. I'll see to the rent. I'll give you spends. And I want sight of the insurance policy you go on about.'

'You've no concerns on that account. We've enough in the bank for a bungalow at Bridlington.'

'Well, where's the bank book, what would I do on my own in Bridlington, and does this life insurance policy rule out payment on suicide?'

He had no answer to that. Gloria sometimes felt she lost her way in arguments. She should ask one question and not settle on another until she had the answer to the first. He always insisted on taking care of the money side of things. That was a man's job, he said. Gloria knew it wasn't.

She must find out if he'd been up to summat foolish. There was the time when he bought a car – or parted with money for a car that he never saw again. The men who conned him were caught. He got a car in the end.

He said, 'I might not be well enough for Amanda's wedding.' So that was it. She'd known all along.

'Yes you will be up to it, so shut up.'

Norman's cough started up again. His small, deep-set eyes watered. The whites had turned pink.

Gloria patted him on the back. 'You will be there. You will see Amanda in my wedding dress.'

Norman kept on coughing. Gloria patted him on the back and then dished out the last of yesterday's rice pudding and poured on evaporated milk.

Norman did as he was told.

Gloria wanted to shake him, but he was too big. She said, 'Deliberate suicide by someone in their right mind is a crime. I read up. Suicide. The word makes it sound slippery and French. Suicide. As if there is no great consequence. It's slaughter. Self-slaughter. Look in the dictionary. At one time, you would have done what you tried to do, and you'd be buried at the crossroads with a stake through your heart.'

'You're thinking of vampires.'

'I'm thinking of you.'

'I've tried to do right by you, love. There's a bank book.'

'Then give it me, instead of your malarkey. From now on you do as I say, or I'll swing for you.'

'Then it's a good thing they've stopped off hanging.'

'Aye. I'll let the government take care of me. Because murder is a sin, but putting a stop to a nut case who tries to take his own life isn't, so think on.'

'Is there any more rice pudding?'

What was wrong with him that he could go from head in the oven to wanting rice pudding? Gloria went to the cupboard. She took out the new salad cream.

'No, rice pudding.'

She took the top off the salad cream, poured it over his head and down the back of his neck before he knew what was coming. 'Now go get a bath, wash your hair, and let me hear you singing. If you stop singing, I won't come to pull the plug and save you from drowning.'

He did as he was told.

He's got me as mad as himself, Gloria thought as she listened to him climb the stairs. It's more than attention he's after. He doesn't like me working for the Chapins. She went up to wash his back.

'I'm sorry,' he said.

'You will be. Because from now on, you hand over your

51

earnings to me, and I see to things. I don't want housekeeping. I want your earnings. I can't trust you. There's summat up that you're not telling me.'

'It's called despair.'

'Don't give me that. I'm not going to be left like some idiot wondering do we have money in the bank, can I pay for a funeral or bury him in the garden, are we up to date with the rent? You've kept me in the dark too long. What is it? What's up? What is it you won't tell me?'

'Nothing. I have no secrets from you.'

When Norman was clean and dry and had his suit on, Gloria took him to the doctor. Again. She picked a time when the surgery hours were almost over, so she wouldn't have to sit in the waiting room with him and draw stares from all and sundry.

She knew this would do no good. But it would be in the notes. It would be on the record.

Dr Hampshire had always been very good over childhood ailments.

They were the last to go in. Dr Hampshire pulled his trick again. 'Would you like to wait outside, Mrs Thwaite?'

'No I would not, Doctor.' She brought a second chair to the doctor's table. 'And with all due respect, I am the one who had to pull her husband from the gas oven.' She turned to Norman, indicated the chair and said, 'Sit down. Tell the doctor what ails you.'

Norman sat down. He had developed an odd habit of holding his hands in a prayer position, against his mouth, and blowing through them. He did that now. It was instead of speaking. Gloria moved a chair and sat down beside him.

The doctor waited.

Gloria waited.

Norman cleared his throat. 'It's as Gloria says. I let her down, Doctor. She came home and—'

'And?' prompted the doctor.

'Gloria came in and smelled gas. I, erm, I'd thought of ending it, my life I mean. She pulled me out. I'm over it now.' He turned to Gloria. 'I let you down.'

Alongside her anger and loss, Gloria felt pity for Norman. He had admitted he let her down, but did he mean today? That's what the doctor would think. Or did he mean all those years ago? People said, 'It's never too late.' Well sometimes it was, but maybe not. Let him tell the doctor. Let him tell the truth, have it out in the open, and see where that led.

'Did you take the tablets I prescribed?' Dr Hampshire asked.

'Some. They didn't agree with me.'

The doctor made a note in his book. He then reached for his prescription pad and did that fast scribble. When he had finished writing, he said, 'I'm going to refer you, Mr Thwaite, to another kind of doctor. I know people hear the word psychiatrist and don't like it, but I recommend this man. You'll be able to talk in confidence.'

'No,' said Norman. 'I'm not mad. I'm not seeing no shrink.'

'Do it for your wife, if not yourself.'

'You must try,' said Gloria. 'We can't go on like this. You won't say it aloud to me. Tell the doctor what ails you.'

Dr Hampshire gave Norman that 'I'm ready to listen' look. When Norman did not speak, Gloria said, 'It's what I said years ago.'

The doctor now ignored Gloria and spoke to Norman. 'There may be a wait to see the psychiatrist. Give it a try, Norman. He won't bite. And start with the tablets. Gloria is doing her best for you.' He now looked at Gloria, saying, 'You'll encourage your husband to take the tablets, Mrs Thwaite.'

Gloria put her hand on Norman's arm. 'I don't believe in tablets, but if it'll make a difference, I'll put them out for you. I can't swallow them for you.' She turned to the doctor. 'How long's this waiting list to see a psychiatrist?'

'Norman would be seen within a couple of months. I also have a telephone number and address for marriage guidance.' He passed Gloria a leaflet.

The waiting room would be empty now and someone would have closed the blinds. Gloria could not fault Dr Hampshire. He was very good on measles, tonsillitis, and chicken pox. He could not be expected to turn back time, to a night of snow drifts and blizzards. He could not be expected to believe badly of one of his own. Doctors stuck together.

Norman had partly admitted what gnawed at him. He had said it, and it was true, that he let her down. Perhaps Norman would tell the doctor the truth if she left them alone. Gloria stood. 'I'll be in the waiting room. Tell the doctor what went wrong that night. I'm not trying to turn back the clock. I just want you to face up to what happened and try and get over it.'

Gloria knew very well when life had gone wrong, and so did Norman, only he told the tale differently. He said the nurse would not have made a mistake. A doctor would not lie. He believed the doctor, who was so kind and full of regrets. Her baby was alive when Gloria leaned into the cot to kiss her goodnight before she was wheeled into the nursery. God's will, the vicar had said. God's will! She didn't believe him. He had no monopoly on God or the truth. The baby died in her sleep, they told her. She would have felt no pain. It was a tragic loss. She made them show her the baby. That little creature was not hers. Norman did not take her part. A doctor would not lie, he said. A nurse would not lie.

'You'll have another child,' he said.

She pushed him away. 'Never touch me again.'

Then the doctors and Norman seemed to agree she should go for a short stay in what was called a hospital but what Gloria knew was a funny farm. There were women there who were locked up for years. Gloria had Steven and Paul to think of, and nowhere to run. When the National Health came in and Dr Hampshire arrived in the village, Gloria registered herself, and Norman and the boys. She did not straightaway tell Dr Hampshire, but later, when he knew her, and knew she was a good mother who took her children to him over childhood ailments and for their inoculations, she told him.

He sent for her notes from the maternity home.

Nothing came of it then. Nothing would come of it now, but if Norman was talking to Dr Hampshire, and would talk to another doctor then there would be some hope for him.

When they were outside, she said, 'We were outnumbered. We were half frozen, made the best of it, and can't turn back time. Live with it. It's too late. If I can live with it, so can you.'

Eight

Officially, residents of HMP Brackerley heard about the wedding job from Officer Kitteringham. Cherry said Miss Kit was trying to look more severe by having a bubble cut perm. Opinions divided. Home perm or a hairdresser job?

Looking flushed with importance, Miss Kit gathered her catering group around the deal table in the centre of the kitchen.

Residents listened politely in case there was something Miss Kit knew that they did not already know. There was not.

As to the perm, Cherry knew this was a professional job or Miss Kit wouldn't have got the bubbles at the back of her skull so neat. Diane disagreed. Miss Kit was careful. She could have done it with mirrors.

Diane fancied a perm, but she needed to look the same for her children on visiting day. On the next visiting day, she intended to tell them that, when she came home, they would

56

have a holiday in a caravan. They would paddle in the sea, make sandcastles, and have ice creams every day. But what Ruby and Albert wanted was a date for the calendar. They wanted to know how soon their mam would be coming home so that they could tick off the days.

Linda worked on her three-prong avoidance plan. She had already urged her friends to be not just willing, but enthusiastic about the wedding. She would now speak, in a casual way, to Miss Kit, whom Linda had come to regard as Chief Girl Guide. First, Linda would drop big hints regarding which residents would be perfect for the catering team because a) they had worked on school dinners; b) served in a Lyons café; or c) intended to make a career in catering.

If this tactic failed, Linda would say how she would love to serve on the catering team but, for the sake of HMP Brackerley, must voice her concerns. What if she were to be recognised, and photographed? This would stir up newspaper interest, leading to a re-hash of the 'student killer' stories, and create notoriety for HMP Brackerley.

If the big hints and notoriety tactics failed to convince that it would be advisable for Linda to be absent from celebrations, then she would be forced to make herself very ill indeed, throwing up and having a serious bout of the runs.

Unfortunately, Miss Kit thought Linda was simply making conversation when she praised her fellow prisoners.

She said, 'That's a very kind thought, Linda, but I already have three girls in mind, including you, and I can't put a new girl on catering.'

Just do it, Linda told herself, as she was putting away the scales. She played the notoriety card.

'Miss, there will be people with cameras at a wedding,'

Linda said. 'Someone is bound to recognise me, take my picture, send it to the papers, and it will all start again.'

'You have nothing to worry about,' said Miss Kit, sounding less than certain. 'There will be rules regarding photography.'

Rules! Miss Kit could oversee the preparation of a tray of jam tarts fit for a queen while giving instructions on the production of a giant trifle, but she did not grasp subtext or danger.

In some ways, Linda envied this officer, not so much younger than herself. She saw no evil, not here. We are her girls. We, us lot, are all progressing, rehabilitating, preparing to take our place in the big wide world of Them.

Linda cleared her throat. Her voice surprised her. It was louder than she intended. 'Permission to see the governor, miss.'

In a look that reminded Linda of comic book surprise, Miss Kit's eyes grew large and round. Her mouth opened wide enough for a swarm of flies.

They both knew that Linda did not need permission. The governor kept an open door. Linda had only once knocked on that door, when summoned regarding her father's illness. Until now, she had not needed to. Now, she sensed danger. Someone would snap a photo as she filled a plate for a wedding guest. There would be a headline: 'Schoolgirl killer grows up.'

Linda approached the governor's door. She made three rapid taps.

'Come in!'

Linda stepped inside. The governor smiled, as she always did, and indicated for Linda to take a seat.

'It's about catering for the wedding, ma'am.'

'I thought it might be.'

'I'd rather not be present.'

'Why is that?'

'Because there will be people there with cameras and someone might take my picture.'

Linda's spirits sank when the governor explained that there would be no photography allowed in the marquee.

'May I ask how that will be enforced, ma'am?'

'There will be notices. A member of staff will be on hand. Some servers may take trays around the grounds, but you need not do that.'

'There was something about me in the paper in May this year, ma'am, when word was leaked about my transfer here.'

'Look at yourself. You are a different person. You are also much stronger. Be brave.'

'Ma'am, I can't be brave when the thought of being on show fills me with dread.'

'Try. There's time yet. If when the day approaches you feel the same, see me again. But I feel confident that you will tackle this event as part of your rehabilitation.'

There was only a certain amount a person could say to the governor, usually. But this wasn't usual.

'Ma'am, I look in the mirror. I'm the same. It will all be dragged up again. That time a photographer found his way into the grounds—'

'And he was swiftly thrown out and the film taken from his camera. There will be security at the manor house for other reasons, but I will be sure to emphasise that residents must be treated with respect.'

Linda thought of Brendan's placard and guessed that in

mentioning 'other reasons' for security, the governor was referring to Mr Chapin's plan to sell the meadows. That might sell a few newspapers locally, but it was the red-top rags that Linda feared.

The governor did not give an inch. 'Look at it this way, Linda, you will be part of Brackerley Catering, a group of competent women doing a professional job. People will be concentrating on the food, the drink, other wedding guests.'

Linda recognised defeat. She was against the ropes. 'Yes, ma'am. Thank you, ma'am.' The thank you was for the governor's time, not her answer.

Cherry was standing in the hall. 'What's up, Linda?'

'Governor won't let me cry off the wedding.'

'Poor you. I'm the opposite. The manager of Bon Boutique has asked me to do a fitting for her friend, Amanda Chapin, and make any necessary alterations to a family wedding dress. I want permission to do that, and then to attend the wedding, sit in the balcony and watch the proceedings.'

'Good luck,' Linda said.

'Thanks. And listen to me. I was caught bringing in top-grade cannabis. It's medicinal. It's recreational. I would've made a lot of people very happy. Yes, I "imported" drugs as the judge chose to put it. So, call me an importer. I was attempting to provide a public service while being a good capitalist, intent on setting up my own business. We must all make the best of a bad job. You're doing what you can – a National Extension College course, and a Citizens Advice course?'

'Yes.'

'Believe me, the staff here will look out for you.'

'But I'm in for murder.'

'We all know you must have had a reason for what you did. You chose not to tell. Hold your head high. The criminality is that you and I ended up inside.'

Linda laughed. She didn't do a lot of laughing. It made her feel better.

Nine

It began to rain on Nell's early morning walk. She spotted Susan, walking more slowly than usual. She was dressed for the weather in raincoat and wellington boots.

As they drew closer, Nell saw that Susan was holding a hanky. She was crying and blowing her nose. At first, she did not notice Nell.

'Susan, what's the matter?'

Susan then came out with one of those involuntary sounds that a person might try and stop, a catch in the throat that turns into a sob.

'Monica is dead.'

Nell had neither met nor heard of Monica. 'I'm sorry to hear that. Were you close?'

'We were friends. You missed her on the Sunday of Victor's birthday tea. But you were at the prison gates the next day, when Victor, Emma, Monica and I passed by in the taxi.'

Nell remembered seeing the old London taxi. 'Yes, we waved to each other. Monica was wearing a blue hat?'

'Yes, she was.' Susan cried, wiped her tears, and cried again. 'We went to Blackpool, where Monica lived all her life.'

'That must have made Monica happy.'

'Oh it did.'

'Was her death sudden?'

'Our deaths are often sudden. I think we told you that a person at Brackerley Home for the Elderly may be quite likely to sleep and never wake.'

Nell was unsure how to respond, but Susan did not seem to notice.

It pained Nell to see Susan so upset, having become used to seeing her striding out so confidently. Death must be a familiar visitor at the home but that didn't lessen the pain at the loss of a friend.

They set off back, walking in silence for a while until Susan said, 'I should like to speak to the nurse. Florence.'

'Susan, Florence moved from the village, to Filey. Remember?'

'Of course. She wrote to me. I sometimes forget but I am not doolally.'

'I didn't suppose you were.'

'Can I can trust you, Nell?'

'I like to think so, or I wouldn't be in charge of a prison.'

Susan reached into her coat pocket. 'I should be much obliged if you would see to a task for me.' She brought out a sheet of paper. 'These are names and dates of deaths at the home for we oldies.'

Nell did not reach out to take the paper from Susan.

Undeterred, Susan said, 'A person's last will and testament becomes a public document does it not?'

'Yes, it does.'

'Once, I would have been able to do things for myself but that has become tricky for various reasons. Would you please enquire from the appropriate authorities, Somerset House I think, which of these people remembered Dr Block or Brackerley Home for the Elderly in their will?'

'Why would you want to find out?'

'Because Victor, Emma and I are investigating premature deaths. We are looking for a pattern.'

'Susan, I've never heard an ill word about Dr Block. If anyone does leave something to the doctor or the home, surely that will be out of appreciation.'

'Perhaps. We are curious. Nosey, if you like. Before you say it, yes, we have time on our hands. We should like to know what last messages our friends leave behind. Did you know that Ethel Winterbottom bought every lady in the home a box of chocolates and every gentleman a cigar?'

They had reached the gate of the home for the elderly. Susan became suddenly unsteady on her feet and leaned in towards Nell for support, saying, 'Never mind. I would leave it to Victor who has all sorts of contacts among the higher echelons, but Whitehall – well the whole of government – is notoriously slow.' She gave a small smile as she unlinked her arm from Nell. 'Thank you.'

Nell could not become involved in what sounded a delusional idea dreamed up by three elderly people with time on their hands. 'Susan, I believe the postmaster is good at handling all sorts of questions for villagers.'

Straightaway, Nell knew that was the wrong thing to say.

'That wouldn't do,' said Susan. 'We are entitled to public information. Information is power. Lack of information may lead to loss of life.'

Nell watched her friend walk up the path to the door. Susan turned and waved.

By the time Nell arrived back at the prison, Daisy, the admin officer, had already arrived and was on the telephone. Nell went straight into her office. A moment later, Daisy tapped and opened the adjoining door.

'Ma'am, that was Florence. She's heard that one of the elderly residents at the home has died. Monica Mason, who was a good friend to the borstal and equipped the sports centre. Florence can't come over for the funeral and wondered if someone would attend to pay respects.'

'Call Florence back,' said Nell. 'Tell her that I will go.'

'Yes, ma'am.' Daisy turned back at the door. 'Oh, she did say that she's looking forward to Fred and Amanda's wedding and will see us all then.'

It wasn't until later that evening, when Nell hung her coat in the wardrobe, that she saw the sheet of paper in her pocket. It was neatly headed 'Brackerley Residents Deceased'. On one side of the page was a list of names. Alongside each name was the date of birth and death. Nell put it in the drawer with the lock, where she kept her diary. She had no intention of doing anything about this and thought it likely that Susan would forget.

Ten

Amanda Louise Chapin opened her eyes and looked at the clock until numbers came into focus. Time to get up. A front desk receptionist must not be late for work. She closed her eyes. The sounds came from above, clog dancing around her brain, blasting her ear drums.

A pause.

There it was again. Thump, thump, thumpity, thump, coming from the ceiling. A hammer, or the stamp stamping of boots?

Suddenly, the hammering on the ceiling stopped. Another sound took its place, the rhythmic tapping of a walking stick, first on the stairs and then on the door of the flat. Him upstairs, on the warpath.

Beside Amanda, Fred stirred and mumbled.

Him upstairs was now tapping on the door. When they did not answer, he shouted. 'How do you like it?'

Amanda slid out of bed. She pushed her hair out of her eyes

and put on the satin gown that had been her mother's. She opened the door and smiled at the man with the walking stick.

'What were you doing, Mr Pearson?'

'Taste of your own medicine. Hammering the floorboards.'

'I thought perhaps you'd fallen, wanted some help.'

'The help I want is a good night's sleep. Well, you'll be gone soon. The owners are coming back, and I've notified the authorities. You are here illegally.'

Amanda made a sad face. 'I'm sorry the music disturbed you, Mr Pearson. Fred and his group are rehearsing for a concert.'

'Concert, with that racket? Pull the other one.' He produced an envelope. 'Are you Miss Amanda Louise Chapin?'

'I am.'

'You will all be evicted and taken to court. Squatting is a serious offence.'

He waited for a reaction. Amanda simply smiled. A smile often did the trick.

'I would not like to see you dragged to prison, Miss Chapin,' said the enemy from above, speaking with a relish that suggested he would like nothing better. 'You seem like a nice girl who's fallen in with the wrong crowd.' He thrust the envelope towards her but did not let go. 'Get out before the police come flashing their blue lights outside that front door.' He nodded at the door of the flat and for emphasis jerked his thumb. 'That lot in there, your musical friends,' he pursed his lips and shook his head. 'You can do better.'

Amanda took the envelope from him, recognising Auntie Gloria's writing. 'Thank you, Mr Pearson.'

'I hope it's an eviction notice.'

She watched him steady his stick before turning away to

make his slow way up the stairs. What was it about old people who thought young people must be on the verge of doing something shady or making too much noise? What was shady about occupying an empty flat? She called after him, 'Mr Pearson, Fred and his band just like to make music. There'll come a day when the owners of this flat say, "This is where the Northern Knights used to rehearse".'

Either he was too deaf to hear, or he didn't want to.

Amanda went back inside. She stood with her back to the door and looked at her Auntie Gloria's familiar writing on the envelope. It couldn't have been an eviction notice anyway, since nobody except Mr Pearson suspected she, Fred, Tim and Bob were squatting.

Amanda sat on the end of the bed and opened the letter. Mrs Thwaite had been Amanda's Auntie Gloria since Amanda couldn't get her tongue around 'Mrs Thwaite' as a child. She was the housekeeper who had taken care of Amanda when her mother died and continued to do so when Penny had come along and married Dad.

Amanda opened the envelope. The letter was dated yesterday. The first side read:

> Dear Amanda,
>   I am sending you this invitation because you did not see the finished version with gold lettering. All invitations posted today! I stood by the post box and watched until the postman emptied it. We are all most exited.

Amanda felt a little exited herself, but she knew that Auntie Gloria meant excited. The letter continued, the writing growing smaller to fit the page.

All is well here. Everyone in the village looks forward to your wedding.
Your Uncle Norman has not been himself lately. He will be glad to see
you and it goes without saying that so will I.

   Do not feel obliged about the wedding dress. I have had it dry-
cleaned as you always said you would wear it, but I will not be hurt if
you change your mind and decide on something new and up to date.

No, I will not change my mind, said Amanda to herself. She
would have something old, something new, something borrowed and something blue. The something old would be the
wedding dress, worn by Auntie Gloria.

Amanda had come to an arrangement with her friend Sarah
who managed Bon Boutique in Harrogate. Sarah had written
to tell her that the new 'Saturday Girl' was none other than
Cherry, the designer who had been transferred from Holloway
to HMP Brackerley. When Cherry heard about the wedding
dress needing alterations, she had offered to do it, saying that
Mrs Thwaite should bring in the dress and Amanda must come
to Harrogate on a Saturday. They would do this on the quiet.

Yes! said Amanda and then turned her attention to the
invitation card.

Mr and Mrs Chapin request the pleasure of your company at
the marriage of their daughter Amanda Louise to Frederick
Rudyard son of the late Major and Mrs Harding at 11 am
on Saturday, twentieth of September, Nineteen Sixty-Nine

at St Michael and All Angels Church

and afterwards at the Manor House, Brackerley

RSVP

Amanda bit her lip. She glanced at Fred. He was snoring gently. She dropped the invitation onto the counterpane and gripped the end of the brass bedstead. Her knuckles turned white. She wished she could be a person who screamed and yelled and shouted, but she was no such person. Dad said she was like her mother, self-contained.

Amanda did not quite know what she felt and what she ought to do. She looked at Fred, the rise and fall of his chest, the calmness of a man without a care. There was something about seeing Fred as a sleeping log that gave her a moment's doubt, not about whether she loved him but whether she, Fred, Tim and Bob believed their own publicity for the Northern Knights. They were relying on Dad's wedding present, some money to tide them over, and she needed to win Dad round to the idea of building a recording studio in the manor house grounds.

Fred was the one so anxious to be wed. Why, when he was planning a tour and wouldn't be here? To be sure of her, or to be sure of . . . what? A wedding present and a recording studio?

The embossed wedding invitation made what had so long seemed a distant prospect loom scarily close. *I'm not ready*, she thought. *I'm not having cold feet about Fred, but I'm not ready for this.*

She washed and dressed and went into the kitchen. Tim had made a pot of tea. He poured her a cup. 'What's up?'

Amanda handed Tim the invitation card.

Tim looked at the card. 'That's great.'

'No, it's not.'

'You're not having second thoughts?'

'Not about Fred.'

'Then what's wrong?'

'Penny. She's calling herself my mother.'

He read the card again. 'Well, isn't she?'

'She's my stepmother. My mother died when I was six.'

Tim handed back the card, 'Yes but she has been, well, like your mother for most of your life?'

'No. She was like a big sister. Feels weird seeing her name there. It was my Auntie Gloria who looked after me – no relation. I deliberately asked Penny to talk to the printer about the best way to word the invitation. I should have done it myself.'

Tim said, 'Don't let it upset you. Your mother will be talked about on the day. You're bound to be nervous. Everything will go well.'

Amanda didn't want to be late for work. 'I'm not nervous, just looking for my bag.'

'On the chair.' Tim handed her the bag. 'You and Fred, you're right for each other.'

'You're best man. You have to say that.'

'Bob is best man.'

Amanda brushed her hair. 'Fred asked you.'

'And he asked Bob.'

Amanda sighed. 'Two best men? Who'll take charge of the ring?'

Tim gave a 'search me' gesture.

Amanda picked up her jacket. 'We might just cancel and go to Chelsea Register Office, pull someone in off the street.'

Tim grinned. 'Do it! Let that someone off the street be me!'

Eleven

Amanda hurried across the road to the bus stop, causing a car to screech to a halt. The driver opened his window and yelled at her. Amanda wasn't listening.

She wasn't late for work, not in a rush, and couldn't think what had made her put on a spurt. Nobody was chasing her.

Arriving at work, she sat down at her place in the reception area of the Royal Academy. She loved being here, being part of London life, centre of her universe, feeling there could be nowhere else like this. She picked up her pen and wrote her reply to Auntie Gloria at 33 Willow Lane, Brackerley, via Ripon, Yorkshire.

> *Dear Auntie Gloria,*
>
> *It is a turn-up for the books to have an invitation to my own wedding! I hadn't seen it. You, Uncle Norman, Paul, and Steven (if he can tear himself away from Manchester) must sit in the front pew alongside Dad, Penny and Fred's auntie from Filey. His London auntie from his mother's side can't make the journey.*

About the dress. Thanks for having it dry-cleaned. Yes! I am going to wear it! Please bring the dress to Bon Boutique on Montpelier on Saturday, 23 August at noon. Get Uncle to drive you. Tell no one. I will do a try-on. It's a flying visit. I'm coming by train. Do not breathe a word. This is our secret!

Love,

Amanda xxx

Amanda then wrote a polite note to Penny, reminding her that the Thwaites must have pride of place next to the family on the front pew.

It was the Thwaites, Auntie Gloria and Uncle Norman, that Amanda had gravitated to. Auntie Gloria had worked for the family for a long time and looked after Amanda when her mother was sick. After her mother died, Auntie Gloria brought Paul to keep Amanda company. Paul had been her playmate and best friend. Amanda never felt lonely when Auntie and Paul were in the house. She used to wish the Thwaites lived with her all the time. But they had their own cottage in the village that was cosy. The manor house was quiet and sad. The wallpaper made noises. Windows rattled. After mummy died, three more stairs began to creak. Amanda was afraid until she and Paul jumped on every step and told them to creak as much as they liked.

The house did not like that Amanda's mother was gone.

When Penny came to live at the manor, and look after Amanda and be there all the time, Amanda still saw her Auntie Gloria and Paul. She was big enough to walk up to the village and knew how to cross the road.

After Dad married Penny, he cheered up, and the house

seemed to cheer up. Crofty, the maintenance man from the borstal, came to fix the doors and windows. Crofty whistled while he worked, and Penny sang along as he whistled. They laughed a lot. Amanda joined in, singing, 'Once I had a secret Love'. When she saw them kissing, Amanda didn't tell. Dad went out a lot or would go in his office and shut the door.

Penny told Auntie Gloria that she need not stay so long. Two hours in the mornings would be sufficient. Auntie Gloria took no notice.

When Penny married Dad, she told Amanda that she need not call her mother because they would be more like sisters. Amanda had never called Penny mother and never would. She and Penny got on all right, and Penny took her to singing lessons and dancing lessons. Amanda went on her own to the village to be with Auntie Gloria and Uncle Norman and the boys, Steven and Paul. Uncle Norman made jokes. He said things like, 'Hey-up, our little lass,' and 'Move in, kid, we'll budge over.'

Dad said how spruced-up the house looked. Crofty had saved them money. That was always to the good. But then there was some shouting.

Crofty stopped coming. Penny stopped singing.

Amanda looked back on that time differently now. She had been the young chaperone, the alibi who never minded popping into the village for a hazelnut chocolate bar and a Crunchie and leaving Penny and Crofty together. Sometimes when she got back, she had trouble finding them.

As soon as she was old enough, Amanda took a secretarial course and left for London. It was Mrs Grieves, the vicar's wife from St Michael's, who told Amanda that Frederick Harding was in London, and she would put them in touch.

Amanda forgot about it, but one day Fred telephoned, having been given her number by his aunt, who got it from Mrs Grieves. He said, 'Mrs Grieves won't be satisfied until we can say we went for a cup of coffee.'

He waited for her the next evening outside the Royal Academy.

Oh, and by the way, he intended to go by the name of Rick, Fred being out of fashion. Amanda said, 'Fred is a good name.'

As they walked to the closest café, Fred said, 'Amanda, how come we never got to know each other in Brackerley?'

'I went to boarding school.'

'What was it like?'

'Okay. Lots of games. I made some good friends. What about you, Fred?'

'The same – away at school. My mother sang and played the violin. She got me in at St Paul's School. I sang in the choir.'

'How fabulous.'

'Not that fabulous. I was busking, but now I've formed a band, with a couple of mates from the choir. We have gigs lined up.'

'I'd like to come and hear you.' Amanda suddenly realised how bored she had been until now.

Within an hour, Fred knew that Amanda Chapin was the girl he must marry. It was fortunate indeed to have fallen in love with the daughter of Brackerley Manor House.

Dad and Penny came to London and took Amanda and Fred out to dinner. Penny wanted to meet the other two band members, Bob and Tim. She stayed on for one of their gigs. The next day, Bob took Penny to Carnaby Street and on a shopping spree.

On a glorious Sunday, Amanda and Fred peeled away from the others and took a boat trip to Greenwich. Sunlight glistened on the Thames. They looked at the other passengers and made guesses about what they did and why they were there. The lone man in the black coat and pulled-down hat was most definitely a spy and worked in the MI6 building. A light breeze turned blowy. Amanda combed her hair when they got off the boat. They walked to a café where they ate bacon sandwiches and drank coffee. Without words, both knew that they would be together forever.

Amanda moved into the squat, which was far superior to the room she had rented.

She unpacked her belongings.

Sitting at the dining room table, she took out her writing case. She had bought postcards of Greenwich and the Observatory, one for Dad and Penny, another for her schoolfriend and the third for Auntie Gloria and Uncle Norman.

She wrote just one letter.

> *Dear Auntie Gloria,*
>
> *I had the most marvellous day along the River Thames to Greenwich and wanted you to have this postcard. You and Uncle Norman must visit one day. You would love it. You'll never guess who I was with! Fred Harding whose dad was governor of the borstal. Fred is very sad about his dad, and his horrible death. Fred's mother died years ago, but he does remember her. Fred says that what saves him and keeps him going is his music. He is such a good musician and singer, with his own band.*

Must go as I have to iron my dress for work tomorrow.
Lots of love to you and Uncle and Steven and Paul.
Amanda, xxx

On the nights Penny was at the hotel, Bob didn't come back to the squat. Amanda told herself that here was nothing unusual about that. There had been other nights when he stayed out.

Twelve

As Nell was about to leave the office to attend the funeral of Monica Mason, Kit came knocking at the office door. She looked flushed and upset. 'Ma'am, sorry to barge in. Something shocking has happened.'

'What?' asked Nell.

Kit explained how she unlocked the cupboard to bring out ingredients. 'All the dried fruit for the cake has gone.'

'Did you say anything to the women?'

'Not yet. I didn't want to look foolish. I thought, have I made a mistake? Did I put the dried fruit somewhere else?'

Kit had a lot to learn. Nell said, 'Kit, you'll know that fruit can be the basis for liquor.'

'Ah, yes.'

'I'm sure you didn't mislay the dried fruit. The women have taken it to make hooch. It's something we need to be careful about. Go back to the kitchen, as if nothing has happened. I'll speak to the chief officer. She'll take over in the kitchen. Say nothing about dried fruit. Search the house from the cellars up. Search the grounds. You are looking for a barrel or a large container. It will be well hidden. It will contain dried fruit and water and may already have begun to ferment. Drain the barrel, empty the container. Say nothing. Leave the empty container in place. One nil to us.'

'Don't I tell them off?'

'No. When contraband comes over the wall, we don't make a song and dance. We confiscate. We must always be one step ahead.'

Nell arrived at the church as Dr Block was helping Monica Mason's friends into their usual pew. The elderly residents wore their funeral apparel with an odd 'I am still standing' sense of pride. Nell and her new friends from the home, Susan, Emma and Victor, acknowledged each other. Dr Block twinkled a greeting to Nell.

Sometimes, a funeral was the only opportunity to learn about the life of the person who died. This was no exception. The vicar chose appropriate passages from the Bible and the Prayer Book. He had also gathered knowledge of Monica Mason's life from her friends.

'Monica was born in Blackpool where she helped run, and then took over, her parents' bakery. She developed the business and ran it successfully for many years. She sold the business when she no longer had the energy to be up at four o'clock in the morning six days a week.

'Monica was generous, kind, had a jolly sense of humour. She came to Brackerley to be inland, away from the roar of the sea and the throngs of holidaymakers.'

Mr Grieves concluded his eulogy saying, 'Monica Mason died peacefully in her sleep after a short illness. May she rest in peace.'

The main area of churchyard that fronted the church was now full. An area had been given over to burials at the back of the church. The congregation made their way there, and to the newly dug grave. Nell and Penny Chapin escorted Susan and Emma. Victor steadied himself with the aid of a silver-topped walking stick, alongside Lance Chapin.

'It's very sad,' said Lance. 'All the old people of my youth are leaving us. It makes me contemplate my own mortality.'

'For heaven's sake, Lance,' said Penny. 'Don't talk yourself into a decline.'

Susan, Emma and Victor stood side by side.

All the right words were said by the vicar. Undertakers lowered the coffin.

A dish of earth was passed hand to hand, giving each mourner an opportunity to drop a sprinkle, or a handful, into the grave.

Nell watched as Susan and Emma removed their black felt hats, revealing slightly squashed paper hats beneath. They passed the black hats to Victor, who now held three hats above his heart. In her best thespian voice, Emma said, 'Excuse this informality. We are fulfilling Monica's request that we wear "Kiss Me Quick" hats at her funeral.'

Emma allowed a pause, waiting until she had everyone's attention. 'Monica left Blackpool in her later years, but it was the place she was happiest. One week ago today, four of us took a taxi there on a nostalgic journey. We went to Blackpool Tower, walked by the sea, tried our luck in the amusement arcades, and went on an errand.'

Emma gave a deep sigh, and then gazed lovingly at the coffin. 'Goodbye, dear friend, may you find a heaven where you may once more bite into a stick of rock.' She then began to cry. Susan passed Emma a lace hanky.

Penny escorted Emma back to the path. Victor returned Susan and Emma's felt hats.

As they moved from the grave, Susan took Nell's offered arm. She leaned close to Nell and passed her the seaside hat. 'This is for you,' she whispered. 'Monica wanted you to have it. I told her about you and that I trust you.'

'Thank you,' said Nell. She had never had a 'Kiss Me Quick' hat. There was a first time for everything.

Emma gave a 'Kiss Me Quick' hat to Penny Chapin who did her best to act as if this was precisely what she had expected to receive at a graveside. As they moved from the graveside, Dr Block spoke to the mourners. 'Do join us at Brackerley Home for the funeral repast. Monica lit up our lives. We shall miss her greatly.'

Nell arrived back at her office. She hung her coat on the hook behind the office door and turned her attention to the waiting telex messages and letters. It was not until early evening that she took the coat upstairs to her flat, hung it in the wardrobe and then remembered the paper hat in the pocket.

She took it out, tried it on, smiled at herself in the mirror and took it off. As she put it down, she noticed the note written inside the hat. The writing was a little shaky, but clear. It read, 'Contact Jacob Cleverly Esquire, Solicitor, Blackpool.'

It was initialled MM.

Was Monica Mason giving Nell an instruction? Susan had said she wanted Nell to have the hat. More likely, Monica had lacked a piece of paper at the time she wrote herself a reminder in her hat.

Nell thought back to Victor's birthday party. Victor, Susan and Emma had hinted that Dr Block was persuading residents to leave him a legacy. Susan had put the list of deceased residents' names and dates of death in Nell's pocket. None of this added up. It was Dr Block who had suggested Nell come to the party. He would not invite outsiders if he had been up to something shady. Besides, if that was a rumour among the residents – leave the good doctor a legacy and he will bump you off – no one would sign a will. Someone as well-heeled as Victor appeared to be would move out. Emma the well-connected actress would take a bow and make her entrance at the home for retired theatricals.

Nell hesitated. Still, the person was a solicitor. He would be discreet. If she did nothing, Nell would always wonder why she was given the hat with the solicitor's name.

She rang directory enquiries for his number.

She telephoned and was put through.

'Cleverly speaking.'

'Hello, Mr Cleverly. I am Miss Helen Lewis. I attended a funeral today at St Michael and All Angels in Brackerley. It was the funeral of Miss Monica Mason. One of Miss Mason's friends from Brackerley Home for the Elderly gave me a "Kiss Me Quick" hat that Miss Mason wanted me to have. On the inside rim, she had written James Cleverly, Esquire, Solicitor, Blackpool.'

'Oh, well you are talking to the right person, Miss Lewis. I am Miss Mason's solicitor, but you take me by surprise. I have had no news of Miss Mason's death.'

'The hat took me by surprise.'

'Your name is Miss Helen Lewis.'

'Yes. Nell Lewis.'

'May I have your contact details, Miss Lewis?'

'Mr Cleverly, I am making this call reluctantly because of my position.'

'I will respect your confidence.'

'I am governor at Her Majesty's Prison Brackerley, telephoning from my private flat within the building. There is no connection between my post here and Miss Mason and her friends, except that Miss Mason was generous when the prison was a borstal.'

'Thank you for notifying me of my client Miss Mason's death. She was a most generous woman. I'm very sorry to hear this news. I am Miss Mason's executor and will follow her instructions.'

Politely, they ended the call.

Nell went to the locked drawer where she kept her diary. She took out the note of names and dates given to her by Susan on their walk. The fact that Miss Mason's solicitor had not yet have been informed about her death may not be suspicious, though she would have expected him to be informed. Perhaps there was a delay in obtaining probate, or locating the copy of her will.

It was not Nell's business, and yet something prompted her to act. She picked up the phone again and telephoned her 'niece' Roxana. The deception had gone on since Roxana's birth. Nell could no longer imagine how she would ever be able to tell her daughter the truth.

Roxana worked for an American journalist on Fleet Street who took long lunches and went out for lots of meetings. As Nell expected, Roxana was alone in the office.

'Roxana!'

'Hello, Auntie Nell! Glad you've rung, I'm bored out my skull. How are you?'

'I'm fine. Done anything interesting?' This was a good question because now that Roxana had made a few friends, she usually had done something interesting.

'We went to see *Hair* at Shaftsbury Avenue. Utterly brilliant. It blows your mind. You should see it.'

'I'm not sure that show is aimed at me.'

'It's for everyone, it really and truly is.'

'Well, I'm glad you saw it.'

'And I'll be going again, if we can get tickets.'

'Do you have time to take on a task for me?'

'Of course. Your tasks are always interesting. I might not be able to do it straightaway because my boss has finally recognised my talents and given me some proper research to do. And – wait for it! – my friend along the corridor invited me to go with her when she visits her parents in Devon for a week.'

'That's great. Hope you'll have a wonderful time.'

A delay would suit Nell very well, given her misgivings about poking her nose in. But as Susan had said, wills are public documents.

'I'm going to post a list of names to you, with births and deaths. I want you to go to Somerset House, see if those people left a will and, if so, who are the beneficiaries.'

'And it's confidential.'

'It's confidential,' said Nell.

'Got to go. Footsteps on corridor. It may take me a while, but yes. Oh, and come to London again soon.'

Thirteen

Saturday, 23 August

Gloria Thwaite took the wedding dress, still in its dry cleaner's cover, from the wardrobe in the little bedroom. She felt nervous. Her mouth was dry. What if Amanda was being polite about wanting to wear the dress? What if she had forgotten what it was like, or now thought it shabby and old-fashioned? It would be too late to find another dress. Of course, she could hire one, Gloria supposed. It was one thing for Amanda to have loved the dress as a child when she liked dressing up but another thing altogether to wear it on her big day. The hem had a tear from when Amanda had tripped over it.

Norman was no great help. 'What's not to like about it?' he had asked. 'It suited you. It will suit Amanda. Just let me get on with polishing the car if I'm to park near Montpelier.'

Gloria had thought about taking the album, with the photographs of herself and her mother wearing the dress, and her grandmother too. No, she wouldn't take it. No one would want to look at that. Except that Cherry girl might, the one who raffled a dress at the village fête. Gloria picked up the photograph album to pop into her shopping bag.

Norman took it from her and opened it at the page where the two of them stood on the church steps, she in her wedding dress, he in his new suit.

Gloria would not say it aloud. They never did.

She said, 'We'll meet in the café on Parliament Street when we're done with the fitting.'

Norman dropped Gloria off at the top of the street, refusing to come in with her, saying, 'A boutique's no place for a feller. There's no size to any of these pokey shops. I'd end up knocking summat over and having to pay for it, and isn't it bad luck to see a bride in her wedding dress?'

'That just applies to the groom,' Gloria said.

Gloria walked down the street feeling self-conscious. She looked at the other strolling, window-gazing women and then at herself in a shop window. She wasn't a stroller, she was a hurrier. The windows reflected not the person she felt inside, but a dowdy woman, in a coat that was too long, and wearing her best hat, which was her funeral hat. Gloria realised that she must do better than this for the wedding, but she had not been to a wedding since 1962.

As she stepped into the shop, a young woman with long straight hair that shone like a guardsman's boots looked at Gloria and at the clothing bag with its coat hanger that held the wedding dress. This person wore silky trousers and a silk blouse with a wide, beaded belt. Was she the owner, or the manageress?

'Hello,' smiled the silky person through brightly painted lips, her eyes lighting on the clothing bag.

Gloria remembered to put the aitch on her 'Hello. I've brought the wedding dress.'

'Fabulous! Cherry can't wait to see it.'

Gloria didn't like shops like these, small shops where staff had too much attention to shower on the unwary. You had to be ready to say, 'Just looking.'

'You must be mother of the bride,' said whoever-she-was as she led Gloria up a spiral staircase where a person might lose her footing.

'I'm Mrs Thwaite, Amanda's Auntie Gloria.'

'Sorree! Amanda did say I should expect Auntie Gloria. It's the likeness that threw me. Come this way, Mrs Thwaite. I'm Beatrice.'

Gloria's awkwardness disappeared the moment she saw Amanda, who barged across, grabbed her auntie, and gave her a kiss. 'You can't believe how excited I am. Not just dressing up, but wearing this dress for real!'

Beatrice unzipped the cover and held out the dress for inspection, calling 'Cherry!'

'Gorgeous!' said the girl with the short hair who appeared from a cubicle. 'I'm Cherry.' She held out her hand. I'm pleased to meet you, Mrs Thwaite. I remember you from the Brackerley village fête. You bought a raffle ticket for a dress I'd run up and helped raise money for a good cause. Thank you!'

Gloria felt at ease now. She liked Cherry. She seemed down to earth, a worker. If anyone was to make alterations to the wedding dress, it ought to be her.

Amanda and Cherry went into the fitting room and closed the curtain behind them.

'Mrs Thwaite, while you're waiting,' said Beatrice, 'would you like to look at wedding outfits for – well, suitable wedding outfits?'

'Thank you, not now,' said Gloria, feeling proud of herself for not being mowed down. She went to sit in the chair by the window.

When Amanda came out of the fitting room, she looked glum. 'I've put on weight.'

'It's perfect,' said Cherry. 'It's not you. The seams have frayed. I suggest a panel on either side, in the same sort of satin as the neckline and the cuffs, which I will also replace. I can source exactly the right material, probably right here in Harrogate, and I will tidy the hem.'

Amanda groaned. 'I've a train to catch. The boys have a gig tonight and I want to be there.'

'That's fine,' said Cherry. 'You don't need to do anything. Leave it to me. Let me take a measurement.'

When the fitting was done, there was time for Gloria to produce her photograph album and show the pictures of her grandmother, her mother, her sister, and Gloria herself wearing the wedding dress. Amanda turned a page. She looked at the photograph of Auntie Gloria's sister. She turned back and looked at Gloria's mother, and then at Gloria.

'You've never shown me this before, Auntie Gloria.'

'Haven't I?' said Gloria. And then remembered why she had never shown it.

The album was passed round.

There was a long silence before anyone spoke.

Cherry said, 'It is such a privilege for me to work on this very special dress.'

Beatrice seemed subdued. 'And it's an honour for Bon Boutique to supply the veil.'

Gloria and Cherry walked Amanda to the railway station and said goodbye. Cherry waited by the barrier as Gloria bought a platform ticket and walked Amanda to the train. Cherry could see them talking. For a moment, it looked as if Gloria would board the train. The guard blew his whistle. Cherry watched as the train pulled out. The guard had closed the window, but Amanda opened it and gave a flick of her silk scarf before the train chugged out of sight.

Gloria came back through the barrier, blowing her nose. She said, 'Cherry, me and my husband are going to a café for a bite to eat and a pot of tea. Would you like to come?'

'Ee, I would that, lass,' said Cherry. 'I'm a guest of Her Majesty so these days I don't get out over much.'

Gloria laughed. 'Where did you learn to talk like that?'

'Watching *Coronation Street* with my fellow inmates.'

In the café, Cherry and Gloria sat opposite Gloria's husband. Cherry wondered whatever had happened in Norman Thwaite's life to make him appear permanently morose. He couldn't have been born like it, could he? If so, Gloria wouldn't have married him. Gloria was chatty, happy to talk about how Amanda used to love dressing up.

Norman studied the menu. He did not have much to say for himself. It took fish and chips, two pots of tea and an Eccles cake to make him risk a smile and praise the café, saying they did good fish and chips and didn't stint.

Cherry was in no hurry to return to the prison. When the waitress cleared the table, she asked, 'May I take another look at your album, Mrs Thwaite?'

Gloria was quick to agree. 'Of course! You're like me for wanting to look at photographs.'

Gloria took out the album again. Cherry turned the pages, pausing each time she came to the dress, being worn by each generation of the family.

'I could look at these all day,' said Cherry. 'It's an utterly fab album. Are you related to the Chapins? Because there's such a likeness across the generations, even to the way Amanda holds her head.'

Gloria felt the thump-thump of her heart. She spoke quickly. 'I'm no relation to Mr Chapin or his first wife. I've always looked after Amanda.'

It wasn't the right answer. She could not give a true answer when the person who mattered most was in the dark.

Fourteen

Officer Kitteringham's first discovery of home brewing was a scrupulously clean enamel bucket with lid. It was in one of the garden sheds, behind a wheelbarrow. Kit took off the lid. The dried fruit was already beginning to ferment. It seemed a shame to throw the brew away. A lot of thought had gone into this enterprise. Kit tipped the contents of the bucket behind the shed.

Her second find was a catering-size jar behind a chest of drawers in a dormitory. The drawers had been edged away from the wall to create space. There was also a portfolio of Cherry's there, and a folder with Linda's coursework. Diane would not have squeezed into the space, but Linda or Cherry would. Home brewing was obviously a joint effort.

Kit chose her moment, carried the jar into the garden and watered the flowers with the contents, feeling a sense of triumph, but also some admiration, not just for the women's initiatives but for the governor's way of dealing with the situation. Kit hoped that the women would know who found them out. They may show her respect and not try any more tricks as they counted down the days to the wedding.

A week in advance, Kit took her team through the plan for the big day. She knew her stuff and was on safe ground.

Officer Kitteringham was pleased with the achievements of her catering team. They were to share the marquee with the landlady and bar staff from the Hare and Hounds, with a suitable distance between drinks and food.

Kit's stint in the catering trade ended when she made her choice between the Women's Royal Army Catering Corps and the prison service.

Kit was happy in the prison. The women liked cooking. They liked her and she liked them. When they came to the end of their sentences, they would all get good jobs. Diane was particularly capable. Kit had already looked up the best restaurants and hotels in Hull, so that she could recommend her. Unfortunately, catering for a wedding made Diane morose. In fact, she looked on the verge of tears. Kit gave her a little smile. There was nothing she could say to someone whose happiest day of her life was her wedding day, whose husband died tragically, and whose children put on a brave face every visiting day. Diane shouldn't be here, but you couldn't let yourself think that. Ours not to reason why.

The big day came. The hard work was done. There were urns, trays of savouries, trays of sweets. The chief officer made two trips to take the food and the catering team to the grounds of the mansion. Trestle tables set up in the marquee ought to have groaned under the weight. The set-up went like clockwork.

Cherry was keen to be off. She was to be allowed to attend the church because of having altered the wedding dress. A dress always takes on a different look when worn by the right person. Amanda Chapin was the right person. Inspired by that wedding dress, Cherry wanted to get back to her sketch book. She would take a good look at what outfits wedding guests were wearing, not so much to copy any ideas but to decide what they ought to be wearing. This whole prison business was a waste of her valuable time. The only bonus was that she had won over the owner of the Harrogate boutique, and the customers. It came as a pleasant surprise to her that in unexpected places there would be people ready to spend a goodly amount of money on dressing up. Once she was back in the big wide world, there would be no holding her back.

Miss Kitteringham gave the nod, giving Cherry permission to go to the church.

Cherry was alone in the gallery of St Michael and All Angels. She took a centre seat on the first row, leaning on the rail. The church doors were open. Cherry heard the tap of heels and muted voices as the congregation began to enter. The organist was already playing. One of the Northern Knights in his trademark silver suit took his place at the baby grand piano that the group took with them wherever they could. It should be a theatre, there should be opera glasses, but Cherry recognised Tim. He was keyboards. The organist played an introduction, and Tim joined in. Cherry expected a hymn, but it was a Simon & Garfunkel song, 'The Sound of Silence', a song Cherry loved.

'Yes!' said Cherry to herself. She had also loved *The Graduate,* and remembered its wedding scene as Tim and the organist seamlessly began to play 'Ave Maria'.

Vicar, groom and best man Bob stood by the altar rails.

The wedding march had always sounded a bit too 'in your face' for Cherry's liking, but today she thought it a suitable introduction to Amanda in the vintage dress and the hired headdress and veil. Amanda was followed by a grown-up bridesmaid in blue, and two little bridesmaids in cream satin, all carrying smaller versions of the bride's wildflower bouquet. With the permission of Amanda and Mrs Thwaite, the photographer from the *Harrogate Advertiser* had promised Cherry photographs of the dress for when she included it in what would be her wedding collection. The Gloria dress in white, the Amanda version in cream.

The vicar's welcome gave way to a hymn, and then the vicar asked everyone present if there was any reason why the couple should not marry. Cherry regarded this as the 'Jane Eyre Impediment' moment, when a breathless man would barge in and denounce Mr Rochester – or, in this case, Mr Harding or Miss Chapin – as a bigamist.

The moment passed. All, including bride and groom, remained schtum or answered in the negative as to a good reason for forgetting the whole business and going home.

The declaration of vows, the exchange of rings and the vicar's seal on the matter led into a Bible reading. What followed was the miracle of turning water into wine at the marriage at Cana. Cherry felt a great a glow of satisfaction, almost as if she alone had somehow brought about this wondrous event. By the time she had her side view of the dress, as the main players disappeared into the vestry, she had a slight misgiving about whether the veil ought to have been two inches shorter.

As Cherry made for the stairs, to have a closer look at Amanda leaving the church, she spotted Governor Lewis just leaving by the side door. A wave of utter misery flooded through Cherry. For a blissfully short time, she had forgotten she was a prisoner.

Fifteen

Nell liked St Michael and All Angels. She liked the soft light filtered through the brightly coloured stained-glass memorial windows donated in memory of Chapins past, and other local worthies, one of whom had subscribed to the building of the old people's home. She was less enamoured of the white marble figures of two Chapin ancestors, an earlier Lancelot Chapin, and his wife Agatha, confidently supine in their proximity to the altar and to God. Their remains were said to lie somewhere beneath these perfect effigies that lay here like sleeping partygoers, too done-in to pull themselves together and go home.

Nell had entered the church a few moments before a couple in their forties, so about her own age. Nell never forgot a face, and these two were familiar. They stood out because they were from somewhere sunny. Both were tanned. He was dark-haired, with a few grey streaks. The woman's hair was an evenly dyed dark brown. Nell remembered the big blue eyes. It was Lesley! She and Nell had lived on the same street when they were young. Lesley wore an expensive cream silk trouser suit and low heels. He wore a smart lightweight suit and expensive shoes.

They, too, had that moment of recognition but did not speak until the ceremony was over. They were ready to leave as the organist played them out with 'Jerusalem'.

The three of them came to a halt outside the side door of the church.

'Lesley?' said Nell.

'Yes! Nell, how amazing. Mam told me there was a Miss Lewis at the prison, but I never connected that with you. Is that where you work?'

'It is,' said Nell. 'I'm prison governor.'

'Wow! Who'd have thought it?'

Nell smiled. 'Not I, not in those days.'

'Nell, do you remember Peter?'

'Of course. Peter – don't tell me – Peter Kufluk.'

He smiled as they shook hands. 'You haven't changed a bit.'

Nell laughed. 'I'm beyond flattery.'

Nell remembered Peter as young, good-looking but a terrible dancer, always with an extra packet of fags in his pocket. Nell had almost choked on a Lucky Strike the first time she went to a Saturday night dance at the American base. The arrangement was for respectable girls to be taken and brought back on a bus. Nell, still at school, lied about her age. Lesley, who worked at the local newsagents, covered for her.

Nell, Lesley and Peter moved off the path to make space as people were leaving the church.

Lesley said to Nell, 'I'm so glad the church was full.'

'Oh, there was bound to be a good turnout,' Nell replied.

'Not a certainty,' said Lesley. 'Dad told me that a lot of the villagers intended to boycott the wedding, not because of ill-feeling against Amanda, but as a protest against Lancelot Chapin still planning to sell off the meadows, after half the village signed a petition. The other half were too anxious about being evicted to sign or protest in public, but there's a lot of ill-feeling against him.'

'You're well-informed,' said Nell.

Lesley smiled. 'My parents retired to Brackerley. They've always liked the area and wanted to be in the countryside for walks. St Michael's needed an organist. Dad plays the organ. Apparently, Gloria Thwaite told people that Amanda would be gathering her bouquet in the meadows and she would never let her father sell village land. People who might have stayed away turned up.'

Nell, Lesley and Peter made their way to the front steps of the church, confetti at the ready. Nell knew she ought to have a box of colourful confetti, but admin officer Daisy had been saving the contents of the hole puncher.

The last time Nell had seen Lesley and Pete, Nell's boyfriend Roland had been there. Peter and Roland, young GIs, made friends on their journey across the Atlantic shortly after the US entered the war. They were both from California and answered the call, with that youthful certainty that it would be over in no time. The arrival of Americans felt like a big adventure for Nell and Lesley. After meeting at a dance on the base, when they could, they went out and about as a foursome. By the time they had known each other for three years, Nell and Roland planned to marry. The marriage plans were made before Nell realised she was pregnant. The pregnancy simply brought the date forward. Roland had a few days' leave. He had arranged to hire a car. He would pick up Nell up from her mother's house. Nell's sister and brother-in-law would come with them to Gretna Green as witnesses. In Scotland, a girl under the age of eighteen could marry. The shotgun wedding, as Nell's disgusted mother called it, did not happen.

Roland never arrived, never sent a message, never wrote.

Nell's brother-in-law went to the US base, was turned away, and given no information as to whether Roland was alive or dead, posted home or posted elsewhere. Nothing. Lesley's family had moved from the street and not left a forwarding address, or Nell would have written to Lesley. Nell wanted to know – was he posted elsewhere, did he lose his life, or was he injured? She could not believe that he had simply forgotten her. But that was her sister's view. The old story of the girl who was too easy. Nell's mother never had time for Roland. She said he was too free with cigarettes and chocolate and no good would come of it.

Nell had the baby in her sister's house. She named her Roxana after Roland's sister, and because the name meant Light of Dawn. Roxana was born at dawn. Nell created a story for herself about when Roland would come back, setting aside the hurdle of Roxana being registered as her sister and brother-in-law's child and Nell being godmother.

Nell had long ago stopped telling herself the 'Roland returns' story as she made a life, made a career. Seeing Lesley and Peter brought it all back.

Amanda and Fred stood on the church steps. This was Brackerley's wedding of the year, perhaps the wedding of the decade. Nell and Lesley joined in the congratulations and the throwing of confetti, or in Nell's case, the tiny circles of used paper from the office hole punch.

As well as the official wedding photographer and guests,

the *Harrogate Advertiser* and the *Yorkshire Post* photographers were there.

A beautiful bride, the romantic story of the wedding dress and the novelty of having Frederick Rudyard Harding, local-boy-made-good, ought to ensure that no one would pay attention to the Brackerley Caterers. Linda would have nothing to worry about.

A photographer was taking a group shot, with Penny and Lance Chapin on either side of the bride, and including Norman and Gloria Thwaite. When the photographer stepped back, Penny caught Nell's eye and made it plain she wanted a word.

They stepped aside. Penny said, 'A strange funeral and a glorious wedding, all in one week.'

'The funeral was unusual,' agreed Nell. 'Did you have a message in your "Kiss Me Quick" hat?'

'I did.' There was a pause. Penny glanced about. 'Did you?'

'Yes.' Nell hesitated.

'Go on then,' said Penny. 'We'll keep it to ourselves.'

'It was the name of Monica's solicitor in Blackpool.'

'That sounds very definite. Mine said, "Remind Lancelot that he promised."'

'Promised what?' Nell asked.

'I've no idea.'

Before they could say more, Bob, the best man, appeared. 'Come on, Penny! It's my job to keep you all to the timetable. Food and champagne. Speeches at one o'clock!' He took Penny's arm to usher her to the car that would take them back for the reception.

Penny gave Bob a playful push. 'Not so fast! Amanda is about to toss her bouquet.'

As she watched Penny and Bob, Nell had that same feeling as when she saw them in the manor house garden together. There was a closeness between them that seemed unusual between a band member and the mother of the bride. Nell's feeling vanished when Lance Chapin, who was standing nearby chatting to Dr Block, came across to join Penny and Bob. Lance patted Bob on the back. Nell decided that the Chapins were glad to have young company in the house. They must have missed Amanda when she went to London.

There was a delay before Amanda could do the honours with her bouquet. As photographers jostled for position, Lesley came to speak to Nell.

'Wasn't that a lovely wedding?' said Lesley.

'Perfect,' said Nell.

Lesley smiled. 'Gloria Thwaite helped avoid a village uprising. I don't think anyone will be so tactless as to talk about Mr Chapin being manoeuvred into withdrawing the meadows from sale.'

Chapin's land sale plan had created a revolution in the making. Nell doubted that Amanda picking wildflowers and asking nicely would change her father's mind about what must be a lucrative business deal, but she said, 'The wildflowers made a lovely bouquet.'

Lesley whispered, 'The orchids on the altar, that's what Penny Chapin originally ordered for Amanda.'

Half a dozen village girls in their twenties and younger gathered, ready to leap and catch the bouquet. The person who was simply standing in the right place, was suddenly several inches from the ground, raising her arm and grabbing the bouquet.

'Who caught it?' Lesley asked Nell.

'Florence,' said Nell. 'Our nurse.'

Lesley cheered. 'Must've been a good netball player.'

Those surrounding Florence cheered, but heavy groans of disappointment, or pretend disappointment, came from her rivals for the prize.

Nell went across to Florence. 'Well caught! Good to see you again.'

'And you, ma'am.'

'If the folk tale comes true, and you're next down the aisle, be picky. You deserve the best.'

Florence laughed. 'I know that, and you know that. Meanwhile, any chance of my job back?'

'I was hoping you'd say that. We've missed you, and I'm still referring to you as "our nurse".'

'What do I do to reapply, ma'am?'

'You don't. I didn't accept your resignation. I put you on compassionate leave. I was beginning to think you'd left me with more paperwork. Consider yourself back on board.'

Florence beamed. 'Oh, thank you!'

'Do you have somewhere to stay tonight?'

'I'm at a bed and breakfast in the village. I booked Miss Harding in ages ago, and thought I'd book for myself too. Miss Harding didn't want to miss her nephew's wedding. She has a lift back tomorrow with a couple from Scarborough.'

'Well, I'm glad Miss Harding is here, and glad you're back, Florence. But there's something I've been meaning to ask you.'

'Ask away, ma'am.'

There was no one within earshot, yet Nell lowered her voice. 'Something intrigues me. When I first took over here, you told me that you were warned off taking a job in Brackerley.'

'Yes.'

'Yet you took the job, halftime at Dr Hampshire's practice, halftime at the prison.'

'Yes.'

Nell thought that Florence seemed suddenly uneasy. Nell pressed on. 'Can you tell me why you were warned off, and what was the warning?'

'Well, that's just it, ma'am. There was nothing specific. I was given no good reason, no explanation. At first, I thought perhaps the person who told me bore a grudge, or had a friend in mind for the job.'

'Is there something I should know?'

'I was told Brackerley wouldn't be a good place to work, or to settle down, but the person wouldn't say why, just not to come here. She expected me to take her at her word, without further explanation.'

Florence looked around. No one was listening. People were in groups, snapping photographs and chatting. Some had started to walk back to the manor house grounds. A couple of cars drove off. Florence said, 'Something still haunted her from years ago. She said bad things had happened here and she swore me not to tell. Well, I couldn't, because I didn't know what I was supposed to keep quiet about. I find that sort of thing very annoying. It's like, "What's at the back of the woodshed?" And no one knows. Could be a bloodied axe, could be firewood.'

Nell had never seen Florence lose her cool, yet now there was an edge of agitation to her voice as she said, 'You either say something straight out, or you keep quiet, that's my opinion.'

Perhaps this wasn't the time or place, but for the present there was no one in earshot. Nell asked, 'Is that person still in the village?'

Florence nodded.

'Is she here today?'

Florence glanced towards Nell's companion from early morning walks. Susan Taylor was seated in one of the folding chairs. 'Miss Taylor. Susan Taylor. She worked with mothers and babies at the maternity home many moons ago. She's a resident in the old people's home now. She may not even remember that she advised me to stay away.'

'I suspect she will,' said Nell. 'Susan and I both take early morning walks and we've talked.'

'Oh of course,' said Florence, 'and you went to her friend Monica's funeral.'

'Yes, I did.' Nell did not divulge that Susan had played cloak and dagger, giving Nell a list of deceased elderly people's names, and the accusation that they may have been coaxed into remembering Dr Block in their will. Nor did she think it fit to mention the 'Kiss Me Quick' hat, with the cryptic information about Miss Taylor's solicitor.

Nell changed the subject. 'I was thinking we ought to do something for the elderly,' she said. 'Perhaps put on a concert at Christmas.'

'They'd like that.' Florence sniffed her bouquet and held it towards Nell. 'Isn't this heavenly, ma'am?'

Nell sniffed. 'It's gorgeous, and a lovely tradition, to have gathered flowers on the day of the wedding.'

Several of Florence's friends and former patients were making their way over. Nell smiled at Florence. 'Here comes your fan club. We'll talk later.'

Dr Block had also gathered a group of admirers. He waved to Nell. She waved back but decided not to join the throng of villagers. If people were taking sides about Lancelot Chapin and the sale of land, Nell needed to stay neutral. She wondered whether there had always been a 'them and us' feud bubbling below the calm surface of life in Brackerley. Perhaps the long ago 'bad things' Susan once spoke of to Florence might have been connected to the Chapin family. Susan was of a generation who were good at taking secrets to the grave. She had only ever hinted to Florence about dastardly deeds, but she seemed determined to make known her suspicions about the highly respected Dr Block, who at that moment separated himself from the group to talk to Dr Hampshire, the GP.

Mrs Hampshire came across to Nell, saying, 'Wasn't it just the most perfect wedding, Miss Lewis?'

Nell agreed that it was.

Mrs Hampshire looked in the direction of her husband and Dr Block. 'Those two will be talking shop.'

'Do they work closely together?'

'I wouldn't say closely, but if ever there's a poorly patient at the home, Dr Block calls in my husband for a second opinion, and they are almost always of one mind.'

'That's good practice,' said Nell, thinking that if Susan, Victor, and Emma knew about Dr Block seeking a second opinion, they may be less likely to sling mud in his direction.

'Oh yes,' said Mrs Hampshire. 'Doctors can't be too careful. Speaking of which . . . ' She hesitated.

'What?' asked Nell.

'My husband and I often go to Harrogate Theatre and we always support the amateur dramatics. They're putting on *Blithe Spirit*. Might you come along with us? If so, I'll ask Dr Block, if that's agreeable. He works hard and is so dedicated to his residents.'

Nell would have loved to say yes to *Blithe Spirit*, but in

a place like Brackerley, nothing was kept quiet for long. It was too early in her posting to think about socialising and being paired with Dr Block. 'Thank you for the kind thought, but no.'

Mrs Hampshire sighed. Her mouth turned down at the corners. 'I somehow thought you'd refuse. Perhaps you'll change your mind when you've been here a little longer. Dr Block is such a gentleman. He is kept so busy, but he always found time to take the borstal boys on a hike, locally or into the Dales.'

At that moment, Dr Block was talking to an elderly man in a wheelchair. Nell watched as the doctor wheeled his resident from bright sunlight into shade.

Sixteen

After the moment of elation when she caught the bride's bouquet, Florence felt ridiculous. The flowers ought to have gone to one of the village girls. She was relieved when there were a few cheers. Someone called, 'What a catch!'

And then people came to talk to her, patients, parents of patients, staff from the maternity home and the old people's home. It was a revelation for Florence to realise how much the people of Brackerley cared about her. She had been important here, respected, and she would be again.

When she left Brackerley behind Florence had thought she would never return, never face thoughts of what might have been, or be reminded of her loss. Living away, if only for these few months, had made her think again. She was too young to go into permanent mourning for the major, and for what might have been. She had not even said proper goodbyes. Perhaps that was why people were coming to talk to her, as a long-lost friend who hadn't said goodbye. It was as if some of the villagers were expecting her back.

Florence, still clutching the bouquet, feeling rather

awkward and not knowing what to do with it, went to sit beside the major's sister, Miss Harding, who admitted to being occasionally emotional at weddings. 'You have been very kind to me,' said Miss Harding when Florence confided that she might return to Brackerley. 'You would be doing the right thing. Pay no attention to anyone who says differently. My late brother had his qualities, but not enough. And he was too old for you.'

Florence heaved a sigh of relief. It had taken someone else to tell her what was perfectly obvious. She ought to look for a younger man, someone with a bit of get up and go, who wanted to marry, wanted a family. Be brave, not reluctant to start a conversation, she told herself. It was not shyness. She didn't know what it was. When she did speak, she said the wrong thing. When a person, who was perhaps trying to make friends, made an overture she would somehow rebuff them without knowing how she did it or why, as if they could not really want to be friends. Or she would ask herself did she really need any more friends? She had made a foolish mistake throwing her cap at Major Harding. What she was good at was people in pain, people in trouble, people who needed her help.

It was as if the old nurse had read her thoughts. Susan, seated in a wheelchair, beckoned that she wanted to whisper to Florence.

Florence bent to listen. 'My dear,' said Susan, 'I can't face being bumpety bumped along the road to the manor house. I fell while on my walk this morning and grazed my knee. I am perfectly all right but Dr Block insisted on my being strapped into this boneshaker, to curtail my movements and make him appear heroic as he wheeled me through the gates.'

'It's his job. He did it for your own good.'

'Sitting on leather, having my legs covered with blanket, roasting me alive? Please take me into the church to cool off.'

'I'm going to the manor house for a glass of champagne and to toast the bride and groom. I'll take you. Cool off on the way.'

'I need peace and quiet. Let us go into the church. I must think.'

The side door was propped open. Florence manoeuvred the wheelchair through the porch into the empty church. On the aisle, she put on the brake. Susan said, 'Florence, I intend to confide in you something I have never divulged to a living soul. This tale must be told.'

Florence felt a chill. In books and at the pictures, this is where the person about to tell something of great importance would have a sudden heart attack. That would be the start of the story and then there would be the unravelling of the truth in flashbacks.

The verger had splashed out on incense. That combined with the scent of altar flowers was almost overpowering.

'Susan, tell me on the way to the reception.'

The air was still with a silence so deep that it seemed to hum.

'Florence, do you remember that I warned you against coming to Brackerley?'

'Yes.'

'I hope you have not regretted ignoring my advice.'

'Not for a moment. I wouldn't have left Brackerley if not for the major's horrible death.'

There was a long pause. Florence suspected that Susan had forgotten what she wanted to say. That is typical of me, thought Florence. Everyone will be stuffing their faces, drinking champagne, and toasting the bride and groom. The person who caught the bouquet is trapped with her rumbling stomach, a yearning for champagne and an old lady who is trying to put the kibosh on my plans for a second time.

Yet Florence felt rooted to the spot by her sense of duty, until a voice in her head whispered. You have obliged other people all your life.

The voice was right. Even the major's sister had, belatedly, told Florence that the major was wrong for her.'

Susan spoke quietly. 'I told you bad things happened here.'

Suddenly, that was enough for Florence.

It had been years since Susan warned her off coming to Brackerley. Florence had ignored her then, and she would ignore her now.

'Susan, you can whistle, can't you?'

'Oh, yes.' Susan whistled what Florence thought was the opening of a Beethoven concerto.

'Susan, bad things happen everywhere. I wasn't interested back then in who was having an affair with whom or who stole Mrs Molloy's washing from the line, and I'm not interested now.'

'This isn't just gossip.'

'We are here for a wedding. Do you want to come with me?'

'It's too hot. I need a rest, and to talk to you.'

'Enjoy your rest, Susan. The door's propped open. Someone will hear you whistle. I'll call back when I've toasted the happy couple.'

Susan listened to the tap-tap of Florence's footsteps as she left the church. She felt empty inside, her weak arms resting on the arms of the wheelchair. This contraption into which she was strapped had more life and purpose in it than she did herself. If she died here, her tale would die with her. No one would else would come forward to right a wrong, to put an end to lies.

Seventeen

As Nell began to walk back from the church to the manor house, Gloria Thwaite came to say hello, and to introduce her husband to Nell. He was a gaunt man who, despite being immaculately turned out for the day, gave Nell the impression of having been put through a mangle and some essential part of him squeezed out. She had seen this look in male prisoners and wondered whether Norman had ever been imprisoned or spent time as a prisoner of war.

Gloria, Norman, and Nell walked together. Gloria chatted about the wedding, saying how lovely it would be to hear Fred and his band play. She looked forward to that.

As Gloria and Nell chatted, Norman strode ahead. At a bend in the path, he turned back and waved. 'See you in the marquee.'

Gloria waved back.

As they walked, Gloria told Nell the story of the wedding dress, which Nell had heard but this time it was told with a personal slant. 'I said to Norman, "How did I ever get into that? Was I ever that slim?" He said yes, I was, and he was handsome. That made me laugh.'

Nell smiled. 'I hope your dress will go on being worn into the next century.' As she spoke, Nell spotted the bride and groom, standing by an oak tree. The photographer stood a few yards off, taking pictures of them together and then separately.

'I hope the newlyweds are enjoying this,' said Nell.

'Oh, they'll be enjoying it,' said Gloria. 'It's good publicity for Fred and the band, and Amanda always liked having her picture taken. She knows how pretty she is.'

'There he is!' Mrs Thwaite suddenly caught her breath. She called, 'Norman!'

'I don't see him,' said Nell.

'Then, who's that with Amanda?'

'The photographer,' said Nell.

'No. the other one, standing behind her.'

Nell saw no one else.

Mrs Thwaite shivered. 'He's gone. I could have sworn that was Norman.'

Nell had seen only the bride. 'It must have been a trick of the light.'

'Must've been. He wasn't as he is now. He was in his black suit with the thin stripe, and his hair oiled.'

Gloria looked upset. People did become emotional at weddings. Nell tried to reassure Gloria. 'Sometimes our minds play tricks. Norman won't be far away.'

'I was sure he was there.'

'Perhaps you're remembering your own wedding,' said Nell. 'That's a lovely memory to have.'

They were diverted by Fred who went to stand by the 'TRESPASSERS WILL BE SHOT' sign.

'How about a photo here? This would make a good album cover.'

'Don't you dare!' Amanda called. 'People are up in arms about Dad as it is. And he has his speech to give, and so have you! Now come on, we're going back in the car! You, too, Auntie Gloria. Will you come, Miss Lewis?'

'Thank you, but I'm enjoying the walk.' Nell strode out, knowing she would be back quicker that way.

She intended to check on her staff and residents in the marquee, listen to the wedding speeches, and give the necessary congratulations and hellos before slipping away.

Kit and the residents were handling proceedings with military precision. Nell was about to join the queue, but Kit had put a plate aside for her.

'You've all done brilliantly,' said Nell. 'Well done!' She smiled encouragement to Kit and the residents and gave a thumbs-up, feeling proud of them all.

'Where's Linda?' Nell asked.

Kit nodded in the direction of the tent flap. 'I haven't said anything to her because I know how she's feeling. Every so often she seems to think someone is looking at her and she goes as if to straighten the tent flap or check on the urns, keeping her head down and her back to people.'

Nell was pleased that Linda was here, even if anxious. She would eventually know that she could go out without being recognised. As Nell left the marquee to circulate, Dr Block approached carrying two glasses of champagne. 'A toast to your wonderful catering team,' he said. They clinked glasses. 'Let me know when you open the first restaurant in what would be the Brackerley chain, staffed by your former residents.'

Nell smiled. 'I will pass on your compliment, though I have

an idea that our residents will spread their wings wider than Brackerley.'

Mrs Chapin spotted Nell and the doctor and floated towards them, also full of praise for the caterers.

'It was a magnificent wedding,' said Nell. 'Are the happy couple going on honeymoon?'

'They're booked into a hotel by the coast for a couple of nights and then the band are going on tour, and Amanda back to work. They're nothing if not ambitious.'

Nell saw Cherry and thought of complimenting her on the alterations she had made to the wedding dress, and then thought better of it. There was a coolness in Cherry's manner. Nell wondered was Cherry playing a part while screaming inside to be elsewhere. An award-winning designer did not need to be told that she did a good job letting out a couple of seams on a wedding dress and tidying a hem.

There was sudden activity around the stage, where the bride and groom together with Bob, Tim and Mr Chapin gathered. Bob and Tim took to the stage and played a dramatic introduction, with a roll of drums.

Bar staff from the Hare and Hounds continued circulating with trays of champagne, ready for the toast. It was one o'clock. Time for the speeches.

The father of the bride took the microphone. Mr Chapin made the perfect speech, thanking everyone for coming and making this day so memorable. He praised Amanda, welcomed his son-in-law into the family, and remembered the groom's late father with affection. He expressed great pleasure that Miss Harding, the groom's aunt, could be here with them today. It was a great sadness that Amanda's mother could not witness this happy event, but he felt sure that she was smiling down from heaven.

Lancelot Chapin raised his glass to the two ladies of the manor, his daughter Amanda, and his wife, Penny.

He ended on a note of warning to the Northern Knights. 'Frederick, Tim, and Bob learned their technique as choir boys at St Paul's Cathedral, but Amanda was lead singer and soloist in her school choir.' Chapin bowed in Amanda's direction as he waited for an appreciative cheer. He continued. 'The Knights had better watch out, or they may soon need to change their name to Amanda and the Northern Knights.'

He was greeted with applause. First the groom and then the best man responded.

Nell watched as Penny said something to her husband. Mr Chapin went back to the microphone.

'One final word that won't be the final word. I know you are all concerned about the possibility that the meadows will be sold. I think you also know that Amanda and friends went to the meadows this morning to gather flowers.' He paused for a round of applause and cheers. 'I am exploring possibilities to save the meadows. It would be remiss of me not to say that, at present, we have no satisfactory alternative to the sale, but I am investigating every avenue. Be assured that if there is to be development, it will be done in a sympathetic manner, and you would all be kept informed and consulted.'

Chatter stopped. A hush fell. One person pushed back his chair and walked out. Nell watched and counted. Four more villagers followed.

Bob, the best man, quickly leapt to the rescue, shaking Mr Chapin's hand and at the same grabbing the microphone. 'Thank you to our host and father of the bride, Mr Lancelot Chapin. Ladies, gentlemen, boys, and girls, we Northern Knights have two new songs for you, before we hand over to the DJ.'

Nell watched. Other guests had righted the chairs that had been pushed over as the angriest of the guests left. A few more guests departed in a more peaceful fashion.

Nell admired Lancelot Chapin's honesty. He could have kept his mouth shut about the sale of land, but his timing was bad, and his management must be worse. He owned the village. He hosted shooting parties. There were rumours that he had fingers in other pies and a directorship of a bank. Something must have gone very wrong for the Chapins. It couldn't just be the cost of a wedding. Charges for catering were modest. The bar, the marquee, erecting a stage, hosting the band and all their equipment would have mounted up, perhaps alongside concerns about how Fred would provide for himself and Amanda. In a village where, for generations, people had thought of the land as shared, as part of their heritage, Lancelot ought to have anticipated fierce opposition. Protests, petitions, and graffiti might be just the beginning. No villager would think, 'Our landlord Mr Chapin is hard up.'

Eighteen

When Florence left the church, she did not know what to do with herself, or where to go.

She had done as she intended – spoken to the governor. She had her job back and knew that her old workmates would be pleased to hear the good news. On her way back for the wedding, Florence had promised herself that in future she would look after number one, and not be drawn in by other people's sob stories. Time for a glass of champagne.

She would go back to the manor house by the road, not wanting her heels to sink into grass and be ruined. She kept to the path, carrying the bouquet. Wildflowers. Already wilting. She must put them in water.

Someone was on the move. Florence caught sight of her out of the corner of her eye. A natty waitress uniform. For a person wearing heels, Diane was certainly moving. The new determined Florence ought not to feel sorry for a prisoner, but Diane had arrived at court with just her bus fare home expecting a fine and to be back with her children when they came home from school.

Diane was making for the road. Straightaway, Florence set off after her, knowing exactly what Diane was up to. She had absconded once before. The governor had driven to Hull and brought her back. A second time would not be tolerated. Diane would be found and shipped off to a closed prison miles from her kids. But Diane was not behaving rationally. It was a busy Saturday. There would be a lot of traffic on the road. How was it some people could run in heels? Diane was racing as if chased by demons. She would do what she did before, show a leg and thumb a lift. Some people never learn. Florence ought to know. She included herself in that. By the time Florence reached the road, Diane would be sitting in the cab of a lorry, enjoying the scenery, looking forward to seeing her kids and sending her sister out for fish and chips. Florence could sympathise with a person who acted impulsively. She had done so herself.

Florence had gone to Filey nursing a hurt, but not entirely broken, heart. She saw now that marrying the late Major Harding, her major, would have been disastrous. By moving to Filey she had harboured hopes of starting again. She had delivered the major's dog to his sister. She was soon on good terms with almost everyone, in every shop, and with the con-gregation of the local Catholic church. People were friendly, particularly a certain Claude Kettlewell. Claude was born with one arm but did not let this impede him. He was halfway intelligent, had the sort of sense of humour that showed itself in quick, clever quips. Marriage to a nurse was his childhood dream. But he did not want children and Florence did, before it was too late, so that was that as far as she was concerned.

Diane had reached the road. Florence paused to take off her shoes that were now crippling her. 'Oh, sugar me,' she said when a lorry stopped. She ran into the road, arm extended, thumb pointing skyward as she shouted and waved. A car swerved. A bus driver hooted his horn. A motorcyclist yelled and called her a rude name.

When the lorry started again, Diane was nowhere to be seen.

Florence told herself to calm down. She stood sedately. She stuck out her thumb. A car with a couple in sped by.

She stuck out her thumb again. A woman with kids in the back and an old fellow in the front shook her head, mouthing 'Sorry'.

Florence stepped back as a bus approached.

A white van came into view. Florence stepped onto the road, wildly waving her shoes at the driver. The van braked quickly in order not to run her over. The driver wound down the window to swear, but she climbed in before he could open his mouth.

'Sorry to stop you, driver—'

'You gave me no choice. It was stop or run you down.'

Florence felt sick. She had hoped to catch up before Diane reached the road. There would be no keeping this quiet now. 'I am a State Registered Nurse, and this is an emergency. I need you to please follow that lorry. The passenger is my patient.'

'You could have got us killed.'

'Her name is Diane. She is my responsibility.'

He was a pleasant-looking man, and though she had taken him by surprise, he set off, but perhaps because the driver behind was angrily thumping his horn.

'Where is your patient heading?'

'Hull.'

'I'm going to York,' he said. 'I can't stop now. I'll drop you off at the next lay-by.'

'If you put your foot down, you'll catch up with them within a mile. It won't take you out of your way. Hoot your horn, pull in front, set your blinkers going and hoot again. I'll be waving my scarf out of the window.'

'Are you always this bossy?'

'Please, this is important. Future happiness or misery depends on you.'

'Oh.' He frowned. 'You're very dressed up or I'd say you and your patient have just been let out of that women's prison.'

'I've been to a wedding at St Michael and All Angels.'

'That's nice.'

'I caught the bride's bouquet, but I dropped it while chasing after my patient.'

'It's catching the bouquet that matters, isn't it?'

'How do you know that?'

'I'm well informed about certain matters. I listen to the radio all day.'

'You're not listening now.'

'I switched the radio off when I saw you, carrying fancy shoes.'

'You're driving too fast. Overtake slowly. Sound the horn. Give me time to wave this scarf.'

'Yes, nurse.' He took his hand off the steering wheel and saluted. 'My name's Howard. Any further orders?'

'Keep your hands on the wheel.'

'I've told you my name. Howard. What's your name?'

'Florence – and that's it, that's the lorry!'

He indicated and pulled in front of the lorry, forcing it to halt and saying, 'You'll lose me my licence!'

Florence was out in a flash, round the passenger side of the lorry, where the door handle was just out of reach. Then Howard was beside her, opening the door,

Diane screamed, 'No-o!'

Florence said, 'Come back while you have the chance, or it'll be Holloway and you can kiss your home visits goodbye.'

Diane hesitated. The lorry driver gave her a sad smile. 'You better go, love. I can't have the cops on my tail for abduction.'

Diane, clinging onto her shoes, climbed out.

'So, Nurse Florence, where now?' Howard asked as Florence and Diane squeezed onto the front seat.

'Brackerley Manor House,' said Florence, and then suddenly clapped her hand against her mouth as she remembered. 'Call at the church first. I left an old lady in her wheelchair. Somebody might lock the door and she'll die overnight.'

Nineteen

Officer Kitteringham had scheduled fifteen-minute breaks. They had also taken turns to walk around the grounds gathering empty plates. Linda did not want a break. She preferred to stay in the marquee with her back to everyone, stacking plates or filling the urns. Suddenly, Miss Kit said, 'Where's Diane?'

The others looked at each other. They had taken turns on breaks, stretching out the time before going back to the prison. Kit looked at her watch. It was twenty past two. The speeches had ended. The band had played and then handed over to the DJ. Diane ought to be back, but she didn't wear a watch. Kit would give her just a little longer.

It was half past two. Cherry was serving. Linda was near the tent flap, having just refilled an urn. Kit said, 'Linda, go and see if Diane is all right.'

'Yes, miss,' said Linda. It was reassuring that Miss Kitteringham, Chief Girl Guide, always stayed the same. Only she would have added, see if Diane is all right.

Linda glanced through the tent flap to check the coast was clear. So far, so good. None of the guests paid her attention.

No one had come into the marquee with a camera around their neck, looking for the most notorious prisoner.

Linda crossed to the Portakabin and into the Ladies section.

Two lavatory doors were Engaged. Linda waited. Two women came out and washed their hands. Linda sensed nothing dangerous about them. One of them redid her lipstick and combed her hair. They both said hello. That was nice, thought Linda. They don't know who I am or where I'm from.

The third loo was empty.

Linda guessed where Diane was. She would be behind the marquee, sitting on the bench by the old red brick wall. When this marquee was taken down, there would be a view of the lawn, the flowerbeds, and the house.

Linda walked to the bench. At first, she could not tell who it was, only because the sight of the knife and the blood on his shirt stopped her from seeing anything else. She would have turned and run back into the marquee, but she could not move. She stared, expecting some change, expecting to see only a bench and to know this was a figment of her imagination. But there was nothing imaginary about the big red face of the man seated on the bench in his black suit and white shirt that was covered in blood, or about the knife protruding from his chest. Blood made a pattern around the knife, not dried blood but fresh blood like something from a joint of meat. Linda's brain was doing funny things. It told her this was one of those trick knives where the blade retracted, and red ink had been spilled on the white shirt. He was playing a game.

Just as she realised this was no game, he moved.

Linda felt the scream in her throat but did not hear a sound. What made her scream and swallow that scream was his movement. She thought he was going to get up, but he simply slid sideways towards the arm of the bench and his body moved forward a little, as if he might fall. The arm of the bench held him. On his little finger was a barrel ring with a diamond. She had noticed it this morning when he came to the marquee to say hello and jolly them along.

It was Mr Chapin, the father of the bride, the man who had given the speech. Linda had gone to the marquee entrance, to hear some of the speeches, just to know what people said now, how they talked in that world she had left behind. It was safe because everyone was looking towards the stage.

Seeing him, seeing the blood, this was too much like before, only this time, she didn't do it.

If she went back through the flap into the marquee, Miss Kit would fuss. There would be a commotion. Linda couldn't go forward, and she couldn't go back. She raised the flap a couple of inches, to take a look, praying no one would see her. She saw Miss Kit and heard her saying, 'Where have you been?' But Miss Kit wasn't speaking to her. She was speaking to Diane who was being brought in by the nurse. Diane was pushing an old lady in a wheelchair, and the old lady was saying, 'I'd murder for a cup of tea.'

Linda thought she might catch the nurse's eye and signal, but the nurse was talking quietly to Miss Kit, who suddenly looked upset, as if she might start to cry.

Linda dropped the flap.

Taking a step back, she walked sideways, fearing that if she turned her back the dead man would rise and grab her by the throat. She walked the narrow path that had been left between the Portakabin and marquee until she came into sunshine, and then she stepped back. Being in the sun would expose her. She would be stared at.

Wedding guests were by the marquee's main opening, in twos and threes, happy and smiling. No one turned to look at Linda in her waitress uniform.

She dared not take the couple more steps from that narrow corridor between the Portakabin and the marquee. If she did, she would be in full view of everyone on the lawn. Linda knew what she must look like. She couldn't stop shaking. Someone would swoop on her asking what's up, what's the matter. She wanted to run and hide but there was nowhere to run.

She stood for a moment, trying to catch her breath. Across the lawn, the governor stood with a man and a woman by the door of the manor house. She must tell the governor. She must be believed. There's a dead man behind the marquee and it wasn't me that killed him.

She imagined the responses, she knew what people would say: Well, she would say that wouldn't she?

It wasn't me, ma'am.

Linda felt so cold. She began to shiver. Her stomach churned. Before she knew it vomit came out of her, spilling onto her front, onto her shoes, onto the ground, more vomit than one person could hold. Linda could not move. The DJ was still playing. People were chatting, eating, drinking. If just one person saw her, they all would. There was nowhere to hide.

Cherry was gathering up more plates and glanced at Fred Harding and Amanda. They were talking to a couple of wedding guests. The first time Cherry saw Fred, he was busking for the Wyndham Theatre matinee queue. Now he was gazing at Amanda as if she'd hypnotised him. When would someone look at Cherry like that? If someone did, she would be immediately suspicious and want to know what he was after. It would be 'Go to Marrakech' all over again. 'Just make this one trip and we'll be on our feet.'

Well, Cherry was finding her own feet. She had a dozen sketches of the vintage wedding dress. This would become a staple of her collection, a tuck here, a detail there, and it would be a wow. Her heartbeat quickened at the thought of recreating the gown in her own fashion. Amanda was now dancing with the new husband. Cherry could not decide whether Fred was gazing longingly at Amanda or beyond her at the manor house and grounds. He looked exceedingly chuffed with himself.

It was a crying shame that the catering clan couldn't stay for the evening. Cherry knew Fred and his band through Bob. They'd met at a couple of parties before Bob joined the Northern Knights. Earlier, she had escaped the marquee for ten minutes, dumping her tray so she and Bob could find a quiet corner round the back of the house, share a spliff and reprise a happy memory.

As she crossed the lawn back to the marquee, Cherry stopped and stared. Linda was by the side of the marquee, on the path. She was shaking and looked disoriented. Cherry banged down the tray on the nearest table and hurried across.

'Bloody hell, Linda, what's wrong? What's happened?'

Linda couldn't stop shaking. 'There's a dead man on the bench.'

'What are you on about? And you can't go back in the tent looking like that. Let's get you cleaned up.'

'No! Just tell someone. Now.' Still shaking, Linda pointed

126

across the lawn to where the governor stood near the manor house door. 'Tell the governor.'

'Come and sit down before you fall down.' Cherry led Linda past the Portakabin and helped her sit down. 'Wait there!'

Twenty

When the call came in on the radio, Detective Sergeant Angela Ambrose had just left the house where she had taken a statement from a woman who had been flashed at while walking her dog in nearby woodland.

'Where are you?' the duty sergeant asked. Angela gave her location.

'We have a reported suicide in Brackerley. Thirty-three Willow Lane. Gas. A Mr Norman Thwaite.'

'Who reported?' Angela asked.

'The neighbour, Ted Platt, Thirty-five Willow Lane.'

'How did Mr Thwaite gas himself?' She had mental images of someone with a canister, or a pipe from a car.

'Head in the oven,' came the reply.

'How could that happen? I thought all the gas supplies had been switched?'

'Not everywhere, and not in Brackerley.'

'I'm on my way.'

Angela set off. She groaned. Why was it taking so long to make the switch to natural gas and be rid of carbon monoxide?

Why did we still have what people saw as a painless way out in the corner of every kitchen in the land? This would be Angela's second call to a gas-oven suicide. The first time she hadn't even been a PC. She was eighteen, working in a motor firm and volunteering as a special constable. A bailiff called to her from a yard. He was there because a tenant had not paid her rent.

'Had to break down the door,' he said. 'Left it open because of the stench. She's only gone and gassed herself.'

Angela, hanky over her nose, had gone into the kitchen. She forced herself to take the woman's pulse. No one had told her what to do in a case like this. Now that she looked back on it, she realised she had done the best she could.

Next to the rent book on the table was a biro. Angela read the small, neat handwriting on the cover of the rent book. 'At the end of my tether.'

Angela would never forget that incident, the note, the way the writer had pressed hard on the full stop, so hard that the point of the biro left a dent on the cover of the rent book.

As bad as the choking smell of gas was the thump of despair.

Angela banished the image from her mind by looking up at the bright sky and the dappled pattern roadside trees created on the road to Brackerley.

Angela spoke into the car radio. 'Arrived in Willow Lane. A man has come to the door. I assume he is the neighbour who made the call. Going inside.'

The voice at the other end said, 'Standing by.'

Angela clicked open the low gate. The garden teemed with marigolds. Halfway up the path, red and white roses grew either side of a pergola, their heavy scent giddily sweet. The door stood wide open. The neighbour adopted an at-ease stance. His bushy white eyebrows met as he frowned. Angela introduced herself and asked the man's name. He was Ted Platt, the man who made the call. Angela noticed that he had also opened the window.

They entered the kitchen where, despite the open door, the smell of gas hung heavy. The gas oven door was still open. There was a floral-patterned cushion on the floor nearby and a newspaper on the oven shelf.

'I carried Norman upstairs in a fireman's lift,' said Mr Platt, 'not knowing how long you would take to get here. It wouldn't be right to lie him on the floor or sit him up in a chair, too much of a shock for his wife. Where's the dignity?'

'Where is Mrs Thwaite?' Angela asked.

'She'll be at the wedding. I saw them setting off in the car about half ten. There's a do at the manor house afterwards. I don't know why Norman came back without his missus.'

The why of Norman Thwaite coming back without his wife seemed plain to Angela. He intended to put his head in the gas oven. But what had tipped him over the edge?

There was a note on the table. 'Top up oil.'

Something he wrote earlier, or for this morning, and had done it. 'Did you see any other note, Mr Platt?'

'No and I haven't touched anything.'

Only the body, thought Angela.

'Does anyone else live in the house?' she asked.

'No, not now. But their son Paul is visiting. He's at the wedding.'

'Thank you, Mr Platt. I need to go upstairs and see Mr Thwaite and then we'll talk outside?'

'Aye, we'd better. I'll put a couple of chairs out,' said Mr Platt.

Angela nodded. In a previous life, Platt might have been a stage manager, laying out the body, bringing the chairs.

Angela went upstairs. Someone who left a note to himself to check oil ought to have left a goodbye.

There were two bedrooms, one with a double bed and one with two singles. The deceased, dressed in a black suit, white shirt and blue tie, had been laid neatly on one of the single beds. Ted Platt had closed Norman Thwaite's eyes and crossed his arms on his chest.

Angela took Mr Thwaite's wrist, feeling for the pulse that wasn't there.

She checked her watch, took out her notebook, and wrote the time and 'no pulse'. There were no signs of any injury, nor that this was anything other than suicide.

She looked in the deceased's pockets. There was a handkerchief, a packet of cigarettes and a lighter, and in the inside pocket an invitation card to the wedding of Amanda Chapin and Fred Harding. On the back of the invitation card, in pencil, was a note even shorter than 'top up oil'. It said, 'I'm sorry.'

Before going back downstairs, Angela closed the bedroom window and door. It would be horrible to have flies coming in. She opened all the other upstairs windows.

Downstairs, she looked on the floor by the table in case a note had fluttered out of sight. She looked in the oven to see if Mr Thwaite had tidily placed it there.

Twenty-One

Nell's chosen spot was close to the manor house main entrance. From there, she could see the marquee, guests coming and going.

She had said most of her hellos. All was going smoothly. As she mentally ticked off her list of people to keep onside, Nell surreptitiously checked her watch. Quarter to three. The catering team had done HMP Brackerley proud. Bar staff from the Hare and Hounds would take over shortly.

Nell was just about to go to the marquee when Peter and Lesley appeared.

'Well, hello!' said Peter. 'The elusive Miss Lewis. Everyone wants to talk to you and there's no space for old friends who gatecrash a wedding.'

'Of course there is!' said Nell. 'Especially friends who have crossed an ocean. And Lesley, do tell your dad he played the organ beautifully this morning.'

'I will.'

'I'm sure the congregation are glad your parents decided to retire here.'

Lesley smiled. 'And I'm glad Dad wangled us an invitation to the wedding. It's such a delight to be here.'

'We've been hovering in the wings,' said Peter.

Lesley smiled. 'Where do we start after all these years?'

'How about where you live, do you have kids?'

'We live a short drive from San Diego,' Lesley said. 'We have a boy and a girl, still at college. They don't believe it when I tell them what age we were sent to work. I'm what they call a homemaker, Peter pushes a pen.'

'So you live near San Diego,' said Nell, 'where Roland came from. He talked about the place such a lot. Do you know whether he got home after the war?'

It was a mystery to Nell that a place name, and the name of the boy she fell in love with, could, after all these years, stir feelings in her.

There was a slight hesitation while Lesley waited to see if Peter would answer, and Peter waited for Lesley. In those few seconds Nell knew Roland was dead.

She knew that thought must show, because very quickly Peter said, 'We see Roland sometimes at the reunions. He was shipped back injured, but in one piece.'

Lesley added, 'He's talked about you.'

Nell managed a smile and resisted saying, tell him I don't talk about him, or think about him. Instead, she said, 'It was all so long ago, adding, 'Let bygones be bygones,' instantly hating the cliché.

'And what about you, Nell?' Peter asked. 'Do you live in the prison? We passed it yesterday.'

Nell smiled. 'I have a flat there, but I am allowed out.'

'What about your family, your sister?'

'She married, has children.' Nell glanced about, to make

133

sure no one was within earwigging distance. 'I have a niece. Roxana.' She said this in a way that she thought Lesley may understand. Being an unmarried teenage mother would not have been a good choice for Nell.

Peter frowned. 'Ah Roxana, that name's familiar.'

'It means light of dawn,' said Nell.

Lesley would remember that Roxana was the name of Roland's sister.

Lesley suddenly gave Nell a quick hug and a kiss on the cheek. Had she understood? Nell now regretted giving even a hint about Roxana.

Nell straightaway wished she had not said Roland's name or San Diego. The place had sounded so romantic, exotic, when she and Roland first met at the Saturday dance. He had told her where he came from and what he would achieve, and that one day there would be a statue to him in his hometown. Why did American place names resonate as they did? Perhaps because Americans were good at creating songs, stories, fables about the places they set down roots, or simply passed through on a train.

Nell wondered, might she have done something differently, found a way to keep Roxana. But she gave her up. Nell worked, made a career, made a life. She was independent, able to do something for her child, now a young woman.

On an impulse, Nell decided that she wanted to hear about Roland. Did he achieve such great things that there was now a statue for him? Nell doubted it, but let Peter spit out whatever he wanted to say about Roland.

But suddenly Cherry came hurrying towards her. Cherry, for whom the word 'cool' was invented, looked anything but. 'Ma'am, someone needs to speak to you.'

Cherry was drained of colour. She was holding herself very straight, arms at her sides. Peter and Lesley stepped back.

Lesley came close and said quietly, 'We fly home on Monday. Tomorrow, we'll be at the eleven o'clock church service. There is something I must tell you.'

Tactfully, Lesley and Peter moved away.

Nell said, 'Cherry, what's wrong?'

'Ma'am, Linda needs to speak to you.'

They set off towards the marquee and when Cherry was sure no one would hear her, she said, 'Mr Chapin is on the bench behind the marquee. He's dead—'

Nell hoped for another word. Mr Chapin is dead drunk, dead angry. Cherry kept her lips tight shut.

'Where is Linda?' Nell asked.

'At the far end of the Portakabin. Linda's in a bad way. She was sent to look for Diane and found Mr Chapin's body.'

'What makes you certain Mr Chapin is dead?'

'When I saw Linda's face, I didn't doubt it. He's dead, ma'am.'

'What about Diane? Did she see the body?'

'Don't think so. I think she'd, erm, gone for a walk.'

From Cherry's hesitation, Nell immediately knew what sort of walk. She looked about for help. Across the lawn, a small group of people stood chatting.

Nell pushed thoughts of Diane to the back of her mind. 'Cherry, see the man in a dark grey suit, champagne glass in his hand?'

'The doctor?'

'Dr Hampshire. Say, "Dr Hampshire, may I have a word." Draw him aside. This will be for his ears only. Say "Governor Lewis needs to speak to you urgently," and that you'll take him to me. His hearing is good, you can speak quietly.'

'Yes, ma'am.'

'Bring him to the end of the path by the marquee.'

Nell strode swiftly across the lawn, eyes front, on the alert. Surrounding herself with an invisible keep-away-from-me cloak. If Cherry was right, and Nell did not doubt her, they would need to act quickly. Certify death, contact police, secure the scene, prevent people from leaving.

Keep calm, Nell told herself. At the same time, she knew she would stay calm. She always did. She went to the path between the side of the marquee and the Portakabin.

Nell reached the Portakabin. Someone was just coming out of the Ladies. Nell stood aside to let her pass.

At the other end of the cabin, Linda was sitting on the grass with her back to the Portakabin wall. There was vomit down her front, on her shoes, on the ground. She was pale, shivering.

Nell took off her jacket and put it around Linda's shoulders. 'Stay put, Linda. I'll be right back.'

'They'll say it was me.'

'Was it?'

'No, ma'am.'

Nell walked the few yards to the rear of the marquee where the bench stood close to the high wall of the manor house. There was Mr Chapin, as described, with a knife through his heart, blood soaking his white shirt. Slumped sideways, he had tilted over the arm of the bench.

Nell looked at her watch, took a small notebook from her bag, and made a note of the time. Ten minutes to three. She went back to Linda and helped her to stand.

Dr Hampshire appeared. 'Is this the patient?'

'This is Linda who's just had the shock of finding a body.

It's Mr Chapin.' Nell pointed. 'There's a bench behind the marquee.'

Dr Hampshire strode quickly up the path.

Nell turned back to Linda.

Linda looked blank. She was shaking, looking at her feet. 'I've been sick on my shoes.'

'Tell me what happened.' Nell looked at Linda's clothing and at her white plimsolls. There was vomit but not a speck of blood.

Linda parted her lips, but no words came.

Nell prompted. 'You were in the marquee, serving?'

Linda nodded.

'This is no time to lose your tongue. Take a deep breath and speak.' When Linda didn't answer, Nell said, 'I'm going to stand behind you and hold your arms to keep you warm and stop you shaking. Is that all right?'

Linda nodded.

Nell stood behind Linda. 'Be steady.'

'They'll think it was me.'

'No one will jump to conclusions. Tell me what happened.'

'Miss Kitteringham sent me to look for Diane. She wasn't in the Portakabin. I called her name, tried the doors. And then I came out and went up the path, thinking she'd gone for a smoke.'

'And?'

Linda's face crumpled. Nell thought for a moment that she would not speak.

'I saw Mr Chapin, with the knife in him.'

Dr Hampshire walked slowly towards Nell. He opened his mouth to speak but looked at Linda and then simply nodded confirmation of the death to Nell, not that she needed confirmation.

'Doctor, would you please find the vicar. I'll call the police. We need to keep this quiet until the police arrive. They'll want everyone to remain on the premises. We're all potential witnesses. Let's not alarm anyone. I'll call from the manor house.'

Dr Hampshire said, 'I'll find the vicar and I'll be sure he and I are with the family before the police arrive.'

Cherry was waiting at the top of the path. 'Ma'am, the chief officer is here. She asked where you were and said to tell you she will be on the lane with the minibus to take us back.'

'Where is she?'

'By the manor house big window, because I whispered that there has been an incident and that you would want to speak to her.'

'Good thinking, Cherry. Tell her I'll be right with her, and then stay with Linda in the marquee.'

Cherry nodded and was gone.

Nell lifted the flap for Linda to go into the marquee. 'There's a free table in the corner. You're on a break, all right?'

'Yes, ma'am.'

'If anyone asks, say you were sick. Don't wipe your clothing. Keep your nerve. People will keep away from a person with sick on her. Linda, no one is going to blame you.'

Nell hoped to God that would be true. She went to the long table, where Officer Kitteringham was instructing her team. 'Kit, there will be short delay before we return. Linda has been sick. See that she and Cherry are given cups of strong sweet tea.'

'Of course, ma'am. I wondered where they'd got to.'

Nell walked across to the table where the landlady of the

Hare and Hounds was serving a drink. Mrs Dale had her head screwed on right and Nell needed her on side. 'Mrs Dale.'

'Miss Lewis.'

'I can rely on you?'

'You know you can.'

'There's been a serious incident. I'm going to call the police. Have your waiters pile beer crates, blocking both entrances to the Portakabin and to the rear of the marquee. No one must enter. Direct staff and guests to the toilets in the Portakabin behind the stage. If people have questions, say the toilets are out of order – an overflow, plumbing problems.'

Mrs Dale nodded. 'Consider it done.'

Nell glanced at the rear of the marquee. There would be a spot where she would be able to bob through to cover the body.

Nell went back to Kit. 'I'm going to tie this tent flap. The Portakabin is out of bounds. Direct people to the toilets behind the stage. Slow down the packing up but behave as if we are making ready to leave on schedule.'

Kit frowned. 'Yes, ma'am.'

As she left the marquee, Nell kept a pleasant look on her face, as if everything was all right. People were still listening to the DJ. Some were dancing.

Twenty-Two

Calling the police meant venturing into the manor house without having told the people most concerned that their loved one was dead. Nell was relieved to see Chief Officer Markham hovering near the manor house, seemingly admiring a potted plant. Always good to have back-up. Nothing phased Nell's chief officer. She had served in the war. The 'Keep calm and carry on' slogan might have been coined by her.

There was no one within hearing distance but, despite that, Nell kept her voice low and conversational. 'Brace yourself for a shock, Chief. Linda was sent to look for Diane. At the rear of the marquee, on the bench, she saw Mr Chapin's body.'

The chief's eyes widened, her lips parted, but it took a few seconds for the question to come. 'Is she sure?'

Nell took a breath. 'I went to see for myself. He has been stabbed through the heart.'

'My God, how awful.'

'Yes.' Nell paused. 'I need to call the police, and then the prison for freshly laundered sheets to cover the body and a change of clothes and shoes for the residents, and shoes for me.'

The chief said quietly, 'Who else knows?'

'Linda, Cherry, and Dr Hampshire. We keep a lid on, until the police arrive.'

'Quite so!'

Nell needed to do this quietly and quickly. The door to the manor house was not locked. 'Let's go,' she said.

Nell stepped inside, remembering the telephone on the hall stand. They paused in the hall, hearing voices from the sitting room on the left, where she and Kit had sat with the Chapins when planning the wedding. The door was slightly ajar. The first voice was Penny's. The answering voice was male. Nell and the chief officer exchanged looks.

'It's Bob, the best man,' Markham whispered. 'I spoke to him after the ceremony.'

If Nell could hear Penny Chapin and Bob, they would hear her making a call. Nell remembered seeing a wall telephone in the kitchen. She put a finger to her lips. This was no time for disturbing the occupants and breaking bad news to Chapin's widow. Everyone present was a suspect. Those close to Lancelot Chapin would be top of the list.

Relying on her chief officer's lip-reading skills and nous, Nell mouthed, and mimed, that she would make the call from the kitchen and for the chief to ensure no one picked up the phone in the hall.

Nell went to the kitchen. She took the precaution of checking the doors that led off — a pantry and a storage cupboard for brooms and mops.

Nell lifted the telephone from its wall cradle and dialled 999. She looked at her watch. Ten minutes to three. Less than four hours after walking his daughter down the aisle, Lancelot Chapin was dead. This was hard to take in, and what a devastating blow for Penny and Amanda. Then came the more practical thoughts – the who, the why, and how bloody awful.

'What service do you require?' asked the voice at the end of the line. 'Ambulance, Police, Fire.'

'Police. I need to report a murder.'

The connection was quick.

'I understand you are reporting a murder. Is that correct?'

'Yes.'

'Your name please.'

'Nell Lewis, governor at HMP Brackerley. I am calling from Brackerley Manor House, home of Mr and Mrs Chapin. Mr Chapin has been fatally stabbed.' Nell paused, to give the call handler time to write. 'There's a wedding reception going on. Mr Chapin is on a bench behind the catering marquee.'

'Who else knows of the death, ma'am?'

'To my knowledge, two prison residents, Dr Hampshire, and my chief officer.'

'Time of death?'

'The body was discovered around two forty pm.'

'Who discovered the body?'

'Linda Rogers, prison inmate.'

'The deceased's next of kin?'

'His widow, Penelope Chapin. His daughter Amanda has just married in St Michael and All Angels. I'm speaking quietly because I've come into the manor house to make this call. The widow is in a room down the hall with one other person. I haven't informed Mrs Chapin of her husband's death because I intend to ensure everyone remains on the premises without disturbance or panic.'

'And are you able to secure the scene until police arrive?'

'I'll do what I can to contain the guests, keep the scene clear and have the gates shut. There are upwards of sixty people here. Some left because of ill-feeling regarding a land development plan.'

'Anything else, ma'am?'

'Police permission to cover the body with a sheet from the prison laundry. There will be no space for a tent.'

'I can't officially authorise, but I can think of no better idea. Can we contact you on this number?'

'After the family know.'

'We'll get someone out to you quickly.'

'Will you use sirens?'

'Yes. For speed.'

When Nell ended the call, she rang the prison. Officer Friel answered.

'Governor here. There's been a major incident in the grounds of the manor house. We need clean sheets from the laundry, paper sacks for residents' clothes, and a change of clothing and shoes, including size five for me. The chief will collect. Be at the main door to save time. Alert the farm to stop and question any strangers that come sniffing about.'

Friel was the most loquacious of the officers. For once she simply said, 'Yes, ma'am.'

Nell hung up and went back into the hall where her chief officer stood sentry by the phone. Nell hesitated at the drawing room door. She felt torn. The widow ought to know, but if she did, there was no telling how she would react. Nell and her chief officer left the house as quietly as they had entered.

'Chief, back to base. Collect sheets to cover the body,

changes of clothes and shoes for the residents and clothing and shoe bags. We'll need authority figures on every exit, with a reason for people not to leave.'

The chief nodded. 'Yes, ma'am.'

A moment later, Cherry was beside Nell.

She said, 'I've told the DJ to lower the volume and be prepared to wind down.'

Twenty-Three

Norman Thwaite's neighbour had placed kitchen chairs on the concreted area outside the back door of 33 Willow Lane. He was bursting to give his account of finding Norman's body.

Police Sergeant Angela Ambrose produced her notebook as Mr Platt said, 'I saw Norman coming back from the wedding. There's his keys on the table. He just drove up and parked in his usual place. I noticed Gloria wasn't with him, but women like weddings. I supposed she was staying on and he'd had enough.' Ted Platt sighed. 'Poor Norman. What came over him?'

'Please confirm your name, sir.'

'Ted Platt, well, Edward Platt.'

'Address, Mr Platt?'

'Next door. Thirty-five Willow Lane.'

'Did you notice what time Mr Thwaite came back from the wedding?'

'Well, I'd just switched off the radio, the one o'clock news, so I suppose about half past.'

'And what brought you to call on your neighbour?'

'Norman had lent me his hedge clippers. I'd cleaned them and put them in his shed, and then I came to tell him.'

'What time was this?'

'Oh, I don't know. I haven't been a clock-watcher since I retired. When he didn't answer, I pushed the door to give him a shout. Something was stopping it, so I pushed again, a good push. That's when I got the stench. I saw that he'd sealed the door with gaffer tape. I dashed in, turned off the gas, dashed out for air, keeping the door open, came back when I'd had a breath of air and took him from the oven. It was too late. That's when I dialled 999.'

'You had a shock, Mr Platt, and you did what you thought was right. I hope you'll never experience this kind of situation again, but please remember that you should call the police straightaway. You did the right thing turning off the gas, but the scene of death should remain as found. You ought not to move a body.'

'Oh, what, just leave him there?'

'Yes. Until the police and ambulance arrive.'

'Well, I was flummoxed, wasn't I?'

Had Norman Thwaite really committed suicide, or did someone want him gone? 'Was there anyone else in the house or garden?'

'No. Mrs Thwaite and Paul must still be at the wedding.'

'Paul?'

'Their son.'

Angela made a note. It would be helpful to have Mr Thwaite's death confirmed by the local doctor.

'Mr Platt, is there a doctor nearby, in the village?'

'No. Dr Hampshire is our GP. He lives outside the village, and I know he's at the wedding.'

'Do you have keys for this house?'

'The back door is always open. There is a key in the shed for the front door.'

'Thank you, Mr Platt. Please bring me that key. I'll write you a receipt.'

He produced two keys from his pocket and handed them to Angela. 'I took them just in case.'

She gave him a receipt, and a card. 'If you think of anything else, ring this number. Thank you for your help. I won't keep you any longer.'

He looked surprised and a little disappointed, but after offering a few words of advice left by the back door. Angela locked it behind him. She got into the car and put in the call. The duty sergeant answered.

'Where are you? I've been trying to contact you.'

'On Willow Lane. Just taken the neighbour's statement. Mr Thwaite's next of kin, his wife and son, are at a wedding reception at the manor house. I'll find them and bring them back.'

'You're needed at the manor house. There's been a fatal stabbing. The bride's father, Lancelot Chapin.'

'When?'

'Sometime before two forty pm. The prison governor will do her utmost to keep guests on the premises until we arrive. We're taking all uniforms off the street and directing them to the manor house to secure the scene and for witness management. We're calling in special constables. The DCI and DI Dennis are on their way. If you arrive first, look for Miss Lewis, prison governor. She made the call. No one must leave or enter without authorisation. There's a marquee. Get everyone in there and keep them there until the DCI arrives.'

'How many?'

'According to the prison governor between sixty and seventy. A handful left early.'

With those numbers, it would be brief interviews: just names, addresses, where were you, what did you see?

'Okay.' Angela looked in the rear-view mirror. 'Hang on. I can see someone hurrying in my direction, wearing a suit and tie. Looks like he's come from the wedding. There could be a connection. Norman Thwaite came home alone from the wedding and put his head in the gas oven.'

'Listen! The deceased is Lancelot Chapin. Brackerley Manor House. He's an important man. Go now!' said the duty sergeant.

Angela had been part of the investigation team into Major Harding's death, shortly after the borstal closed. Brackerley was beginning to feel like a risky place.

'I'm on it,' said Angela. 'I'll be first on the scene.'

The young man coming down the hill was putting on speed. Angela got out of the car, knowing Governor Lewis would do the right things. The young man was middle twenties, around five foot nine, dark hair, dark-blue suit, white shirt, red tie – and he clearly wanted to speak to her. A murder at the manor house, the suicide of a guest and someone running down the street. Catch him while you can.

It was time to have everyone in the marquee. Nell had told Kit and the catering team to suggest to guests that they may wish to stay in the marquee because there would be an announcement. Naturally, they asked what announcement. Nell said, 'Tell them you don't know, but you know there will be an announcement.'

As she walked in the direction of the stage, Nell spotted the vicar and his wife, Mr and Mrs Grieves. Dr Hampshire must have gone to the house without finding the vicar. Nell walked in their direction. She needed to speak to them, somewhere they might be private.

There was no one in the summerhouse. Nell waved and beckoned. She opened the door and went inside.

A low red-brick wall gave rise to high windows, the whole surrounded by tall plants with huge leaves, giving the place a tropical feeling and creating shade for the four benches. Unless other guests felt a sudden urge for a taste of the tropics, this ought to be a good place for quick and quiet talk.

Mrs Grieves came in and sat down, and Nell did the same. Mr Grieves followed and sat beside his wife.

'Oh Miss Lewis,' said Mrs Grieves, 'I was just saying what a wonderful day this has been, and then Dr Hampshire told me you wanted a private word. He was going into the manor. There were a few people nearby and I got the impression it was something important.'

Nell came straight to the point. 'It *was* a wonderful day, a memorable day, but I'm sorry to say that in future we will remember it with mixed feelings. I have some shocking news.' She waited for her words to register. 'Brace yourselves, Vicar, Mrs Grieves.' Nell paused, her tongue in a knot. But the deed would not be undone by silence.

'It's Mr Chapin.'

'What about him?'

'I'm very sorry to break the news that Mr Chapin was found dead, and his death was violent. He has been murdered.'

The vicar palmed his hands in prayer and leaned his head against them.

149

Mrs Grieves turned pale, trying to take her husband's arm as he rose, saying, 'It can't be murder. Not here.'

'Yes, here,' said Nell. 'While we were all celebrating.'

For a moment the vicar and his wife just looked at Nell. Then he murmured a prayer, before saying, 'I must go to Mr Chapin. Where is he?'

'The area is a crime scene and blocked off. None of us must go near. I've notified the police. What you can do, Vicar, is go to the house. Dr Hampshire is there. He was looking for you. He wants you to be with the family. The police are on their way. They may turn up with sirens blazing. It's heartbreaking that the family will have to hear such news. They'll need all the help you can give.'

The vicar patted his wife on the back. 'I'll go to Penny and Amanda.' He strode out.

Mrs Grieves leaned forward. She had begun to shake. 'It can't be true. Amanda and Fred are getting changed, ready to set off for the hotel.'

'I know it's hard to take in,' Nell said, 'and now Amanda and Fred won't want to go anywhere.' Mrs Grieves took out her hanky, dabbed her eyes and wiped her nose. 'No one must enter or leave the premises,' Nell continued. 'You'll notice gatemen arriving, and constables and specials brought in off the streets. The police will need everyone in the marquee. It will be easier to have them in there now, rather than turned back at the gate. The police will want guests' names and addresses and to speak to everyone. Mrs Grieves, this is where you can help. Would you please go to the stage and ask guests to gather in the marquee for an announcement, without saying why.'

Mrs Grieves looked blank.

Nell said, 'People are beginning to leave. The constables on the gate will stop them from leaving but it really would be better if it doesn't come to that.'

Mrs Grieves said, 'What'll I'll do, is, well, I will go round and tell the groups of people that they are asked to gather in the marquee, and to pass the word.' She nodded in agreement with herself and left the summerhouse.

Angela got out of the car and waited for the man hurrying along from the top of the street towards her. If she were right and he was coming from the wedding, he had come a roundabout away.

The man drew level, asking, 'What's going on?'

Why is he alarmed? Angela wondered. I'm in civvies, unmarked car. Is it obvious that I'm a cop?

His run down the hill had not left him out of puff but he began to breathe heavily. 'I thought you were outside our house and that you were going to drive off, because there's no one in, but Dad's car is there. He might be next door.'

'Which is your house, sir?'

'My parents' house is thirty-three. I thought you'd come from the wedding and that something had gone wrong. I wasn't expecting to see the car back so soon.'

'Sir, I'm Sergeant Ambrose, CID. And you are?'

'I'm Paul Thwaite. Has something happened?'

'Have you just come from the wedding reception?'

'I went to the church, didn't stay for the reception.'

'Could you tell me, sir, what time you left the church?'

'Same time as everyone else.' He was biting his cheek. 'I don't think the whole thing took more than half an hour. I left before the photos. It didn't take long for them to marry.' He paused. 'I wished the bride and groom well, and then I went for a walk. Why do you want to know?'

At the house opposite, curtains twitched.

'What's going on?' Paul asked again. 'Has something happened?'

Angela said, 'Let's step inside for a moment, sir.' He was agitated. Angela looked for signs that he had been in a struggle, for traces of blood. From the look of his shoes, he had stepped in mud. Did Norman Thwaite come home and commit suicide because he knew his son had killed Mr Chapin?

They walked down the path. The moment they stepped inside the house, Paul sniffed. 'Someone left the gas on.'

Angela said, 'I have some bad news for you, Paul. Will you sit down?'

'I'll stand.'

Keep this normal, Angela told herself. Don't scare him off. 'Do you mind if I sit down?'

'Go ahead.'

Of the two chairs, Angela sat in the rocking chair, guessing it would not be Paul's choice.

This was best said quickly. 'I'm very sorry to tell you that your father took his own life this afternoon. He was found by your neighbour, Mr Platt, who turned off the gas and opened the windows. Mr Platt was too late to save your father.'

Paul sat down heavily on the nearest chair, gripping the edge of the chair arms so tightly that Angela could see veins trying to burst through his skin. His appearance appeared to confirm that he had been walking. Sweat on his brow, mud on the bottom of his trouser legs as well as on his shoes.

She knew she ought to be at the manor house, but if ever

a person looked guilty, that person was the man in front of her. But guilty of what?

Angela went to the kitchen sink, filled a mug with water and handed it to Paul. He drank the lot in one go.

'Where is he? Where's my dad?'

'He's upstairs.'

'Upstairs?'

Better get this out in one go. 'Your neighbour Mr Platt carried your father upstairs, not wanting your mother to come back and find him as he was, and perhaps not knowing how quickly we would be here. An ambulance will come to take your father's body to hospital for examination. That is the procedure in a case of suicide.'

'You can't just come in here and take over. Where's my mother?'

'As far as we know, she is still at the wedding reception.'

'I should've stayed with Mam and Dad.'

'Was there a reason you went for a walk alone?'

'Because I felt like it. And I can't stand listening to speeches.'

'Did you tell anyone that you were going?'

'I told Mam. If I'd told Dad, he might have come with me.'

Paul Thwaite blinked rapidly. He sniffed again and began to cough. When he got his breath he said, 'How did next door know about Dad?'

'Mr Platt came to return some hedge clippers. He would have been asked by the operator to be sure, to feel for a pulse, to look for signs of life.'

Angela did not say that he also would have been told not to touch anything and to leave the body as it was.

'Do you wish to go up and see your father?' Angela asked. Paul nodded.

Angela rose and walked up the stairs ahead of him. Paul said nothing. He followed her. She opened the bedroom door, remaining on the landing.

Paul took his father's hand. 'Why, Dad? Why would you do this?'

Since waking this morning, Paul had had a bad feeling, a feeling something was wrong. His dad was edgy, telling his mam to calm down and not be a bag of nerves. Mam was so careful, but she'd dropped a cup, a favourite cup. Dad had cut himself shaving. Paul wouldn't say this to Amanda, but he remembered Fred Harding from when they were kids. He'd thought Fred a twerp. He thought Fred was marrying Amanda for her money. And where was Steven? He hadn't even bothered to put in an appearance.

Angela went back downstairs. She would not leave Paul alone in the house. He would have time to change his clothing. She checked her watch. She may not now be first on the scene, but she had Paul Thwaite, a potential suspect. She went back to the car and put in a call.

'Before you ask, I'm still on Willow Lane. I have Paul Thwaite, son of the suicide. Paul approached the car erratically. He claims to have been at the wedding but not the reception. I don't want him to have time to clean himself up. I'll take him with me to the manor house to find his mother. Two specials live in Brackerley. Who's available?'

'No one. Call's gone out, everyone to the manor house.'

'I have two potential suspects here, wedding guests, one alive, one deceased. I can't leave the house unattended or open to entry by the nosey neighbour. I need someone here.'

Angela stayed put. She watched from the window. It took seven minutes for the special constable to appear.

He knocked on the front door.

'Special Constable McKenzie,' he said, showing identification.

'Sergeant Angela Ambrose.' Angela closed the door.

McKenzie spoke quietly. 'Just had a call to send me to the manor house, about to put my uniform on. I told them I'd seen Paul coming back and then another call came in telling me to be on duty in the Thwaites' house while Sergeant Ambrose goes to the manor house and takes Paul to the marquee for questioning – and to break the bad news to his mother, poor lad.'

At the bottom of the stairs, Angela pointed. As they went through to the kitchen, she said quietly, 'Paul's upstairs. The neighbour carried Mr Thwaite to a bedroom.'

McKenzie pulled a face and shook his head. 'Some people just do as they please. And muck it up for the rest of us.'

They stepped outside the back door. McKenzie said, 'I'm to gather up keys and wait here for instructions. Norman Thwaite's clothes and shoes will be required for forensics.'

Angela gave McKenzie the keys, saying, 'I hope the diligent Mr Platt didn't clean Norman's shoes and brush down his suit before carrying him upstairs.'

'I'll mention that, just in case.' McKenzie looked out into the garden. 'Norman kept it beautiful.'

'Yes.' They stood for a moment, admiring the blooms. 'Tell me,' Angela said, 'is there a reason why Paul would go to the church but not the wedding reception?'

'Amanda and Paul were like brother and sister, along with Steven. My guess is that Paul thought Fred and his rock 'n' roll and his London ways not good enough for Amanda.'

Paul came downstairs. He looked at the special constable. 'Mr McKenzie?'

'Aye lad. I'm very sorry for your loss.'

Angela said, 'Paul, I'm going to the manor house. Will you come with me and find your mother?'

Paul hesitated.

McKenzie said, 'I'll stay here until you and your mam come back, if that's agreeable. I won't be much company for your dad, but I'll stay with him if that suits you.'

'Thank you.' Paul looked ready to say more. 'I, er, I didn't want to——'

'You didn't want to leave him on his own,' said McKenzie. 'Nor would I. I'll sit with him.'

Twenty-Four

As she began to drive, Angela said, 'Paul, there's been a message about a serious incident at the wedding reception. Your mother is not affected but for now everyone is staying on manor house premises until they have been spoken to by police.'

'What incident?'

'I'm not at liberty to say at present. There will be information shortly.'

'What about Amanda?'

'We have no news of Amanda and no reason to believe she has come to harm.'

I'm beginning to sound like a press officer, Angela thought. Let me out of here.

'Brace yourself, Paul.' As she turned from Willow Lane onto the main road, Angela switched on sirens and flashing lights. Vehicles pulled towards the verge to let them pass.

Angela turned onto the narrow lane that led to the manor house, switching off lights and sirens. A special constable was opening the gate, having checked her number plates. She spotted a couple of bobbies brought in from patrolling the streets, and a gateman from the prison. Paul said, 'What's happened?'

'That's what I'll find out. Let's find your mother. You'll want to take her home.' Angela let her words hang in the air before saying, 'Was there a reason you gave the wedding reception a miss?'

His jaw tightened. 'Like I said, I don't like speeches.'

Angela had been at the manor house once before, when Mr Chapin made a complaint about trespassers. She had reminded him about rights of way and that those 'trespassers' had complained about the bull in his field.

The gateman let them through. Angela saw that he also let a couple of departing cars go through the gate, one with four bouncing kids in the back seat, the other with an elderly couple in the back.

'Anyone you know?' Angela asked Paul.

'I wasn't looking.'

Don't be an idiot, Angela told herself. His dad's just died. He's not going to look who's driving a car.

Angela made radio contact. 'DS Ambrose with Mr Paul Thwaite, arriving at the manor house.' It was 3.25. Angela was first on the scene.

Across the airwaves, the duty sergeant said, 'DI Dennis is on his way, with constables. The DCI is aware.'

Angela interpreted for herself. They would be pulling in more bobbies off the streets to take statements. No messing about for a major crime scene where the victim is a person of local importance, but she was still first CID officer.

'What's happening?' asked Paul.

Angela drove clear of the gates and rolled down the window. She spoke to the gateman, showing her ID. 'Sergeant Ambrose, CID.'

'Bernie, prison gateman. I've just come on.'

'No one enters, no one leaves without permission, Bernie. Keep track of registration numbers.'

'Will do, just, you know, kids and old people?'

'No exceptions. Who was driving in those cars with the kids and the old people?'

'The man with kids, he works at the bank. Eric Partridge. Dr Block runs the old people's home.'

Angela got out and took the loud hailer from the boot of the car.

'Come on Paul. I can't have a drink, but you can, and you might want to eat.'

'I'm not hungry.'

There was one table free in the marquee. 'Sit down, Paul. I'll put out a call.'

At the entrance to the marquee, Angela raised the loud hailer. 'Will Mrs Thwaite please make her way to the marquee where her son Paul is waiting for her.'

Angela looked across at the food table. She recognised the officer in charge and went to speak to her, ID at the ready. 'Hello, Kit?'

'Yes.'

'I'm Sergeant Angela Ambrose CID.'

'Yes, I remember you.'

'Is the governor nearby?'

'She'll be back soon.'

'Where is she?'

Kit hesitated. She lowered her voice. 'The governor is

159

behind the marquee, covering the body with a sheet from the prison laundry.'

'Okay.' Angela looked in the direction of Paul. 'That chap by the entrance. His name is Paul Thwaite. Would you see he gets a cup of sweet tea and a sandwich? He's had a shock. His mother Mrs Thwaite should be joining him soon, and then an officer will drive them home.'

Angela walked back to the area near the gate, to what was now a huddle of uniformed officers and special constables, waiting for orders. She chose a WPC whom she knew slightly.

'I have a sensitive job for you.'

The WPC brightened up. 'Yes, Sarge?'

'In the marquee, speak to the prison officer in charge of the catering team, Officer Kitteringham. She'll point out Paul Thwaite. I put a call out for his mother, Mrs Thwaite. As soon as mother and son are together, drive them home to thirty-three Willow Lane. The husband, Norman Thwaite, has committed suicide. See them into the house. Local Special Constable McKenzie will be in the house. He knows the family. He will call for an ambulance. Stay with them.'

'Right, Sergeant.'

Twenty-Five

Nell's Plan A did not work. The marquee was too well pegged for her to raise a section of canvas and surreptitiously bob under to reach that part of the path where the bench stood. Having informed Kit that the side flap leading to the Portakabin must not be used again, she overruled herself. She trod the path to the bench for the second time, carrying the clothing bag that contained a newly laundered sheet.

As she reached the bench, a sudden call on a loud hailer made her jump. The call was for Mrs Thwaite to make her way to the marquee.

Nell looked at Lancelot Chapin's body for a second time. As she did so, she had the strangest sensation that he seemed more present, more solid in death than he had in life. She walked to the back of the bench and placed the sheet over the body, tying a corner to a second sheet to secure it to the back of the bench. It took longer than expected. All the while, she harboured a dread that Lance would move, slide, fall. Finally, it was done. As she went back the way she had come, Nell thought that she would never make a bed again without seeing blood and feeling sick.

Kit was waiting for her and handed Nell a boot bag. 'Chief said to give you this, ma'am. Change of shoes and a bag for the ones you've got on.' When Nell had taken the shoes, Kit said, 'The chief called on a retired gateman who's a wedding guest. He'll walk the perimeter because he knows all the ways in and out.'

'Thanks, Kit. Have a cup of coffee ready for me.'

'Yes, ma'am.'

Nell looked at her watch. It was 3.30. Two and a half hours ago, Lancelot was on stage, making his father of the bride speech. Nell's brain would not let her match that confident, happy man to the corpse with a knife in his heart.

Although the Portakabin was now out of bounds, Nell went in, washed her hands. She did a balancing act in the doorway while she changed her shoes.

Back in the marquee, she took her cup of coffee to a table and for the first time in years wished she hadn't given up smoking. The tables were filling up. Mrs Grieves had spread the word. People were coming into the marquee, but not in great numbers. Nell spotted Sergeant Angela Ambrose talking to Mrs Thwaite and to the young man beside her. That must be Paul Thwaite.

Angela could not have been here long. She would be here because of Lancelot Chapin's death. Was something else going on? Angela had her notebook on the table. As she listened to Mrs Thwaite, Angela jotted down a few words. A WPC joined them, and then Mrs Thwaite and Paul left with the WPC.

Angela came across to Nell's table. She said quietly, 'You made the call about Lancelot Chapin, ma'am?'

Nell nodded. 'Yes, from the manor house but out of earshot of the family.'

'Two cars were leaving as I arrived. I've spoken to the gatemen.'

'Mrs Grieves, the vicar's wife has been directing people into the marquee.'

'Who else knows?'

'Two of our catering team, Linda and Cherry. Linda discovered the body at approximately two forty. She asked Cherry to come and tell me. My chief officer and the catering officer have been informed. Dr Hampshire certified the death. He and the vicar are with Mrs Chapin now.'

'I'm glad Mrs Chapin has someone with her. I'll speak to her first, let them know we're here. The DCI and DI are on their way. I'll need to speak to your officers and the catering team.'

Angela hesitated. 'That was Mrs Thwaite and her son Paul who just left. The WPC is taking them home. Do you know them?'

'I haven't met Paul. I know Mrs Thwaite slightly. We met at the Chapins' when discussing catering. She introduced me to her husband Norman as we walked back from the church.'

'What time was that?'

'After the photographs, going on for twelve. The Chapins had their photos taken with the family. Our nurse, Florence, caught the bride's bouquet. I can barely take it in, this shocking ending to what ought to have been the most marvellous day.'

Angela leaned closer to Nell. 'I might as well tell you. You'll hear soon enough. Mr Thwaite went home and committed suicide.'

The words hung in the air for several seconds until Nell grasped them. 'How awful, and for poor Gloria. Does she know?'

'Her son will break the news when they get home.'

'How did he die?'

'He put his head in the gas oven. A neighbour made the call. I've arranged for Mrs Thwaite and Paul to go home.'

Nell could barely speak on hearing of this new calamity. 'Poor Gloria.'

'Did you happen to see what time Mr Thwaite left the reception?'

'No I didn't.'

'Can you think of anything significant about that walk back from the church?'

Nell shook her head. 'Only that Norman seemed detached, keeping to his own path as Gloria said.'

Angela took a deep breath. 'I must go into the house and talk to Mrs Chapin.'

'Right.'

Nell walked with Angela to the marquee entrance. She watched Mrs Grieves making her way to the stage. She must have realised that her softly, softly approach of passing the word hadn't done the trick.

Twenty-Six

The mood changed. Mrs Grieves felt it. The DJ had lowered the volume of his records. The family was out of sight. The Brackerley caterers had cleared every finished-with plate. Staff from the Hare and Hounds were wiping tables.

Mrs Grieves had passed the word for people to be in the marquee. She told herself that she must be more positive, get on that stage, stop the music and take the microphone.

'Daydream Believer' drifted quietly into the air. Someone had got to the stage before Mrs Grieves. A slight girl of about fourteen, wearing a bright summer dress, hair in a ponytail, sat at the front of the stage swinging her legs and clutching the microphone.

The DJ stood at the rear scratching his head. Mrs Grieves walked round to a set of portable steps at the back of the stage.

The DJ, his hair standing on end, gave her a hand up, 'What's going on? A bossy waitress tells me to wind down. I'm contracted to play until six, and I'm being invaded.'

The invader in the bright dress strode across, still clutching the microphone. She spoke to Mrs Grieves. 'Missis, I'm

Shelley. Fred said I could sing a song. I sing "Ol' Man River", unaccompanied.'

'Not today, dear.' Mrs Grieves reached out for the microphone. 'I'll take that.' She turned to the DJ. 'When this record ends, switch off the music, dear boy.'

Shelley groaned her disappointment. 'I was here first, Miss!'

Mrs Grieves felt sorry for the girl. 'Be patient, Shelley. Everything comes to those who wait.'

'I'm fed up of waiting. Waiting for Shirley Bassey to answer my letter, waiting my turn for the microphone.'

Mrs Grieves switched on the microphone. 'Ladies and gentlemen—' There was one of those awful screeching noises. Mrs Grieves moved the microphone a few inches from her mouth. 'I am Mrs Grieves, the vicar's wife. May I please have your attention for an important announcement.' She had spoken clearly and loudly. As heads turned to look, she took a deep breath. 'Ladies and gentlemen, dear guests. I hope you have all had a most pleasant day. I have an important announcement to make. Some of you are now preparing to leave. Please remain in the grounds. Make your way to the marquee. Do not be alarmed, but no one must leave the premises. There has been an incident that you will be made aware of.' There were churchgoers nearby, members of the Mothers' Union. With her very being, Mrs Grieves signalled to them. As one, the Mothers' Union transformed into Mrs Grieves' brigade, carrying all before them in the direction of the marquee.

Shelley took the opportunity to snatch the microphone. Mrs Grieves grabbed the microphone back with one hand and took Shelley's hand with the other. She was reluctant to move as people began heading towards her, coming closer to the stage, as if expecting enlightenment from the vicar's wife. Before she could say anything else, Mrs Grieves was relieved to experience one of those moments familiar from children's Saturday matinees at the pictures, when the cavalry comes riding over the hill.

The tall man in plain clothes parted the crowds as he strode towards the stage. She felt relief at remembering his name and continued, 'Detective Chief Inspector McHale of CID is here to make an announcement.'

The DCI took the microphone, with a polite nod. He cleared his throat. 'Ladies and gentlemen. It is with great regret that I must inform you of the sudden death of Mr Lancelot Chapin.'

There were murmurs of shock and cries of disbelief.

'Please remain calm.' Julian paused. 'I know that you will join me in extending condolences to the family. We will be gathering information, and ask for your cooperation with enquiries into the circumstances of Mr Chapin's death.'

Someone put up their hand. Julian said, 'I won't take questions now. If the officers on duty can answer a question, they will.'

He waited until the shocked response subsided, and then said, 'Please remain where you are. We will hold a moment's silence for Mr Chapin.'

When the silence ended, he said, 'Please make your way to the marquee. My officers are on duty, ready to take your details. Please make your way to the marquee now and remain on the premises until you have spoken to a police officer and been given permission to leave.'

Mrs Grieves, still grasping the wrist of her young friend

167

the songstress, went to the back of the stage. The DJ stared at Mrs Grieves. 'What am I supposed to do?'

'Pack up. Go to the marquee. Speak to the police, send in your invoice for the required amount. Include a note of condolence. Do you need any help? I can ask one of our parishioners?'

The DJ did not need help. Mrs Grieves climbed down from the stage, Shelley jumped down, and stared. 'I was promised a spot.'

Mrs Grieves once more took the girl's hand. 'Did you know that Fred and the band sang in a church choir before they became famous?'

'No.'

'Well, they did. And I think it's time that we had girls in our choir. Will you come and see me after church one Sunday?'

'I might.'

'Are your parents here?'

'No.'

The air was still. Conversations dipped or petered out. People were moving towards towards the marquee, some still clutching drinks.

Shelley whispered, 'It feels creepy.'

She was right. Mrs Grieves felt herself among sleepwalkers, in a dream.

'I knew it was about Mr Chapin when you got on the stage,' said Shelley.

'How did you know?'

'Brendan was at the protest meeting about Mr Chapin and his big swiz, selling off our meadows. He told me Mr Chapin is down to die if he doesn't change his mind. The meadows aren't his to sell.'

'Where is Brendan now?'

'Getting us a piece of wedding cake.'

'Let's go find him, shall we?'

But the marquee was filling up, and Shelley could not spot Brendan. And then Mrs Grieves could not spot Shelley.

Twenty-Seven

The policewoman who drove Gloria and Paul home spoke quietly and politely, not saying much at all, just being so very nice to them.

For Paul and Gloria, time stood still. They sat in the back seat of the unmarked police car. Paul had the sensation of a long-ago dream where he held onto a balloon as it rose, carrying him into the sky and all below him became remote, and small. He forgot how to breathe.

We are cut off. We are set adrift.

The car they were in had been nodded through at the manor house gates, when others were not allowed to leave. The car turned onto the road. Do it, Paul said to himself, just do it, take her hand. He took his mother's hand.

When Paul had spoken to his mother in the marquee, to give her the bad news, all he said was, 'It's Dad.' He watched the colour drain from his mother's face, so rapidly. Her lips turned white. She asked no questions. She knew. How could she know?

What made their news so unreal for Paul was that his dad and Amanda's dad had both died on the same day.

An ambulance was parked outside their house. When Paul and Gloria got out of the car, Paul saw the driver and another ambulanceman sitting in the front seats, waiting.

Mr McKenzie, postmaster and special constable, was at the door.

Everything will start to happen now, Paul said to himself, and all sorts of things will happen that never did before. I don't know what to do.

'I've put the kettle on,' said McKenzie. 'Oh, Mrs Thwaite, Paul, I'm right sorry for your loss. No one is going to rush you.'

'Where is he?' Gloria asked.

'Your neighbour, Mr Platt, carried Mr Thwaite upstairs to the bedroom on the right.'

Paul made to take his mother's arm. She shook her head. 'I'll go up on my own. I need to have a word with him.'

'Will you have a drop of brandy?' McKenzie asked.

Gloria shook her head. 'Nay, I won't want to be breathing fumes on Norman.'

When Mrs Thwaite had gone upstairs, McKenzie chatted to Paul. Was his dad in a poor way, had he ever attempted such a thing before. Paul could not say whether his dad had attempted to take his life before. That question came like a blow. He would have known, wouldn't he?

'Not that I know of,' he said, 'not while I was living at home.'

'We couldn't find a note, not something that gave an explanation, just a short apology in the top pocket of the suit your dad wore today.'

Paul said nothing. He would look himself, but it would be like Dad to do something and let the action speak for itself.

'Your dad was still working at his garage, not retired?'

'You know he was.'

Paul thought he knew what Mr McKenzie was getting at. Why didn't Dad do the deed in his garage.

Paul's Mam was a long while upstairs and while she was gone, Paul became upset and annoyed by Mr McKenzie. *What's he up to?* Paul asked himself. When the sergeant asked how long they'd known the Chapins, and was there anyone in particular with a grudge, and other questions that he must know the answer to, then the penny dropped. Mr McKenzie wasn't being the good neighbour, the helpful postmaster, he was being the special constable.

'Dad never had a bad word for Mr Chapin. Dad stuck up for him when other people called him every name under the sun.'

'I know that, Paul.'

'If anyone's saying Dad would have done for Mr Chapin and then come home and topped himself, they're mad. If there'd been anyone there today that Dad thought planned to harm Mr Chapin, Dad would have throttled them.'

'Aye lad. I know.'

'People boycotted the do because Mr Chapin was going to sell off the meadows to a housebuilder from Leeds for blocks of flats and parking space for commuters. Dad told me that he took a lot of flak for not signing the petition. Me, I see the point of wanting to keep the meadows. Maybe the old villagers are right when they say that Chapin ancestors stole land from the peasants. Eliminating Mr Chapin isn't going to change the fact that something's got to give in Brackerley. Nothing stays the same.'

There were footsteps on the stairs, his mother coming back down. Paul said quietly, 'I don't know who killed Mr Chapin, or why Dad took his life, but for God's sake leave us alone. Look somewhere else.'

'You're bound to be upset, Paul. Your dad was a good man. I know that.'

Gloria stood at the bottom of the stairs, staring at nothing, as if not knowing where she was. Paul guided her to the rocking chair and sat her down. Mr McKenzie came to sit by her, putting a cup of tea on the little table.

Paul went upstairs to say goodbye to his dad.

The windows and back door had been left open for hours but still Gloria thought she smelled gas. She had been sitting in the chair, by the open back door, for an hour or more.

She smelled gas when she went into the kitchen and opened a cupboard door, forgetting why she had opened it. She smelled gas when Paul decided he would lay a fire and took a newspaper from behind a cushion.

It was a warm evening, but Paul was laying a fire.

He was good at laying fires. He had never needed to use the gas poker, not even when coal was damp.

Norman had gone, taken away in an ambulance, as if going to hospital to be made better.

The police came, a man in a black-leather jacket, apologetic, saying the usual things about shock and sorry and it would be helpful if—

Gloria couldn't remember exactly what she said, but she did tell the man in the black-leather jacket that Norman had tried to take his life before, and the doctor had seen him, and they could speak to the doctor. After the last time with the doctor, Gloria had told herself that Norman would not do it again. He promised. And now, on this day of all days, on

Amanda's wedding day — Gloria stopped herself at that. Of course. The wedding day was his trigger. The only other day would have been Amanda's birthday.

All she need do was make it clear that Norman was not a murderer. He had not killed Mr Chapin. She could say that she had done it, and with good reason. I killed him because he stole my child. But she did not know how Lancelot Chapin died. The police knew how he died. The prisoner who found him knew. The prison governor knew. Gloria did not know how Lancelot Chapin, the amiable, wealthy, caring, generous child thief, met his end.

Chapin was bigger than Norman. Norman could not have overpowered him. Norman brought back a gun from the war but had no ammunition, and his spirit was broken. That was a combination of the war, and his own doing.

Later, Gloria wondered whether she might have done things differently and kept Norman alive. What would that difference have been? To be kinder, angrier, firmer in the face of doctors. But people think in black and white when they don't know the full story.

Might she, years ago, have written to the problem page in her magazine, enclosing a stamped addressed envelope for a personal reply that could have saved Norman's life? Well, no. Because she knew what had been done when she was shown an empty cot and a dead child, and they all had their stories straight, Dr Block, the nurses, Dr Hampshire. A sudden infant death. A cot death. And, behind their words, the threat of an asylum for a woman half mad with grief, and for the sake of Steven and Paul who needed her.

And Norman knew. Did he know from the beginning? Or did the truth dawn on him slowly, when he began to call

Amanda 'our little lass'? Gloria had to believe that it dawned on him slowly. Was that behind his gas oven capers? Was this final time a deliberate suicide, or did he once more think she would miss him at the wedding reception and come to save him as she had before?

Now everything changed. People, might think, oh, on the day of Mr Chapin's death, Norman Thwaite went home and gassed himself. What did he have to hide, to fear, to regret? No one must ever know.

If people slung mud, she would sling it back. She would protest her husband's innocence. She could explain to Paul and Steven that their father had bad experiences in the war that gave him nightmares. She had tried to help him. So had the doctor. That Norman left them in the way that he did was not through lack of love but because he did not have the words, he did not have enough left in him to carry on. Part of him wanted to stay in the world, go on being their dad. He tried to help himself, but that wasn't to be. Something had happened that could not be put right, something he blamed himself for. A lesser man would have shrugged it off.

Or she could tell the truth.

Gloria went to the sideboard and opened the deep drawer. When she did, she smelled gas. She might forever smell gas. Gloria brought out her photo album. She would rearrange the pictures. The wedding pictures were on the same two pages. Grandmother, mother, sister, Gloria, each wearing the same wedding gown. Gloria had written names and dates under each photograph. There would be one more photograph to add.

She would write Amanda, Saturday, 20 September, 1969 to Frederick Harding at St Michael and All Angels, Brackerley.

Paul brought two bowls of soup to the table.

It was not yet dark, but the curtains were drawn, out of respect.

'Come on, Mam,' Paul said. 'We're going to have this soup. You haven't eaten.'

'I don't want to.'

'You must.'

They sat down. Gloria picked up her spoon, surprised to be hungry. She had meant to eat at the wedding and couldn't remember why she forgot.

They finished the soup in silence.

'I found Dad's note,' Paul said.

'The police showed it to me,' said Gloria. 'It was in his suit top pocket. Said he was sorry.'

'Not that note.' Paul picked up the soup dishes and took them to the sink. 'I knew he'd leave a note for me. It was in the toe of my old wellington boot in the shed. It might have been there a long time.' He unfolded a sheet of blue writing paper and placed it on the table. The paper had been folded into six. It opened like a concertina.

Gloria looked at the note, but Paul was not sure that his mother's eyes would tell her brain the words, and so he read the note to her. It said, 'Steven we are proud of you. Go on doing well. Paul we are proud of you. Look after your mam. Gloria, sorry I let you down in the end. You did your best. Love, love, love. Xxx'

And Paul said to himself, *it's me. He's telling me. He wouldn't tell Steven, to look after Mam. There'd be no point.* After pouring them glasses of brandy, Paul said, 'Tell me. I have to know what was up. I've always known there was something the matter, something wrong.' When Gloria stopped crying, when she could speak, she said, 'He meant to write more. He wouldn't have used a sheet of writing paper for so few lines.' That was not the whole truth. Gloria could see this note was old, had been in the toe of the wellington boot too long. It must date from a time when he was about to take his life, and then changed his mind. They should have spent more time at the seaside. That might have made a difference.

Twenty-Eight

For Amanda nothing felt real. When Dr Hampshire came to the house she had changed into her blue dress and sandals for the journey to the coast. Dr Hampshire asked to use the bathroom, and for Amanda and her stepmother to meet him in their sitting room in a few minutes. By the end of those few minutes, the vicar was also there, and then a plain-clothes sergeant called Angela; Amanda knew it was bad when the vicar asked for Penny and Fred to be present.

This day should have been so different. The day she had imagined, and expected, forced its way into her thoughts. Dad had said Fred could drive to Scarborough in his car, which was a big deal. Uncle Norman had serviced the car and filled the tank. When Amanda asked, 'What about me driving?' Dad had put both their names on the insurance. Frederick and Amanda Harding.

Now here they were, she and Penny, with this plain-clothes police sergeant called Angela, and they agreed to whatever she said, about a room for interview and a room where inter-viewees might change their shoes, which would be required for examination. Nothing made sense, except glasses of brandy poured by the doctor.

Where was Uncle Norman? Where was Auntie Gloria? Amanda had heard the announcement for Auntie Gloria to go to the marquee where Paul was waiting for her. Amanda hadn't seen Paul since she left the church.

Penny went upstairs to put on a black dress and a mournful face.

Later, it was Penny who said that they ought to go out, go to the marquee where there were so many people gathering, and police. Penny said they could not send people away without the right word and that the vicar thought it would encourage people to help the police. Lance would want them to do the right thing.

Fred agreed with Penny about doing the right thing. That would encourage people to come forward. Amanda said nothing. She did not know how there could be a right thing, and the police were not letting anyone go anyway. Afterwards, she would think she had done as they said because she'd slid into a waking nightmare.

Angela stayed with Penny and Amanda, talking to them, saying she was sorry to be asking just a few questions. A constable talked to Fred, Bob and Tim in the library.

Bob and Tim went across to the marquee first. Tim took his guitar. Did he think someone would come into the house and steal it? Amanda's head felt split in two, one side blank and disbelieving, the other side saying why, why? Why would anyone hurt Dad, why can't we see him? And there was that part of her that would not go away, that voice in her head saying, I am too old to be an orphan child, too young to be without parents.

As she, Fred and Penny came from the house, Fred took Amanda's hand. Penny made a tight grab on Amanda's arm, saying she did not know if she could do this.

Amanda said, 'You suggested it.'

'No I didn't.'

The walk to the marquee felt weird to Amanda, as if she were floating, then suddenly she feared the marquee. What if the ground opened and swallow her?

Bob was by the entrance. Tim was tuning his guitar. A plain clothes man ushered them in.

You will go in, you will go in, you will go in.

No, Amanda wanted to say. *Let it be before. Whisk today away. Let it be yesterday.*

The light in the marquee seemed filtered and soft, shutting out the harshness of a sunny Saturday. The place hushed, as if everyone in there held their breath. So many. She did not know one big tent could hold so many. She remembered the smell of a circus, sweat, straw, animals and fear. Here, the smell was trampled grass, beer and icing-sugared wedding cake.

Penny whispered, 'I can't do it.' She who wanted the right word to be said now had no words at all. Penny nudged Amanda. 'You speak.'

People's faces were big and tight, they would not look away. Amanda sensed rather than saw Bob staying close to Penny. Tim stayed put with his guitar. He began to play the George Harrison song, 'While My Guitar Gently Weeps'. Over the music was such silence as Amanda had never heard.

Waitresses stopped picking up plates of half-eaten food, empty cups, empty glasses.

Some guests openly stared at them. Fred was squeezing

Amanda's hand too tightly. They had agreed that Penny would speak. It was Fred who had said, 'Best let it come from Penny.'

Amanda wondered how Fred suddenly knew what to do. But she supposed he was right, and Penny had agreed.

Now, Penny looked at her feet and gave the slightest shake of her head to confirm that she was too distraught to speak.

For now, silence from Penny did not matter, because of Tim and his guitar. Amanda was suddenly aware of the ring on her finger. Chelsea Register Office popped into her head. If they had married there, might her dad still be alive?

A child wriggled out of the tent flap. Amanda saw an arm encased in a police blue jacket sleeve push the child back. The mother scooped it up.

They had come across to the marquee because Mrs Grieves, the vicar's wife, backed Penny's idea, assuring Amanda that it was the right thing to do – if she felt up to it – and no one wanted to leave until they saw the bride and groom once more.

Fred did a slight clearing of his throat, as if to remind Amanda of the silence and expectation. 'Shall I?' he whispered, without moving his lips.

'No.' Amanda squeezed Fred's hand, and then let go.

She let her hands slide across the smooth fabric of her dress and kept them by her side to steady herself. She wanted to run. She wanted to be out of here.

The words 'Be brave' came into her head, her mother's words. Be brave, the last words she remembered her mother saying.

Amanda looked around the marquee for a familiar face, so that she could pretend that was the only one she must speak

181

to. She looked for Auntie Gloria, Uncle Norman, or Paul. She settled on her best friend from school.

'Thank you from me and Fred and Dad and Penny, for being at my wedding. Dad didn't let us listen to him rehearse, so I first heard his speech when you did. You'll know that he mentioned my mother, whom some of you remember, and my stepmother, Penny, who brought songs and smiles into Dad's life, and Auntie Gloria who looked after me when Mum died, and who has been here for me always, along with Uncle Norman and Paul and Steven, who are like family. Some of you know that my wedding dress was Auntie Gloria's. I'm proud to have had the loan of it, and to have Fred beside me. I can't say more about Dad as I can't believe he's not here.' She looked at the marquee entrance, and really did expect to see him.

Fred put an arm around Amanda and hugged her. Amanda didn't want to be hugged, not here. But a person must remember her manners. She said, 'Our world has turned upside down and inside out today, so we are glad that you came to give us your love and support. We return your love and wish you a safe journey home. I can't take in what I'm told has happened to my dad. But I know that the police want to speak to you. Please help the police.'

As if Penny suddenly realised they were done, she gave a little wave, as if from a royal car passing at five miles an hour, and said, 'God bless you all. Safe journey home, everyone. Don't forget your slice of cake.'

As Amanda and Fred left the marquee, a police officer was telling people to remain seated.

Amanda strode across the lawn. She would have broken into a run, but Fred gripped her hand too tightly.

She was five years old. She had clambered on the bed, although someone – a nurse, or Auntie Gloria? – had told her not to. Her mother had hugged Amanda and said, 'You're a big girl now. Be brave. Auntie Gloria loves you. She will take care of you.'

So her mother must have expected to die. Amanda could understand that now. But Mummy went on living until she crossed the road without looking right, left and right again.

A speeding motorist knocked her mother down. It was thought she would mend. Amanda heard them talking. They talked about a blood clot on Mummy's brain. They told Amanda Mummy had gone to heaven. Where was Mummy going on the day she was knocked down? Amanda now wondered. Perhaps she was going to collect me from Auntie Gloria's.

Amanda knew that buses went everywhere. She asked what bus they would catch. Buses going everywhere turned out to be a lie. Buses did not go to heaven.

At the door, Fred released his grip on Amanda's hand. She glanced back. Bob was linking Penny's arm, as if for support. Amanda frowned. 'Fred, tell Bob and Penny to lay off.'

'It's not like that.'

'Oh, come off it. Tell him to lay off or clear off.' Amanda hurried along the hall. She ran up the stairs to her room, calling, 'I'm going to lie down and I'm shutting the door.'

Fred came up the stairs after her.

'I need to be on my own.'

Amanda closed the curtains. She put a chair behind the door, tilted so the back was under the doorknob. She kicked off her shoes and disappeared under the eiderdown.

What if Dad had left this house to Penny? Amanda had

told Dad she didn't want the house. She knew it would be a millstone around her neck, as it was around his.

Amanda would have no home. Penny and Bob would take over.

Perhaps that was what Penny had planned. Penny was not clever, but knew which side her bread was buttered. Bob was clever.

Tim stayed by the marquee, playing his guitar, singing almost to himself, until uniformed constables came. He and Bob had been spoken to briefly, given their details to a uniformed officer, and told they may be interviewed again later.

Tim expected their tour would be cancelled, but it would be Fred who had the say-so. The plain-clothes man in a black-leather jacket said. 'Ladies and gentlemen, I'm Detective Inspector Ian Dennis. Thank you for your patience. Please remain seated while officers come round to speak to you. The WPC here' – he turned to a woman in uniform who raised her hand – 'along with Tim, who plays the guitar and has volunteered to help, will escort mothers and young children to the summerhouse.'

Twenty-Nine

Police constables worked their way around the marquee, taking details from wedding guests. As Nell moved towards the catering table, she heard some of the questions: Name, address, telephone number. Do you have the formal invitation? Who were you with, who did you see, at what time and where? Did you take photographs?

Nell turned her attention to her catering team. Linda, usually clockwork precise, wound to a halt. Kit had to encourage her to take a drink of tea. Cherry soldiered on. Diane had combed her hair and washed her face. She looked anxious, as well she might after her disappearing act. Nell would keep her here for now. All would return to the prison together after police interviews.

As Nell was about to speak to Kit, a WPC approached. 'Miss Lewis?'

'Yes.'

'Ma'am, Sergeant Ambrose requests to speak to you. She has two rooms available for witness interviews and is ready to begin when you are. She has the library, second on the right as you go in the manor house, a cloakroom with changing facilities on the other side.'

'You'll need the women's clothes and shoes for forensics?'

'Yes, ma'am.'

Arriving at short notice, and probably from different directions, Nell knew the police would not have all their usual equipment. 'I sent for prison clothing sacks, shoe bags, and a change of clothing. Take these for the cloakroom.' Nell handed the WPC bags of overalls and plimsolls and the clothing and shoe sacks. 'I'll follow you shortly. Tell the sergeant that I need to bring Linda to the cloakroom to change. I'll bring her first.'

That would be better than Linda sitting at the farthest point of the marquee, hoping not to be noticed.

The chief was by the entrance to the marquee. When the constable had gone, Nell asked her to take over.

'That's why I'm here, ma'am. I saw you give the prisoners' change of clothes to the WPC.'

Nell noticed that it would take the chief a while longer to remember to call prisoners residents.

Nell gave the nod to Kit. 'Time to talk to Sergeant Ambrose, Kit.'

Not surprisingly, Kit looked a little sheepish.

'I know I should have kept a closer eye on Diane, ma'am. We had breaks morning and afternoon, and she was back on the dot from her morning break. She's saying that this afternoon, she was completely overcome by the urge to go home.'

At this moment Nell felt the same, but her home was still the top floor of the prison.

Kit said, 'Diane owned up when she came back, that she'd thumbed a lift, meaning it to be just a quick visit. Apparently, she thought she could be home in an hour and that her sister's boyfriend would drive her back.'

Calmly, Nell asked, 'How do you know this?'

'Florence told me when she brought Diane back. And they brought back an old lady in a wheelchair. She's by the side of the bar, with a glass of brandy. She's saying she's all right to stand now if someone will find her walking stick.'

'Who is she?'

'I heard one of the drinkers at the bar call her Susan. She says her knee clicked back in place. She held onto the bar and swung her leg a bit, but I think that was the brandy. She's back in the chair.'

'And where is Florence?'

'Florence went to the summerhouse and took her first aid bag. One of the mothers was upset about her child climbing into a plant pot that cracked. Florence says it never ceases to surprise her how quickly a child can recover if they have a decent sticking plaster plonked in the right place.'

'And Diane?'

'Collecting plates.'

'Kit, Diane has just attempted to abscond for the second time. Collect Diane. Do not let her out of your sight. Keep her in the marquee until the chief officer takes over. Sergeant Ambrose is about to start witness interviews.'

Kit lowered her voice. 'Cherry said there was a serious incident. I thought she was having me on.'

'Everyone is entitled to have someone with them during the interview.'

'Ma'am, I should like you to come in with me to my interview. And I think I did one thing right.'

'Oh?'

187

'When Cherry told me about an incident, I said none of them should speak about it.'

'That was a good move.'

Nell knocked on the manor house door. It was opened by the WPC who had taken the bags of button-through overalls and footwear.

Once she and Kit were inside the manor house, Nell caught the familiar whiff of lavender polish. A mixed bunch of flowers in a Chinese vase had shed petals on the inlaid mahogany table.

They passed the door to the drawing room where she guessed the family may have gathered, but there was an air of deathly quiet.

The cloakroom reminded Nell of cloakrooms in the ballrooms and clubs where she once went to Saturday night dances.

There was a counter for the passing across of coats. Beyond that were coat rails. The hangers rattled on the rail as the WPC hung the grey overalls that the women would change into. Nell raised the counter and walked through. Plimsolls were already on a shelf, neatly placed in order of size. The whole business made Nell's spirits sink. This was to have been such a glorious day.

Nell turned to Kit. 'It's a precaution, changing into plimsolls and overalls, important for Diane and Linda who walked up the path and behind the marquee. Did you go across to the Portakabin by way of the path, Kit?'

'I did.'

'There may be no trace, it's been a dry day, but let's take the precaution.'

Nell handed her shoes to the WPC for labelling. 'These are what I was wearing when I went round the back of the marquee.'

Sergeant Angela Ambrose was waiting for them in the library. Kit went into the library first, to give her name and ask that the governor sit in with her.

Nell followed and took the vacant seat in a reassuringly solid captain's chair. The room was quiet and had the soothing air that libraries acquire over time. After the madness of the marquee and the busyness of the day, Nell was suddenly in no hurry for the interview to begin. She welcomed a pause.

Angela thanked Nell for arranging the change of clothing and footwear for residents.

'What about officers' clothing?' Nell asked.

'Orders are to examine only residents' clothing. After that, we'll be guided by scene of crime findings.'

Nell spoke to Kit. 'Kit, I'm here simply as an observer. It's Sergeant Ambrose who'll be asking the questions.'

Angela leaned forward and picked up a pen. 'Tell me, Kit – may I call you Kit?'

'Yes.'

'Kit, do any of your catering team know the Chapins?'

'Only by sight, from church and the summer fête. There might be a nod or a smile.'

The police want to eliminate the residents, thought Nell. None knew the victim or had a motive for wanting Mr Chapin dead but, prisoners being prisoners, members of the public might point a finger. Experience indicated that whoever killed Mr Chapin was someone close to him.

Angela placed a polaroid photograph on the table, a wedding group. 'Did you see Mr Chapin today, Kit?'

'This morning. He came in to say hello and jolly us along with a few cheery words. Oh, and he took a pastry. He didn't need to come in again because we took a tray across to their table, close to the manor house.'

Angela showed Kit a photograph. 'Did anyone from this photograph come into the marquee?'

Kit looked at the photograph that Angela put on the table. It was of the Chapins, the bride and groom, along with Gloria and Norman Thwaite.

'Other than Mr Chapin, Mrs Chapin came into the marquee before she went to the wedding, to say hello and how smart we all looked. I met Mrs Thwaite when the governor and I went to the manor house to discuss doing the catering. I know a call was put out for her to come and meet her son. I saw him waiting but I must have been doing something else when Mrs Thwaite came in.' Kit looked again at the photograph and pointed to Norman, 'If that's Mr Thwaite, well he was one of the first in when people were walking back from the wedding.'

'Did you happen to notice the time?'

'He was here well before the speeches started at one o'clock. I remember him because he looked so sad.' She thought for a moment. 'He went to listen to the speeches. I didn't see him again after that.'

Angela made a note. 'What time did Diane go on her break?'

Kit looked suddenly glum. 'Two o'clock. She was meant to be back at two fifteen and she wasn't. I let myself be sidetracked. A guest came in and was asking about the wedding cake and about the best recipe for egg custard. There wasn't an immediate rush for food and before I realised, it was half past. Linda had put herself in charge of the urn and was nearest the far tent flap. I asked her to go see if Diane was all right because she'd complained of stomach cramps earlier. Then there was just me and Cherry on the counter.'

'And what time did you send Linda to look for Diane?'

'Oh, dead on half past two, as soon as I checked my watch.' Kit blushed. 'Because of Diane's stomach cramps, I thought she might be still in the toilet.'

Angela nodded with real or well-feigned sympathy. 'She might have been.'

'But she wasn't.'

'Kit, you mentioned that Norman Thwaite went to hear the speeches at one o'clock.'

'Yes.'

'Did you see him again? I'm wondering who else was around about that time, in the run-up to Diane going on her break. Do you think Norman listened to all the speeches?'

'He may have done. But after the speeches the band played two numbers before handing over to the DJ. Around that time some guests, men mostly, came up for the bar. Norman wasn't among them, but he knew the bar staff. I saw him talking to them earlier.'

'Thank you, Miss Kitteringham.' Angela put down her pen. 'Is there anything you want to ask me?'

'No, Sergeant.'

Having walked back with the Thwaites, Nell was curious about the interest in Norman.

When Kit had gone, Nell said, 'I walked back with the Thwaites from the church.'

Angela thought for a moment.

'How did they strike you? Mr and Mrs Thwaite I mean.'

What is Angela trying to decide, Nell wondered. 'Mrs Thwaite was chatty. Norman kept step with us for a while and then strode on, saying he'd see us at the reception. They just seemed a normal couple.'

'Ma'am, as you know, Norman Thwaite went home from the reception and committed suicide. The call to Willow Lane meant I was close by and first on the scene. The Thwaites' son Paul came hurrying down Willow Lane to see who was outside their house.'

'What a shock for Paul, and his mother,' said Nell, 'and what a hard task for you, to come from a suicide to a murder.'

'Of course, it doesn't mean there's any connection,' said Angela.

'No.' Two such dreadful events seemed to Nell too shocking to be unrelated, and at the same time too shocking to be connected, especially in a quiet place like Brackerley.

Angela said, 'I'll be creating a timeline. If there's anything you can tell me about your walk back from the church with the Thwaites, please do.'

They sat in silence for a moment while Nell thought back.

'I met Mrs Thwaite at the Chapins. She's their daily housekeeper and seems very close to the family. Today, on the walk back from the church, Mrs Thwaite was concerned about Norman when he went off on his own, even though she said he did that a lot. When she spoke, it felt like something deeper than becoming separated. A photographer was taking pictures of Amanda and Fred. Mrs Thwaite thought she saw Norman standing close by, not as he is now but as he was as a young man. It could have been a trick of the light, or a half-forgotten memory, but it was odd, that's all I can say.'

'Is there anything else?' Angela placed her hands on the table, almost unconsciously pushing the notebook and pen out of the way.

Nell shook her head. 'I wish there were something else, apart from the one big question mark over why Lancelot Chapin would leave his family and his guests and disappear behind the marquee. And who could be so full of anger, hatred or fear that they would kill him so brutally?'

'That's what we'll try to find out.' Angela put away her notebook. 'Is this a good time for me to talk to Linda? Let her give her account again, and get it over with?'

'It might be more helpful to allow her some recovery time.' Nell sighed. 'I'd rather anyone else at all had found Lance Chapin on that bench.'

'Then let's give Linda a while longer. Mrs Grieves came to talk to me. She said a girl at the podium, Shelley, was waiting to sing. According to Shelley, her friend Brendan was at a protestors' meeting and heard of a plan to murder Mr Chapin if he didn't withdraw sale of the land. Do you know either Shelley or Brendan?'

Nell shook her head. 'I don't know them, though I've heard about Brendan. He helps at the farm on Saturdays, so the Ramsdens at the farm will know him. I haven't come across Shelley.'

'Okay. Thanks. I caught up with Brendan briefly, in the marquee, eating cake. No signs that he'd done anything but eat all day. Chocolate sponge on his shirt. He doesn't appear to have the strength to stab a grown man. According to the Hare and Hounds landlady, who knows him well, he's a cheeky chappie whose main interest was in taking home a bag of buns. The special constable will speak to him and let me know if there's anything more than a bit of bravado and bragging but I feel confident we'll be ruling him out.'

Thirty

Diane was most willing to cooperate with the police. She had said yes to having the governor sitting in on her interview with Police Sergeant Ambrose – not that she thought she needed her, but it was a way of giving the governor the simple facts. The main simple fact was that Diane had been overwhelmed by the need to go home. She had once heard someone call the plain-clothes policewoman Angela, but she wouldn't call her that. You had to stay on the right side of them, show some respect. The sergeant seemed quite human, but she didn't look as if she had kids. The easy questions came first. Diane gave her name, date of birth, her address as HMP Brackerley and her home address as her mother's. 'We had the house next door, I kept it on as long as I could pay the rent but after my husband's trawler went down and he was lost at sea, nothing was the same. It was very hard for us, very hard for the children.'

'Yes,' said Angela. 'You suffered a tragic loss.'

Diane waited for her to say that it was understandable that a mother wanted to go home to see her kids.

Angela said, 'I'm here to investigate a crime, the murder

of Mr Chapin. You may be able to help and that's why I'll ask you a few questions. I need to know where people were and what time, and whether anything they saw or heard, which might seem insignificant, may help in our enquiries.'

'Okay.' Diane sniffed. She took out her hanky.

'Diane, what time did you go on your break this afternoon?' Angela asked.

'Two o'clock.'

'What did you do on your break?'

'Went to the Portakabin, to the loo, washed my hands, combed my hair.'

'And then?'

'Walked to the end of the path, came back.'

'Did you go from the path to the grounds, among the wedding guests?'

'No. Didn't want to. I only stopped there a minute, listening to the music, the DJ. I'd been on my feet all morning. I fancied a sit-down and a smoke, so I went round the back of the marquee and sat on the bench.'

'Could you still hear the music?'

'Oh yeah, I could still hear the music.'

'Do you remember what was playing?'

'Yeah. "Cupid", Johnny Nash. You know, "Cupid draw back your bow". Then it was "Aquarius / Let the Sunshine In" and then it was—' Her face crumpled. She began to cry, and couldn't speak for a moment.

'It were The Doors, "Hello, I Love You", our song. Mine and the kids. It was like they were calling to me.'

Angela smiled sympathetically. 'Diane you're doing really well. Take a moment. Have a sip of water. Excuse me.' She went to the door.

Diane continued crying, blowing her nose loudly and, Nell thought, glancing at Nell to see if the governor clocked how distressed she was. Nell heard Angela say to the WPC, 'I need the DJ's playlist, with timings.' Angela returned to her seat. She waited until Diane had composed herself. 'What happened then, after you'd listened to The Doors?'

'I finished my smoke as I listened. It wasn't even a full smoke. It was half a Senior Service. I could picture Ruby and Albert dancing, and then it was if they were calling me. I had to move. I couldn't sit still, and then I was walking towards the road, and I thought, I could be there and back in under two hours, just say, hello, I love you, and I'd be back to help with the clearing up in the marquee.'

'Diane, my main reason for wanting to hear your account of events is because I am investigating a crime,' Angela continued. 'The area where you were sitting is a crime scene. A man was found dead there.'

'Mr Chapin.'

'Yes.'

'Well I'm sorry about that but he wasn't there when I was. I'd have spoken to him, or said something.'

'Did you see anyone else in that area behind the marquee?'

'No.'

'That area is where the crime took place. I need to know what traces you might have left. That is why we needed to have your uniform and your shoes. Tell me, did you smoke your half a cigarette to the end?'

'Yes.'

'And then?'

Diane looked puzzled. 'Well, that was it. My last cig.'

Patiently, Angela said 'What about your tab end?'

'Well, I just dropped the tab end, stepped on it – wouldn't want to set the grass on fire, pushed it under the bench with the toe of my shoe so as not to be untidy.'

'And then what did you do?'

'Went on to the end of the marquee and across the grass and kept going.'

'Earlier, in the Portakabin, on the path, or on the grass, did you see Mr Chapin?'

'No.'

'Did you see anyone else, a stranger, or someone who was familiar to you, or appeared to be acting suspiciously?'

'No, definitely not. I wasn't taking notice of anyone else, except a woman putting lipstick on in the Portakabin. It was pale pink, a colour you might as well not bother with.'

'You noticed no one else on the path behind the marquee, as you left?' Angela asked.

'That path's a narrow space. If there'd been anyone else, I would've bumped into them. I was thinking of my kids. I didn't even realise the nurse was chasing me until she kept calling my name. I'm sorry the nurse had to run after me, and carry her shoes, and ruin her tights and lose the wedding bouquet and flag down a van that overtook dangerously so as to bring me back.'

Diane sniffed and wiped her nose.

'Thank you, Diane,' Angela said gently. 'Your statement will be typed for your signature. If you think of anything else, please tell Miss Lewis.'

Kit was waiting in the hall.

'Take Diane back to the marquee, Officer Kitteringham,' said Nell. 'Ask the chief officer to come across.'

Nell waited as Diane was escorted back to the marquee, and the chief officer appeared. Nell said, 'Chief, looks as if people still want refreshments. Keep an eye on Diane. If she can get on with her work, fine. Otherwise, take her back to the house.'

'Punishment cell?'

'Yes.'

Nell felt a huge surge of disappointment. Diane had done so well. She would have been set to have a responsible job on release.

Thirty-One

Nell was with Linda in the manor house cloakroom, seated on the long bench by the wall. 'I'd rather get it over with,' she had said when Nell asked her if she felt up to being interviewed by Sergeant Ambrose or needed a little more time. 'There's not a lot else I can say, but I'd like you to come in with me.' Gone was her smart waitress outfit, now bagged up to go to forensics.

The grey button-through prison stock cotton overall hung loose on her. The pumps were a size too big, with gapes at the heels. It saddened Nell to see Brackerley's top-notch catering team as a poor copy of their earlier selves. That diminishment ought to have paled into oblivion beside the horror of murder, and yet it was a knockback and made Nell's heart heavy. As soon as they stepped into the hall, Linda said, 'Ma'am, I don't feel up to it. I've turned to jelly. I feel sick.'

'Do you need a drink or the toilet?'

'I want to lie down in a dark place.'

'I know you don't feel up to this, Linda, no one would, but it must be done and so you were right to want it over with.

Sergeant Ambrose simply wants your account of what you saw today.'

'Sergeant Ambrose?'

'Yes. Sergeant Angela Ambrose.'

Linda remembers, thought Nell. Knowing who she will speak to makes her less anxious. Linda was able to provide important information in the enquiry into Major Harding's death.

'You will stay with me?'

'Yes.'

'I feel as if my legs might go from under me. I feel as if – oh I don't know.'

They paused at the library door. 'This won't take long. The sergeant is gathering facts, that's all. You are here as a witness. When we go into the library, I recommend that you sit in the captain's chair.'

'What's a captain's chair?'

'You'll know it when you see it. It's made of wood and has arms.'

'Oh, I know. I didn't know they were called that.'

Sergeant Ambrose looked up as they entered.

'Miss Rogers, thank you for coming in to assist with our enquiries. Do take a seat.'

Nell drew out the captain's chair and nodded to Linda, who sat down. Nell sat a few feet away in a straight back chair.

Sergeant Ambrose picked up a pen. 'Hello, Linda. May I call you Linda?'

'Yes.'

'I'm Sergeant Ambrose.'

'I know,' Linda said. 'I remember you.'

'Linda, we are investigating the death of Mr Lancelot Chapin. Did you know Mr Chapin?'

'No.'

'Had you ever seen him before?'

'I'd seen him in church on Sundays, but I don't usually pay attention to people I don't know. This morning, when we were setting up, he came into the marquee and spoke to Miss Kit and then to us, saying what a good job we'd done and making a joke saying, don't eat all the food before the guests arrive.'

'Will you tell me, for the record, what you were doing today?'

Linda felt confident about saying the kind of thing she might write in her diary. 'We were up early this morning, to prepare the food, like the salad and the fruit salad. Some food was in the manor house pantry from yesterday. We were here at nine. The tables were already up. We put on the big tablecloths and set out plates and cutlery, wiped down the smaller tables for the guests, put the food out, covered it. Miss Kit had filled the urns for tea and coffee. We took a break. A few people came in early for a drink and a pastry before they walked to the church. It got busy after the wedding, from about quarter past twelve. We kept the jugs of soft drinks topped up. Kept dishes topped up. Guests picked up a plate and said or pointed to what they wanted. We served, with spoons or tongs.'

'Was there anyone there that you recognised, among the guests?'

'I didn't look at them. I didn't want them to look at me.'

'Why is that?'

'I didn't want to be here today, in case anyone recognised me and remembered my crime.' Linda looked up. 'After what happened today, they will say, she killed a man. He frightened

202

her and she reacted. Or they will say, there is such a thing as lust for killing. It's in her to murder.'

Nell glanced at Linda who seemed to gasp for breath. As far as Nell knew, this was the first time Linda had spoken of her crime since the day of her father's funeral.

Sergeant Ambrose spoke quietly. 'Linda, that is not how I am thinking. When police say a person is helping with enquiries, more often than not it does mean exactly that. You are here as a witness, an important witness because you had the misfortune to see Mr Chapin's body and the courage to report it. My questions are routine, to establish facts.' Angela allowed a pause.

'Did you have any interaction with Mr Chapin?'

'None. He was walking about while we were setting up. I didn't want to be at the reception. I usually muck out the pigs on Saturdays. That was what I wanted to do.'

'But you were allocated to the wedding reception?'

'As part of my rehabilitation. I wish Diane had come back from her break or that I wasn't the one to be sent looking for her.'

'But Miss Kitteringham sent you to find Diane?'

'Yes. I suppose because I was nearest the tent flap.'

'When you went to look for Diane, did you see any other person on the path or in the vicinity?'

'No one on the path, and no one until Cherry saw me. I don't think I was seeing anything. I was just being sick.'

'You said you didn't see anyone among the guests that you recognised. Was there anyone you recognised who wasn't a guest?'

'Yes. A lad who helps out at the farm. Brendan. He came in a couple of times on his own and then with a girl, helping themselves to food.'

'Did you talk to each other?'

Linda sighed. 'He said they'd come with their banner, which the girl made. It's a protest banner about the meadows and someone at the gate had taken it from them and sent them away. They came back. He said if Mr Chapin kicks the bucket, Mrs Chapin and Amanda won't sell the meadows. Amanda definitely won't. He asked if we'd poisoned the food. He is an annoying boy. Mrs Ramsden says he's all show, all mouth and too young for long trousers. He made a gun with his fingers and pointed, kidding on that he saw Mr Chapin—'

'When was this?'

'Just before one o'clock.'

'Tell me how you came to leave the marquee.'

'Miss Kitteringham asked me to look for Diane because Diane had said she was going to the toilet, and she was gone ages.'

'What time was that?'

'Diane went at two, for fifteen minutes. I was sent to look for her at half past two.'

'When you went to look for Diane, where did you look first?'

'In the Portakabin.'

'Did you take anything in with you?'

'No.'

'A bag?'

'I didn't have a bag, just a hanky. We'd been issued white gloves, but I left mine on the table.'

'Had you been in the Portakabin before?'

'Yes, earlier that morning.'

'Describe to me what you did when you went to look for Diane.'

'I went through the tent flap across to the Portakabin. I went in the door marked Ladies. Two lavs were engaged. I called Diane's name. I pushed the unlocked door and there was no one there. Two women came out, not Diane. I called her name again. I thought it'd be like her to go into the gents if the Ladies was engaged. That's when I turned and walked as far as the washbasins. It's not straight along, part of the structure drops back. From outside, it looks like a double box shape. There are wash basins in between the Gents and the Ladies. I went past the washbasins and the roller towels. A bloke came out and gave me a funny look. I felt an idiot. Diane had gone for a smoke, obviously, that's what I thought.'

'And what next?'

'I came out of the Portakabin and walked up the path to where I'd seen a bench when we looked round this morning. That's when I saw the body, a man on a bench with a knife in him and blood on his shirt.'

'What did you do?'

'Nothing. I thought it was a trick, or I was seeing things, but he was real. I backed away. I thought someone would come. I wanted to call for help but I couldn't. And then, he moved, kind of slid down towards the arm of the bench, and that's when I turned, back down the path, to the end, and all the time, thinking someone was behind me, to grab me, but nobody was. Just me. And I can still feel on my back as if there's someone there.'

'Was there anything else about him that you noticed?'

'That it was Mr Chapin, from the red face, and from the ring on his little finger with a diamond.'

The sergeant was writing, and then looking at Linda. 'Can you describe the knife?'

'It had a bone handle, or else one of those handles that looks like a bone handle. It was stuck in him, somewhere in or near his heart.'

'Had you seen a knife like that before?'

'Yes. We have them at the prison.'

'Do you happen to know whether the knives you brought with you today are all accounted for?'

'I don't know. After I saw the body, I didn't know anything.'

'What did you do next?'

'Like I said, turned and went back, not the way I'd come out of the side flap. I couldn't go back into the marquee because I knew it would be written all over me, what I'd seen, and I'd been sick on myself. At the end of the path, I looked across the lawn. I saw the governor talking to a couple.'

'What about Diane, the person you went looking for?'

'All I know is that she wasn't there, but Cherry saw me, and she took me to sit on the ground behind the Portakabin and said I had to be cleaned up, I had sick on me, and I said no, just leave it. I asked for her to tell the governor.'

'Thank you, Linda. You've been very helpful. If you think of anything else at all, please tell one of your officers.'

Linda could not say any more, her mouth felt too dry. Outside, Nell said, 'You did very well, Linda.'

Linda still couldn't speak. In any case, she would not have said what was on her mind because it felt like a broken record. She had thought they would blame her. She killed once, she'll kill again. People might pooh-pooh that, but she knew different. She'd learned stuff in Holloway. People who killed might kill again. She'd learned stuff working at the farm. The gardener's grandson was rearing geese for Christmas. He boasted about how good he was at killing them. He liked to shoot.

Rabbits, she understood that. Rabbits went in a stew. He shot birds, and squirrels, before they knew what was coming. He hated Mr Chapin. The grandson was a nasty piece of work or else he made a good show of being the tough guy. No one else thought him dangerous, but Linda did. She knew danger when it reared its head. He'll kill someone, she thought. Perhaps he already had. That was not up to her. That was up to the police. But what if he did kill someone, and she hadn't said?

Linda was glad that Miss Lewis was walking her back because her legs had turned to jelly. Nothing was real. She wanted to be away from this place back to the safety of the prison. Next, it would be Cherry's turn to be questioned.

Thirty-Two

While Sergeant Angela Ambrose waited for the constable to bring the next witness into the library, she set out the polaroid photographs on a table. They were numbered on the back in pencil. A few sticky fingermarks gave the hint that the photographs had already been shown to people at the tables in the marquee. Probably every other copper had already gathered names. The photos all had that slightly pale colour, like a hint that the image would not last as long as the oldest person in it.

There was a knock on the library door.

The young WPC had taken a few steps back from the door and stood in the centre of the hall. She said, 'Sergeant, prisoner Cherry Davenport is in the cloakroom changing. She's made a bit of a fuss.'

'What about?'

'Being asked to take off her waitress outfit and put on the button-through overall. Said she'd rather be naked. She asked if she can be taken back to the prison in a van with blacked-out windows. She said there are people here who know her, and she would rather curl up and die than be seen in workhouse uniform.'

'Don't let her die before the interview. Let her wait for a while.' She beckoned the constable. 'Take a look at these photographs. Tell me if you can put names to faces.'

Angela had acquired a list of wedding guests from the prison catering officer. From a brief chat with the Hare and Hounds landlady, she could make a few connections. Who played golf, who drank with whom on Friday nights.

The WPC tried her best with the photographs. She knew the auntie and uncle of one of the bridesmaids.

'Go back to Cherry Davenport,' Angela said. 'Say that Sergeant Ambrose is ready to see her now. If she's still kicking off, be very polite and say that we'll see what we can do about her clothing.'

'What can we do?' asked the constable.

'Nothing. But we would if we could.'

Angela had realised who Cherry was, and why she would not like wearing a grey button-through overall.

Looking out of the window, she could see that interviews were still going on in the marquee. It was quite likely that some drafted-in special constable would be asking the killer question and make a breakthrough while she, Angela-first-on-the-scene, sat interviewing prisoners who were among the most observed people here and who had no motive whatsoever to kill a man they did not know.

What did keep niggling away at Angela was Norman Thwaite's suicide. It seemed to her that there must absolutely be a connection, but what?

There was a tap on the door. Angela called 'come in'. She

turned to see the constable leading a stylish figure, with beautifully cut dark hair, wearing a gorgeous kaftan.

'Sergeant, I have the next witness,' said the constable.

Angela recognised Cherry Davenport straightaway. She had been featured in all the fashion magazines Angela enjoyed reading, or at least looking at the pictures and marking them out of ten, with ten as ridiculous or unwearable, while occasionally seeing an outfit she marked with a one, two or three that she might ask her mother to run up for her. She had also been into the boutique in Harrogate where Cherry worked on a Saturday. There had been a dress for sale, designed by Cherry, priced at considerably more than Angela earned in a week.

'Hello, Miss Davenport. Please take a seat.'

'Thank you.' Cherry lowered herself into the chair, resting her arms.

'I'm Sergeant Ambrose.' Angela picked up her pen. 'Would you confirm your full name and address?'

'Cheryl Patricia Davenport. Please call me Cherry. Everyone does. I have no address other than the prison. The rental agreement on my flat expired.'

'Do you wish to have another person present while we conduct the interview?'

'Thank you, but no.'

Oh good, thought Angela. I can get on with this.

Angela would not ask her how she came to have exchanged a grey cotton button-through overall for this designer kaftan, or whether she had nipped upstairs and borrowed an outfit from Amanda or Penny Chapin's wardrobe.

Cherry was confident, with a friendly manner, one of those people who would be noticed. She had that something indefinable that Angela thought must be what they called 'presence' or 'charisma'. Angela wished she had it, though such qualities might be superfluous for a police officer.

Oh, that sergeant was hopeless. She asked every question twice and tripped over the murder weapon. But so very charismatic.

'Cherry,' said Angela, 'I'm interviewing you not on grounds of suspicion but as a possible witness. Did you see anyone acting suspiciously, or carrying something that could have concealed a knife?'

'No. Most people had free hands so that they could carry their plates. I didn't notice anyone with a big bag, apart from women from the village who were looking to take stuff home for tomorrow's picnic.'

That's interesting, thought Angela. I was thinking of a man having the anger and the strength to thrust a knife. It could have been a woman wronged. It could have been Mrs Chapin. When better to kill than when a host of wedding guests could share the suspicion?

'Cherry, you were the person Linda talked to after she found Mr Chapin's body. Would you tell me what led up to that event?'

'The reason it was me is that I'd been collecting plates and was on my way back and saw Linda towards the end of the path, shivering, shaking, and with sick down her front.'

Cherry sounded angry as she continued. 'Linda wouldn't let me take her in the Portakabin to clean her up. She pointed to the governor and said for me to tell her.'

'This obviously upset you,' said Angela, while thinking she really ought to find ways of not sounding like mistress of stating the startlingly obvious.

'Yeah, because it just brought it home to me. Again. We

can't react like you would on the outside. We must watch every move. And I'm angry because if Diane hadn't done a runner and Linda sent to look for her, Linda wouldn't have been in that situation. Someone else would have found Mr Chapin. None of us from the prison ought to be going through this. We should have been enjoying the day.'

Having got that off her chest, Cherry sighed. She spoke carefully. 'I was looking forward to this event. It would be a break from routine. Linda did not want to be here. She's very private, prefers to get on with her work and to read and to study, and be the fount of knowledge. She has a dread of the gutter press digging up her trial and dragging her through their mud. On the day we were told about the catering opportunity, Linda went straight to the governor and asked to be excused. But we all, including Linda, wanted today to be a success and the start of new opportunities for Brackerley inmates. Linda would simply rather not have played a public role. Diane didn't run off because of anything she saw or heard, but because she becomes irrational about her children. But we are being rehabilitated and must experience "the real world", including other people's kids running wild. I am not complaining about the outside world because I love going into Bon Boutique in Harrogate. Also, I have a professional interest in the wedding because of having made alterations to the family wedding dress.'

'Was the wedding dress the first Mrs Chapin's?' asked the sergeant.

'It belonged to the auntie.'

'And who is the auntie?'

'Gloria Thwaite, though apparently, they're not related. I thought I saw a family resemblance between Gloria and

Amanda, particularly after looking at the family album, but I was wrong.'

Angela suddenly thought of a possible link. If there was a resemblance between Mrs Thwaite and the bride, might Mr Thwaite go to the wedding, see the resemblance in a different light, and think back to a time when he felt sure there was something going on between Gloria and Lancelot Chapin?

Like the bar staff, and the prison catering officer, Cherry had not heard any sounds from behind the marquee, no raised voices, no sound of a struggle.

Angela thought that whoever killed Mr Chapin must be known to him, someone he had arranged to have a chat with. But why? The manor house was close enough for them to go inside. Angela knew from a previous visit, when Mr Chapin had complained about trespassers, that he had an outbuilding behind the house that was equipped as an office. He could have arranged to speak to someone there.

Angela stood. 'We have several polaroid photographs. Would you take a look and tell me if you recognise anyone in those photographs.'

Angela led Cherry to the table where she had set out the photographs.

Cherry stood looking at the photographs, pointing out who she recognised, 'Oh, she's been in Bon Boutique. That is Dr Hampshire, the village doctor. That's the prison nurse, Florence Carreras who went off to Filey to find a home for a dog and didn't come back – except for this wedding. This couple, Mr and Mrs Thwaite, very kindly took me to lunch and dropped me back at the prison. The urchin squeezing in next to the bridesmaid and pulling a face is Brendan who helps out at the farm. He kept popping into the marquee and grabbing food for himself and his friend.'

Angela had a feeling there must be a clue to something or other here, but she couldn't think what. Cherry, like Angela, seemed to have a thoughtful moment. She looked at the photographs again.

'Of course I know the Chapins by sight and I'd seen Mrs Chapin when she came up to London. There's a boutique in Chelsea, on the King's Road, that stocks my designs. Penny Chapin came in with Bob and bought this kaftan – that ought to have been on a hanger, not on a hook in the cloakroom. She also bought a shirt for Bob. I didn't know until afterwards that Penny was Fred's girlfriend's stepmother.'

'You know Bob and Fred?'

'Oh yes, and Tim. I'd been to their gigs and saw them at a couple of parties. Bob showed Mrs Chapin around London when Amanda and Fred had something on. That's why I felt entitled to borrow this kaftan just now.' Cherry smiled. 'A person must make a good impression at an interview.'

Angela let this pass. 'Cherry, did you see or hear anything, today or previously, that gave grounds for suspicion or that struck you as odd?'

'No. I wouldn't know what would appear odd in Brackerley. We're self-contained in the prison. We are not up to speed about outside goings-on, I'm a Saturday girl in a Harrogate shop. I could tell you more about London, Thailand or Marrakech than about Brackerley. Mr Chapin politely came to the marquee this morning and spoke to us. I'm sure we're all sorry he is dead.'

Angela was about to bring the interview to a close with the addition of the usual 'If you think of anything else—'

She stopped herself. Something indefinable about Cherry's manner as she hitched up the kaftan, saying, 'I'd better take this off,' made Angela think again about Cherry's performance, for which she had put on a costume to help her play a part. There was something this witness had left unsaid.

Cherry had come into the library keen to put her prison mates in the clear. She cared about clever Linda. She was protective of Diane. Cherry was not to know that neither was under suspicion. Having told Angela that she knew more about London than Brackerley, Cherry was now ready to return the kaftan to its hook. Penny Chapin's kaftan. Penny was escorted about town by Fred's best man, Bob, and had bought him a shirt. Penny stood to inherit. Bob might be more to Penny than simply her friendly escort. Was this Cherry's way of pointing in another direction, away from her fellow prisoners?

Cherry took off the kaftan and folded it, revealing the despised grey overall. 'I'll hang up Mrs Chapin's kaftan and brave the outdoors in my convict gear. Being a trendsetter, I'll probably be snapped by a free-range photographer and in two months, *Vogue* will feature prison attire.'

'I have one more question, Cherry.'

Cherry sat down.

'Did you and Mr or Mrs Chapin know each other, from when she visited London?'

'No.'

'Would Mrs Chapin have known you in London, because of your fashion profile?'

'I doubt it. And on that day in the boutique, Bob was too absorbed to see me. I'd go into the boutiques keeping a low profile, checking out what drew the customers, and what they were wearing. I'd eavesdrop, listen to comments. This kaftan sold out within days.'

'What makes you sure that it was Mrs Chapin that Bob was with?'

'If I said she has a limp, you would think that I noticed that today, or at the fête, which I did, but I also noticed at the time, in the shop. She paid by cheque from a joint account with the name Mr and Mrs Lancelot Chapin. After they'd gone, one of the salesgirls said, "Who'd call their child Lancelot?" And there was a riff on whether Lancelot's mother had an Arthur and a Guinevere in the family.'

It could be nothing, thought Angela. Why wouldn't Mrs Chapin visit London, to see her stepdaughter, and why wouldn't Bob escort Penny to Chelsea, if Amanda and Fred had something on that day. But Angela said this only to quell the excitement of having opened a new line of investigation. Penny and Bob the rock artist may have plans that would benefit from an inheritance from Lancelot Chapin. Penny was closer in age to Bob than to her husband. Going to London to call on Amanda would be the perfect cover for an affair.

Thirty-Three

Angela hadn't eaten since breakfast. As she walked back towards the marquee, she saw the boy from the polaroid photograph, identified by Cherry as Brendan, being walked by a PC towards the gates. He had probably done nothing worse than help himself and his friend Shelley to food and more than a fair share of wedding cake.

Bar staff had taken over in the marquee, the HMP Brackerley caterers had left. The police photographer was by his car, talking to DI Ian Dennis. The photographer took his camera bag from the boot, shouldered it and walked with the DI towards the crime scene. Guests who had given their details to constables were driving off. They would be interviewed at the station, or in their homes, supposedly for their convenience but also to clear the scene and leave the Chapin family in as much peace as might be possible while they put up with questions, searches, and press interest.

DCI Julian McHale was speaking to Governor Lewis. It had been obvious from the previous investigation, into the murder of Major Harding, that the DCI and Miss Lewis had a history. Not that Angela was nosey, but she was curious.

Angela decided to grab a bite to eat, while there was still some food left, despite feeling slightly queasy. Sometimes, hearing the description of a body and imagining it was worse than seeing the body for yourself.

As she helped herself to a ham sandwich, adding coleslaw and potato salad, DI Ian Dennis came to join her, bringing two cups of coffee, setting one down for her.

'Tough day, eh, Angela?' said Ian. 'First on the scene at the suicide, and now here.'

Ian would earn an A plus in stating the blindingly obvious.

Angela muttered an acknowledgement, swallowing too soon so as not to speak with her mouth full. Ian was going to tell her to do something else. She waited for the punchline.

'We have a new blackboard for the incident room.'

Had she heard right? A new blackboard. 'Oh.'

'And chalk.'

'Right.'

'I'd like you to go back to the station and chalk a timescale of events on that board and the names of persons of interest. We'll meet first thing tomorrow, staying local, same room as when we were last here, top floor in the Brackerley Co-operative building.'

Rounding off one helluva day by spending Saturday night in a room at the station, chalking on a blackboard, was not why Angela joined the force. Ian Dennis was married to a teacher. Perhaps she had put the blackboard idea into his head. Angela put on her thoughtfully puzzled I-am-knackered look.

The DI could be perceptive. He smiled sympathetically. 'I

know it's been a hard day, but if it's any consolation, we have coloured chalks.'

Occasionally, very occasionally, Angela wanted to cry. 'Sir, how about having the board delivered to the Co-operative building, this evening or early in the morning? There's a caretaker. His telephone number is on the door. I still have a note of it from our last use of that building.'

'Oh, well, yes, we can do that.'

Angela grabbed a napkin and wrote the number, copying it from the back of her notebook. She smiled. 'Will you ring the station, or will I?'

'You ring. I've one more job to do before I can leave. I have the keys to Mr Chapin's office.'

Angela felt pleased with herself. She would be free to go home and have a good think about what to write on the blackboard in the morning.

When the DI left, she was soon diverted by a smartly dressed man of about fifty years old. Angela had seen him earlier. Where?

He hovered with his tray and asked if he might join her. Since there were now empty tables, Angela wondered why.

When he sat down, she remembered him. He was the man who drove from the premises as she had arrived, when no one was to be allowed to leave or enter. The gateman had let one car with children leave, along with this man because his passengers were elderly.

'I'm Dr Block,' he said, 'a friend of the family and director of Brackerley Home for the Elderly. I was gathering up some of my residents to leave when there was a suggestion that people should remain there but what with getting them into the car and all that was going on around, I didn't realise I

219

ought to stay until a member of my staff told me after I arrived back. I returned to call on Penny and Amanda, kept it brief. Such a shock about Lance.'

'Yes.' Angela took a sip of coffee.

'Apologies for intruding on your lunch. I was told you are Sergeant Ambrose and that there are constables taking statements.'

'That's right.'

Dr Block glanced about. Angela followed his gaze. There was now just one uniformed officer, busy taking a statement.

'I don't have a great deal to say,' said the doctor. 'I was a guest at the wedding and when I heard the dreadful news it occurred to me that you would want to take statements.'

Angela produced her ID. 'I'll take your statement, Doctor.'

'Oh, thank you.'

'Did you hear the request that people remain in the grounds and gather in the marquee?'

'I caught part of it, but my old people are not easily gathered, and they were talking, the engine was running and someone was having a coughing fit. I didn't catch what was being asked of us.'

Angela took out her notebook. 'Do you have your wedding invitation?'

'Yes.'

The doctor put his hand in his inside pocket. He then checked his other pockets and shook his head. 'I must have left it back at base. Sometimes I think my residents send me as absent-minded as they are themselves.' He shook his head and smiled at his own forgetfulness.

'It's all right.' Angela smiled back. She remembered his name from the invitation list. He seemed just the right sort of person to work with the elderly – amiable and unhurried. 'Would you tell me what time you arrived at the church, and at the reception, who you spoke to during the course of the afternoon and what time you left, and whether you took any photographs.'

He smiled. 'There's a tall order! I spoke to so many people. As to our arrival, we were at the church about ten forty-five, in good time to take our usual seats which had been reserved. I bought three frail residents. Miss Taylor stayed in the church grounds to talk to a friend who was to bring her back. Miss Whitaker never says no to a glass of champagne. I brought her and Mr Hawthorn straight to the reception after the ceremony.'

'And what time did you leave?'

'Now you have me. It's not the sort of do where one looks at a watch. I know my residents were flagging by mid-afternoon and so I drove them back to the home. As to who I spoke to – well, hellos to everyone. I congratulated the bride and groom, the parents, the groom's aunt. I exchanged a few words with Dr Hampshire, the Reverend and Mrs Grieves, Miss Lewis the prison governor, the girls at the catering table.'

'Thank you, Dr Block.' Angela closed her notebook and put it away. 'If there is anything else, we'll be in touch. May I have your telephone number?'

I have a card. He slid thumb and finger into his waistcoat pocket, found no card, and then reeled off the number. Angela made a note of his telephone number.

Thirty-Four

After the warmth of the day, Nell welcomed the cool air in the basement of the prison. On the original plans of the house, this six by nine feet space was a pantry, set against a wall, the bricks whitewashed. During the building's use as a borstal, the pantry became the secure cell, the punishment cell. Nell renamed it 'The Room'. At some time, the pantry door was removed, and a gate added, so the inmate was always visible. Slivers of natural light came from a window on the opposite wall, but it was now dusk. Nell had ordered a classroom-style light shade to cover the solitary bare bulb that hung from the ceiling.

A bench ran the length of one wall. On the other side was a single iron bedstead with narrow mattress. An enamel basin and jug stood on a rough-hewn table, along with regulation scrap of soap and small towel.

Diane was seated on the bench, legs outstretched, wrapped in a blanket, her back to the wall. As Nell approached, Diane swung her legs from the bench and stood.

Nell unlocked the door and went inside. She sat on the other end of the bench. 'Sit down, Diane.'

'Ma'am.' Diane sighed. 'I messed up.'

'Yes, you did. You put lives at risk on the road, your own, the nurse's, other travellers. You undermined the work of Miss Kitteringham and your fellow residents.'

'I know.' Diane sniffed. 'I lost my hanky.'

'There's toilet roll on the shelf.'

Diane reached for the toilet roll and wiped her nose.

Nell said, 'This house is for women who want to make the most of their opportunity to leave prison with better prospects than when they came in. It is not for absconders.'

'I can explain. It was that record by The Doors, coming on just as I saw a boy and girl playing tig and—'

Nell held up her hand. 'Stop there, Diane. You are serving a prison sentence. No Saturdays off.'

'What's going to happen to me?'

'What do you think will happen?'

'I'll be transferred to a closed prison.'

Nell let the reality sink in. HMP Brackerley must not gain a reputation for prisoners to come and go as they pleased. Hard-line politicians and stir-it-up newspaper editors would love to write about this open prison as a second and third chance saloon.

'Diane, your behaviour today shows that you have not yet adapted to serving your sentence in an open prison. If you are unable to adapt, you leave me no choice. Think about that.'

And it's not just your fault, thought Nell. Diane was perfect for the catering team. Today gave her a new opportunity to prove herself. But she is a widow with kids, at a wedding – kids running around, a semblance of normality. The Doors might have reached the hit parade, but they had a lot to answer for. Today ought to have counted towards parole.

Nell felt sick at heart that she had not foreseen Diane might do another runner, not sent two more officers from the house to the marquee.

'We'll talk on Monday.'

'I only ever tried my best. I told that judge the real villain wasn't on trial. No one listened. And it's not just me being punished, it's Ruby and Albert.'

'I understand your feelings,' said Nell. 'I know you miss your children.'

'You can't know what it's like to be separated from your kids, to not see them off to school, to not be the one who takes them to town and buys them ice cream cornets on a Saturday in the market.'

'Diane, I do understand but you broke the law.'

'Ma'am. You can't know what it's like.' Diane began to sob loudly, perhaps too loudly, with a touch of the dramatics.

Nell did not know what it was like for Diane to be suddenly taken from her children. Nell knew what it was like to wean her baby daughter and then to hand over that baby like a parcel, taken from her, without ceremony. To be at her own baby's christening, but as the godmother, as the 'auntie', choose her baby's name, Roxana, and to be cornered into agreeing with her sister and brother-in-law that it made sense for Nell to go out to work and pay for her daughter's keep, while Roxana was brought up to call Nell auntie, and Nell's sister and brother-in-law were mum and dad. That way, there was no disgrace on the family, and on Nell, who would 'meet someone else', and could start again. The sensible thing. The only way in the 1940s, when the threatened alternative was a home for unmarried mothers, and adoption of her baby.

Some girls did not escape such institutions.

Nell spoke quietly to Diane. 'Your children are safe and well, looked after by their aunt and grandma. You are the grown-up. You need to stay in one piece for them, until it's time to see them again. You behaved recklessly. There are consequences. You won't help yourself by getting into a state.'

When Diane was finally calm, Nell stood.

'An officer will bring you an extra blanket and a cup of cocoa. I will see you in my office on Monday morning.'

'I feel sick.'

'There is a bucket in the corner, and water on the shelf.'

Tonight, observation of Diane would be a task for Chief Officer Markham, all stiff upper lip and no nonsense.

Tomorrow, Betsy Friel would be on duty, with her air of consolation, telling stories of childhood resilience and the ingratitude of grown-up children who between them would not go to the trouble of producing a single grandchild.

As Nell turned the key in the lock, Diane called, 'Ma'am, don't send me to the other end of the country.'

Nell took it as a good sign that Diane had something to say for herself. Hopelessness would be worse. Nell put her hand in her pocket. 'Here, I have a spare hanky.'

She passed it to Diane through the bars.

Diane called again as Nell walked away. 'Will I be let out for church in the morning?'

Nell did not answer.

Sunday, thought Nell. Lesley and Peter would be there, probably primed to talk to Nell about Peter's former comrade-in-arms Roland Herbert, the father that Nell's daughter Roxana would never meet.

Still, Lesley and Peter would be gone soon, back to America. It was unlikely that Nell would see them again

225

after tomorrow. She could put up with a brief chat about the old days.

Nell made her slow way back up the stairs. Saturday night. What would Roxana be doing? She was a smart girl, wouldn't get herself into trouble, though someone else might. Nell wondered, did Roxy smoke pot? Probably. It wasn't the kind of thing you could ask about, or warn against. And was it really that much worse than choking on a Lucky Strike? At that moment, Nell wanted to kick off her shoes, put her feet up and drink a tot of Jameson's.

First, she must go to her office, pick up the phone and report to T5. There was much to tell. She would follow up with a telex.

As Nell walked the corridor, Kit appeared from the library. 'Ma'am?'

'Yes Kit?'

'How is Diane?'

'Secured.'

'Is it my fault?'

'Kit, you did an excellent job today. Your catering was first class. You were on your own. What happened was outside your control.'

Kit was still learning. She would be more careful from now on.

Thirty-Five

It was dusk. An eerie quiet filled the empty marquee, the silence broken by the sudden rattle of empty bottles as bar staff from the Hare and Hounds carried crates to their waiting vehicle. There were constables on duty, and they would stay on the premises overnight. Searches would begin again in the morning. Ian had said goodnight to Angela as she went to her car. The sky was darkening, grey clouds turning black.

Ian Dennis had one more job, to look through the documents in Mr Chapin's office. As well as temporary use of the library and cloakroom for interviews, the family had given the police access to Lancelot Chapin's papers, diary and letters that he kept in a single-storey office, built in the grounds at the rear of the house. There might be some clue as to who he was dealing with, major fallings out, double-crossing, someone with an axe to grind or gains to be made.

Ian would look through the papers before having them itemised and brought to the station. Mrs Chapin had agreed, though he was not sure she was taking in what was being asked of her. Ian was trying to keep an open mind, but something told him that the person who put a knife in Lance would not have been one of the objectors to the land sale. They were out in the open, with their grievances and protests. Knifing Mr Chapin in the heart was a crude and ugly act but what if that was deliberate, in order to make the police miss something else, such as business rivalry, a deal turning sour, a contract about to be reneged on.

Ian had qualifications in economics and law and had worked in finance. The DCI relied on him to spot what other people would miss. Ian had joined the force after spending too long in seminars, libraries and an accountant's office, hoping to be out and about, in some of the knife-edge situations he had read about and seen on the telly. In his first couple of years on the force that was what he did, until his skills surfaced.

'Follow the money, Ian,' said the DCI. 'See where that leads. Who gains?'

Typecast. Again. The man with the calculator for a brain, but by then he no longer minded. Knife-edge situations lost their appeal when he married and he and his wife started a family.

Mr Chapin had a comfortable, well-equipped office. The key to the safe was easy to find. A copy of Lancelot Chapin's Last Will and Testament revealed the expected beneficiaries. Lancelot bequeathed the manor house, a millstone if ever Ian saw one, to his wife and daughter. There were bequests, to his regimental charity and to the golf club's charity. The bulk of his fortune went to his wife and daughter. It struck Ian as the sort of will the writer had planned to revise and refine later, when he had the time. There was no mention of Fred Harding.

Ian had taken the opportunity to speak to Fred Harding's

paternal aunt, shortly after their arrival at the manor house. He asked her about Fred. 'Was Fred always musical?' That was more tactful than asking whether Fred was capable of ever holding down a proper job.

Miss Harding told Ian that Fred's musical talent came from his mother's side. Fred's mother sang in choirs. She was determined her son would have a musical education. They could not send him to the sort of school she would have liked, and so he lived with a maternal aunt in London, auditioned for St Paul's Choir, and sang for his schooling at St Paul's.

Fred Harding, the rock 'n' roll choir boy, had made a good choice of bride.

Penny Chapin would be a well-off widow, though she would probably sell land to survive. Rents from the housing stock in the village were low, and the houses in ill-repair. There were complaints in Chapin's files about leaking roofs, damp and mould.

Chapin's bureaucratic correspondence with the Gas Board had delayed the gas switchover.

Interesting. Mr Thwaite would have been thwarted in his attempt to take his life. This thought intrigued Ian. Had Chapin, during their domino-playing evenings in the Hare and Hounds, ever mentioned that he felt pestered by the Gas Board authorities? Authorities whose ulterior motive may have been to stop the desperate taking of what might be perceived as an easy way out?

There was also a newspaper cutting, without a date or name for the newspaper. The headline read,

'Mother blames coal gas switch delay for daughter's death.'

The gist was that a girl on Poplar Street had taken her own life by gassing herself. 'A broken heart was something she would have got over,' said the mother. 'Now she is gone from me.'

Lancelot Chapin's company owned Poplar Street. If my child died like that, I would've been tempted to put a knife through the guilty landlord, thought Ian, whose wife had produced the most astonishing baby boy, now in his second year at school.

Ian instructed himself not to be distracted. Stick to the money, but he noted the story about the gas suicide and tenants' complaints.

In addition to rental income, Lancelot Chapin's income came from investments, some overseas. You couldn't call it earnings. Someone like Chapin didn't have to work for his living. Two investments were local. He was a director of the Brackerley Maternity Home and the Brackerley Home for the Elderly. These two establishments provided steady and lucrative returns.

Obvious, thought Ian. Chapin invested in life's certainties and an aspiration: birth, old age and keeping a roof over your head. All he had missed out on was a chain of undertakers.

Ian turned his attention to outgoings. Was Chapin paying someone off, overextending his credit, being blackmailed? 'Give me something interesting!' he demanded of the papers spread across the desk of the deceased.

Chapin had a business account, a personal current account, a joint account with Penelope Chapin, and the maximum in Premium Bonds for Amanda Chapin, Penelope Chapin, Gloria Thwaite, and himself.

Gloria Thwaite did not fit into the Chapins' pattern of keeping assets in the family chest.

In the filing cabinet, under the label 'Motoring', Ian saw

that Norman Thwaite appeared to have serviced Chapin's Bentley but submitted no invoice. Lancelot Chapin had bought a Morris Minor, paying cash. The number plate of the Morris Minor was the same as the car Angela had reported seeing outside 33 Willow Lane. There were no payments going from Norman Thwaite to Lancelot Chapin.

What was the link between them? Curious.

They had obviously known each other a long time and had some sort of relationship. Mrs Chapin or Mrs Thwaite might be able to cast light on that.

Ian wished he had a theory, but at least he had some possibilities to follow up.

A romantic triangle; a tax avoidance scheme by supplying a gift, or payment in kind. If Norman Thwaite was to be suspect number one, they would need more than that. The rear window of Lance Chapin's office looked out onto the area behind the manor house that led to woodland.

He looked out at the white suits surveying the area. Would they bring in lights, or start their fingertip search tomorrow morning? Two uniform constables were waiting on a decision.

Ian added Lance Chapin's diary to the list of items to be taken to the station. The entry for today simply read: 'Wedding'. Tomorrow was blank and so was Monday. For Tuesday, the entry was: '10 am, Tom Jackson, Surveyor.' On Wednesday at 4 pm, he had 'Mr Kempster, Golf.'

Ian closed the diary and completed the list of the documents he wanted to have boxed up and taken to the station. It just remained for him to return the keys, thank Mrs Chapin and seek her agreement to have the key documents taken to the station.

Thirty-Six

Ian prided himself on being able to get on with women. His wife knew her own mind, and sometimes everybody else's. Top of the list of things that annoyed and irritated her was being patronised, next was being ogled.

He rang the bell at the manor house, hoping someone would take the key from him and say that Mrs Chapin had gone to bed, but knowing he ought to speak to her.

The door opened. One of the musicians stood there with his shirt hanging out.

'I'm Detective Inspector Ian Dennis. Is Mrs Chapin available?'

'Hello, I'm Bob, Fred's best man. Penny's upstairs. She said you'd be returning a key.' He waited, expectantly.

'Would you let her know I'm here.' Ian would have handed over the office key to Amanda, or to Fred, but not to a long-haired lout with his shirt hanging out.

Bob opened the door to the sitting room. 'Take a pew. I'll fetch Penny.' He paused by the door. 'I can't believe it. Just hours ago, there we all were, on stage together for the wedding speeches. We're all cut up. I spotted Mr Chapin among the guests, and then didn't see him again. So—' Making a gesture of helplessness, Bob left the room.

Ian sat down. He was not simply here to return the key but to begin the process of turning Penny and Amanda's lives upside down and inside out.

A moment later another band member came into the room.

'Tim Fallows?' asked Ian, standing.

'That's me.'

'I'm Detective Inspector Ian Dennis.'

'I've just made a bacon sandwich. Do you want one?'

'No, thank you.' Ian would have loved a bacon sandwich.

'We'll all do whatever we can to help,' said Tim, 'but I don't know how. Right now, I'm feeling useless.'

They both sat down.

'Have you been to the manor house before?' Ian asked.

'No. Bob has. He came up a while ago to sort out having a stage, for the speeches and music. Otherwise, we've met Mr and Mrs Chapin when they came to London. We were looking forward to today. Feels unreal.'

'Tell me, do you have any thoughts at all about who might have borne a grudge against Mr Chapin?'

'I'm guessing there would be a few grudges. A man as well-off as Lance Chapin is bound to have made enemies, or aroused jealousy, but I don't know and to be honest, I wouldn't want to.'

'Have you been spoken to by one of our officers?'

'Yes.'

'So we'll have your address?'

'Erm, no.'

Taking out his notebook, Ian asked, 'What is your address?'

'Now you're asking.'

Ian held his pen at the ready.

'We were squatting in Holland Park. We've moved out. The owners are back.'

'Thank you for being so frank. Is there anywhere we can reach you?'

'We've gigs lined up and we're booked into digs. Amanda and Fred have the schedule. I don't know what's going to happen about it.'

'And when you're not on the road?'

Tim looked about. 'I suppose here, for Fred and Amanda. I don't know.'

'It would be useful to have contact details.'

'This address then. Care of the manor house, unless Mrs Chapin and Amanda say differently. The choirmaster at St Paul's School and Cathedral usually knows where we are. If we need storage, the choirmaster lets us keep our instruments in one of the rooms and so does Fred's London auntie, though she doesn't have much space.' Tim took out a card, wrote on the back, and handed it to the DI. 'This chap is our agent, that's recent, and I hope he won't drop us.'

'You sang in the choir?'

'That's how we met. We three auditioned for the choir, which means a free place at St Paul's School, singing for your schooling, until your voice breaks.'

'And then?'

'Out on your ear, unless you have parents who can afford the fee, or unless you have exceptionally good voices, and the choirmaster speaks up for you.'

'Did you all three leave when your voices broke?'

'We three were allowed to stay on. When we did our turn

at the school show, we called ourselves The Scholarship Boys. It was our "up yours, mate" moment. Fred and I went to art college, Bob worked in a record shop. We got by.'

'You've done well.' Not that Ian felt a flash of resentment. These lads hadn't been afraid to take a chance. He had to hand it to them. They stuck at what they wanted to do.

'I'm being honest,' said Tim, 'because I want you to eliminate us from enquiries – if that's the right wording – so that we can move on. We'll stick together as a band, but it might be different now.'

'In what way?'

'Fred and Amanda have the idea of holding a festival, maybe summer 1970, here in the manor house grounds. That was going to be their big ask of Mr Chapin this weekend. There'd be top names, and naturally we would play. It could be a nice little earner for the Chapins, put Brackerley on the map, and be a boost for our band. Fred's drawn up plans and costings, based on other festivals.'

'Did you have the opportunity to talk to Mr Chapin about it?'

'No. Amanda, and Fred would have brought up the idea perhaps before they set off for Scarborough, giving Mr Chapin time to think it over. Penny has known a while but kept it under wraps. Penny likes the idea. Obviously, we're not thinking about that at present.' Tim lit a cigarette. 'I want this horrible murder solved. I don't know whether our tour will go ahead. It's important to us, but in the scheme of things I can see Fred and Amanda might feel differently. I'm coming round to the idea that we should cancel now, give the venues as much notice as we can.'

The door opened. Bob came in, followed by Fred.

Ian stood and introduced himself, adding, 'Condolences on the loss of your father-in-law, Mr Harding.'

'Thank you, and it's Fred. Mrs Chapin would like to have a word. She and Amanda will come down shortly and see you in the library, across the hall.'

'I'll go wait in the library.'

Ian did not close the door. He waited a moment, jotting the name Kempster and 'Golf Club?' in his notebook. He wanted to know who was the Mr Kempster that Lance Chapin had in his diary. It might be tactless to ask Mrs Chapin tonight, but he would find that out some other way, perhaps from the golf club membership list. He was repaid for leaving the door open by hearing Tim say, 'You've got to tell him.'

Bob said, 'No! It's got nothing to do with what's happened.'

Thirty-Seven

Ian would have waited until morning, but Mrs Chapin and Amanda both said they couldn't sleep, and they might as well talk now. The library was lit by lamps with green shades. The women were seated in a corner by a low table. Penny invited Ian to join them.

Penny wore a kaftan and headband. Her hair was in two plaits, over her shoulders, plaits that were coming undone. Her eyes were red-rimmed. She looked exhausted.

Ian apologised for intruding so soon after Mr Chapin's death. He returned the office key. 'Thank you for letting me look at your husband's papers. With your permission I'll have some of the material boxed up and taken to the station. It will help build a picture of Mr Chapin's interests and associates. We'll itemise documents and give you a signature. Sometimes what might seem an insignificant piece of information can open up a line of enquiry.'

'Whatever helps.' Penny turned to Amanda.

Amanda looked blank, as if coming up with her own name might be difficult. She wore an Arsenal football shirt, her legs and feet bare. She was hugging herself and curling her toes.

She glared at Ian. 'Find who killed my dad.'

'We will do our utmost and will keep you informed.'

Mrs Chapin said, 'Ask us anything you want.'

Ian had not intended this to be an interview. That could wait, but he said, 'Had Mr Chapin quarrelled with anyone recently?'

'Dad wasn't one for quarrels,' said Amanda. 'He always found a way round. It's true that he was slow in doing repairs on the village houses and people used to mention that to me when they saw me in the village. I'd tell him, and it would be done. He could be forgetful. He had a lot on his mind, managing the estate and his business interests.'

'I helped him,' said Penny. 'I typed his letters. I kept his diary.'

'Yes, you did,' said Amanda. 'You did what you could. I know that.'

'I asked him not to stop your allowance. I told him, living in London is expensive.'

'Not expensive if you know what you're doing. Dad talked to me. He said I was educated, qualified and able to stand on my two feet, and so I should. I agreed. I manage very well.'

The DI suppressed a smile. Living in a squat and not paying rent must help.

'Thank you both for your help and giving access to Mr Chapin's files. You must be tired. I'll have the documents collected in the morning. Everything will be returned to you.'

Penny gave a dismissive gesture. 'Take what you want.'

Ian groaned inwardly. Listen to yourself. You sound like bureaucrat of the year. Penny and Amanda were the people closest to Lance Chapin. If anyone had picked up vibes, animosities, worries, it would be them. Otherwise, this became a random stabbing, with a knife that anyone could have got hold of.

Ian decided to ask another question, needing to frame it carefully. He was about to speak when there was a tap on the door. Fred came in, holding a pair of football socks. 'Put these on. It's cold in here.'

Amanda held out her bare feet and let Fred put on the socks.

'Do you want a blanket?'

'I'm all right.'

'Shall I sit in?'

'No, it's okay. Stay with the boys.'

Fred nodded and left.

When he had gone, Ian asked, 'Did Mr Chapin have any enemies?'

'Enemies.' Penny stood. 'I am lame.' She strode across to the bookcase to illustrate her lameness. 'That is thanks to a trip wire that was placed across the path. I believe it was meant to topple my husband's horse when he was hunting. It toppled me instead. The anti-hunt mob care about foxes, not people. I could have been killed.'

'I'm sorry to hear that,' said Ian.

'No one was apprehended. Then we have the right to roam lot. They are very polite but so are tyrants when it suits them. They claim to have read old documents describing how the Chapins took this land by force when King Dick was a lad. Well, let them make a case and put it before a court of law. They bring wire cutters and remove barbed wire saying it's blocking their right to climb over a stile or open a gate. I don't go to their houses saying, "Excuse me, I must break down your back fence so I can walk through to the next street".'

Amanda said quietly, 'Penny, we're all upset. I think the police will look into all that. It's why they want the files.'

'Yes, we will.' Ian took a breath. 'There was another tragic incident today, in the village. It concerns Mr Thwaite.'

Amanda had been leaning back in the chair, looking at her feet. She suddenly sat upright. 'Uncle Norman? What about him?'

'I'm sorry to bring more bad news. Mr Thwaite, your Uncle Norman, went home from the wedding and took his own life. There is no reason to suppose any connection.'

Penny leaned forward. 'No connection? Isn't there? I wouldn't be so sure.'

Amanda glared at Penny. 'Are you mad? Dad and Uncle Norman were friends, long before you arrived.'

'Yes, and Norman did very well out of your dad. Perhaps Lance asked for something back.'

'You've got that completely wrong. You've no idea,' Amanda flared up, 'And what about you? What about you?'

'Me?'

'You know what I'm talking about. Don't you dare say anything against Norman or Gloria.' Amanda stood. 'Excuse me, Officer. It's been a long day.'

Ian leapt to his feet as Amanda made for the door. He followed her into the hall. She took a coat from the hall stand and slipped on a pair of shoes. 'Where are you going?'

She opened the door. 'To my Auntie Gloria.'

'I'll drive you.'

'I'll walk. Don't let anyone come after me.'

'What about Fred?'

'Tell him I'm going to see Auntie Gloria. I'll see him tomorrow.'

Ian followed her out. 'Wait,' he said, signalling to a uniformed constable who was on duty and had seen the door open. 'A PC will follow you to the Thwaites' house and see you in safely. What's the address?'

'Thirty-three Willow Lane.' Amanda strode on, calling back, 'It can't be true. He wouldn't, not on my wedding day. Uncle Norman gave me a wink as Dad walked me down the aisle. He gave me a kiss after the speeches.'

Amanda was walking quickly, and then broke into a run.

Ian went back inside to take his leave of Penny.

'I'm sorry about that performance,' Penny said. 'It's a horrible shock for Amanda. She never usually goes over the top like that. She doesn't like to think I'm right. I was going to take her on holiday one summer, but she chose to go camping with the Thwaites. Lance bought a car for them to go in. I thought that car would be for me when they came back, but Norman kept it. I'd thought I would learn to drive.' She looked suddenly helpless. 'What am I supposed to do?'

'Try and get some sleep, Mrs Chapin. I've asked an officer to keep an eye on Amanda, until she gets to the Thwaites'. He'll report back.'

'Will you wait with me? At least I can then tell the boys and they won't be going out looking for her.'

'Yes of course,' said Ian, who wanted to go home.

He made a mental note. Do not interview a mother and daughter together.

Ian wondered about the relationship between Lance Chapin and Norman Thwaite. One man buying another man a car indicated excessive generosity, tit for tat, or else a guilty conscience.

Ian decided he had made a pig's ear of this interview. The women had wanted to talk but were too tired and too emotional for him to make sense of them.

He thought of the sergeant. Angela was good at glasses of water.

'I'll get you a glass of water, Mrs Chapin.' He was up and out of the room, making his way to the kitchen. He took a good look around, found the glasses, had a drink of water himself, and then filled a fresh glass for Penny.

There was a set of knives in the kitchen, a not uncommon set. The holder had spaces for five knives. There were only four on display. Ian had a set like it at home. His wife liked sets of things, whereas his preference was for oddities. It would take strength to thrust a knife into someone's heart. A woman in a rage could do it, but not without getting blood on her clothing. Ian had looked at photographs of what this now wealthy widow had been wearing during the day. She didn't do it. Ian felt sure – but not entirely sure.

When he returned, Penny had poured herself a large glass of brandy. 'I don't suppose you're allowed to drink on duty?'

'No.'

She gave a winning smile. 'I shan't tell.'

'No, but thank you.' He set down the glass of water.

Ian was relieved when the constable tapped on the door and reported that Amanda had been let in to 33 Willow Lane. She had run all the way.

Penny walked Ian to the door, being the perfect hostess.

In her kaftan and headband, the DI thought she would fit in perfectly with the Northern Knights' plan to hold a rock concert at Brackerley Manor House.

'Do you mind my asking how old you were when you came to the manor house?' the DI asked.

'Sixteen. I came as a companion, and unqualified "nurse-maid" to Amanda. She was six and a half, and motherless. She already had a substitute family in the Thwaites, and I was no nursemaid.'

'You were a child yourself.'

'I suppose I was, though at that age we think we are as old as we ever will be and know everything we will ever need to know.'

Ian had seen the marriage certificate. Penelope was twenty when she married Lancelot Chapin.

Ian thought of his wife, who'd say 'Oh God love you!' when her heart went out to someone. He felt like saying that to Penny Chapin. What sort of life was it for a sixteen-year-old to come to a place like Brackerley and be here decades later, married to a man old enough to be her father.

Ian drove back by way of the prison farm. There was a light on in a downstairs room of the farmhouse.

The farmhouse door opened, and a dog came running out, barking. A woman stood at the door. She called to someone and then waved a walking stick at him. 'Identify yourself!'

'Police.' Ian was not prepared to have a shouting match. 'Just checking.' The gate was padlocked. Climb it, or risk squeezing through the space between gatepost and hedge? He climbed it and stepped into mud.

Of course, there would be mud. This was a farm. It was still light, but puddles and mud had a built-in ability to disguise themselves as safe ground. The damage was done.

Stepping gingerly, he made his way to speak to the woman in the doorway. He remembered the name of the farmer and his wife – Ramsden.

Even by the dim light of the porch, Mrs Ramsden was a startling woman, with big blue eyes and a mass of hair like curled white wire.

'Mrs Ramsden. I'm Detective Dennis.' He showed her his ID. 'Have you heard news of what happened at the manor house today?'

'Summat serious, I know that. One of your lot came but said nothing, only that there'd been an incident and had we seen anyone on the property, which we hadn't.'

'We're conducting a murder enquiry.'

'So he was right.'

'Who was?'

'Young Brendan who works here on Saturdays, he told us Mr Chapin was dead. I couldn't believe it.'

'Was Brendan a wedding guest?'

'No, but he needs no invitation when there's food on offer.'

'And have you had any thoughts since our officer called? Any idea of who would want to harm Lancelot Chapin?'

'No. I'm glad he wasn't our landlord, but I'm sorry that he is dead, and for his loss for his family.'

That was a diplomatic way to not give a proper answer.

Mrs Ramsden added, 'There's ill-feeling and talk about the Chapin plans to sell land, but that's come up before, a few years back, and nothing happened. We'd help you if we could, and we have the station telephone number.'

Ian wished her goodnight. As he drove away, the name Kempster came back to him. Lancelot Chapin's appointment on Wednesday at the golf club must be with Mr Kempster, the new coroner. The coroner who would be conducting the inquest into Lancelot's death.

Thirty-Eight

Gloria had long ago decided to say nothing. It was as if that chloroform-soaked cotton square that she had fought against had slipped invisible tentacles around her very being. As if the distress of that time still paralysed and silenced her. The chloroform was not given when she gave birth. It was afterwards, when she began to protest.

Paul wanted answers. He wouldn't accept that there was no answer. 'What ailed Dad?' he asked. 'There was something. I know there was.'

Gloria knew she had stayed silent too long. 'It was 1947,' she said, 'the worst winter, a cold winter with so much snow.'

Her hands were on the table, palms down. Paul reached out and put his hands over hers. 'I remember the snow,' said Paul. 'And a friend of mine, Shirley, her brother talked about it. He said he was coming home from school and needed to cross the road, but there was a mountain of snow, much higher than him. A man came up behind him and just lifted him across.'

Ah, that's Shirley he goes to the pictures with, she is his girlfriend, Gloria thought. She had told Norman that Paul had changed. This time last year, he would not have placed his hands on hers.

His mother's hands were cold, as if that winter had come into the room.

'The snow was so deep,' said Gloria. 'It was impassable, and the air bitterly cold. A snow plough came up our street and cleared the road. But, just like Shirley's brother said, the mountain of snow on the pavement was so deep that a person could not cross. People came out and made paths so that they could get to work or school, but the buses could not get along the lane.

'Mrs Platt was still alive then, and the plan was that she would look after you and Steven. I wanted to give birth at home. There were so many babies being born after the war and so many returned soldiers still in hospitals needing treatment.

'Your dad had it in his head that I must go to the Brackerley Maternity Home. Nothing was too good for me. It cost money. He said that didn't matter. So that is where I went. All went smoothly. I was pleased to have a girl this time.

'My bed was next to the baby dormitory and so I didn't get much rest. It was bedlam when they set each other off crying. When someone left, I was moved to the quietest place at the top of the ward on the far side. Each morning the babies would be wheeled back in.

'One morning, my baby was not wheeled back. I got out of bed and went to see, looking in every cot on the ward. The usual nurse in charge wasn't there. We heard that she slipped on ice on the way to work. My baby's cot was in the dormitory but empty. I went frantic, looking, asking, "Where is she?"

'Your father was sent for. He and a nurse came to tell me

that my baby had died suddenly in the night and these things did happen and there was not always an explanation. Dr Block came saying how very sorry he was. And I can't remember now because that was when I screamed, and then smelled the chloroform and then a needle in my arm. But I knew my own child and some of the mothers, they would be handed the wrong baby and look hard at it and say, "Oh yes, he's mine. He has his father's eyes."'

Paul poured more brandy into the glasses. 'What happened to our baby?'

'I couldn't find her. They showed me a poor still creature and said that was my baby. I knew it wasn't. I thought I was going mad. Mrs Platt was very good, looking after you all. We wouldn't have coped without her.'

Paul said, 'I remember Mrs Platt giving us our dinner.'

'It was a long time after that I worked out the truth. Mrs Platt didn't tell me out of malice. She fully believed my baby died suddenly. She was one of those women who, whatever tale a person tells her, she has heard such stories before. That was how she tried to comfort me. It was one of those things that happens, that's what she said.

'Mrs Chapin had been in the maternity home at the same time as me, in a private room. Mrs Chapin was lovely, but not a well woman. The Chapins had a grown son who went away, the Caribbean I think they said. He was their only child, and he drowned. They were devastated.

'Mrs Platt liked the sound of her own voice. She didn't always think before she spoke. She said what a strange twist of fate that it should be my baby who died and Mrs Chapin, who was not strong, and had been advised against having another baby, had a healthy daughter.'

'What are you saying?' Paul asked, gently.

Gloria frowned. 'There was like a little click in my head, a thought I couldn't shape. I went to see Mrs Chapin and took her a bunch of flowers. She was ill, sitting up in bed, the baby crawling on the eiderdown. I can still see Mrs Chapin's pale cheeks, pale lips, and so much cream lace that the pillows around her looked like a nest for her and baby Amanda, who was chubby and smiling. I held out my arms. Mrs Chapin said, "She won't go to anyone else, only me. It's a worry." I put out my arms again, and said, "Come on, little one". The baby came closer. Mrs Chapin said, "She'll cry." She didn't cry. She did a little shuffle. I took her in my arms. She snuggled up.

'Mrs Chapin looked tired. She was ill. I said, "Would you like me to mind Amanda for you sometimes?"'

'When was this?'

'1948, early spring. While I was holding Amanda, the bedroom door opened. Lancelot Chapin filled that doorway. He stood with his mouth open. We looked at each other. If I hadn't been entirely sure before, that niggle of doubt about my own sanity, I was sure then.

'Mrs Chapin said, "Amanda has taken to Mrs Thwaite, isn't that amazing? Mrs Thwaite is willing to mind her sometimes." Lancelot Chapin didn't move. He looked stuck between the door jambs. I knew I would lose if I staked my claim. I gritted my teeth and said, "It's all right. I won't steal her."'

'Mam, how could that happen? Dad wouldn't have let it happen.'

'Your dad was a good man, a trusting man, a working man, used to taking orders in the army, used to looking up to people with a badge, or a position, thinking others better than himself, knowing his place. He took my part as best he could.

He enquired. He believed the liars he thought of as his betters. I went on looking after Amanda, and you, and Steven. That kept me sane. I was in a tunnel, and there would be an end.'

The curtains were closed but the windows were still open. They heard the gate click. Paul went to see, expecting some sympathetic neighbour who would leave flowers or food on the doorstep.

The door burst open as Paul reached it. Amanda was crying. She looked as if she had been dragged through a hedge.

Thirty-Nine

Nell checked everything was in order in the prison. Residents were in the television room, apart from Diane Redmond who now languished in the punishment cell in the basement. Nell checked with the duty officer, and then went up to her flat.

She kicked off her shoes and sat down on the sofa, picking up the unopened morning newspaper.

She had barely read the front page when the telephone rang.

No one usually rang on a Saturday night. After this appalling wedding day, ending with suicide and murder – though in which order she was not sure – and the disappointment of having to banish Diane Redmond to the punishment cell, Nell braced herself for some new blow.

Trying not to sound weary, she picked up the telephone and gave the number.

'Auntie, are you all right?'

'Oh, hello, Roxana, yes, I am. Lovely to hear from you. I thought you'd be out bopping on a Saturday night.'

Roxana laughed. 'You're the only person I know who says bopping.'

'What is the word then?'

'Play safe. Just say dancing. Don't say "Twistin' the Night Away". Anyway, it's too early to go out. Do you want a report on that list of names you gave me? I finally went to Somerset House and read those last wills and testaments, and I did some newspaper follow-ups where I could.'

'Oh yes! I do want to know,' said Nell. 'It's long over-due.' Not that she had forgotten but had been glad of the delay. She ought not to have asked Roxana and should have refused to take the list of names and dates of birth and death given to her by Susan Taylor in such a cloak and dagger fashion.

'Are you ready to hear the score?'

'I will be as soon as I pick up a pencil.'

'I won't say all names of the deceased over the phone. I'll just give you the numbers one to ten. Got your list?'

Nell took the list from the drawer. She was not surprised about her daughter's caution. Roxana worked for a journalist whom Nell thought paranoid. His mantra was 'Everything is secure until it's not'.

She picked up a pencil. 'Begin!'

'You wanted to know if any left a legacy either to the home or to the director with the unlikely name of Dr Block. Is that a made-up name?'

'No.'

'Here goes. Numbers one, two and four made bequests to Dr Block for his care and attention. Wording varied across the deceased donors but, basically, he was regarded as a kind, considerate, thoughtful doctor, and an all-round good chap. No bequest was paid from number one's estate because after outstanding fees for the home, funeral expenses, and an IOU to a fellow resident for cigarettes, there was nothing left. Ditto for numbers two and four – zilch left in the pot. Auntie, I felt so sorry for those dead people. They said such nice things in their last wills and testaments. One of them asked for ice creams for his friends in the home.'

'Oh! That's so touching,' said Nell.

'Do you think the others felt like eating ice cream bought by a dead person?'

'It was a kind gesture. Perhaps Ronald loved ice cream.'

'They must have been crying into their cornets,' said Roxana with a sigh. 'Anyhow, legacies to Dr Block increase when we come to numbers three to ten on the list. Bequests from them starting with number three are as follows. Are you keeping up, Auntie?'

'Yes.'

'Number three, four hundred and fifty pounds; then nine hundred pounds; two hundred and fifty pounds; one hundred pounds; one thousand pounds; two thousand pounds. Next comes a flat in Whitley Bay and lastly the proceeds from a house in Buttershaw that hasn't yet been sold. That is the will of deceased resident number ten, and it is being contested. What do you make of that?'

'I'm not sure. A flat and a house seem generous bequests. but if Dr Block has made a resident's final years peaceful and happy, perhaps they want to ensure he goes on doing so for others. I can see why relatives might take umbrage, but we don't know the circumstances.'

'The relatives probably never visited.'

'Anyway, thank you. You've done a great job.'

'Then I'll say no more, Auntie, except, when are you coming to London again?'

'I'll come one Sunday next month, before the weather changes.'

After they had said their goodbyes, Nell hung up. Going to London could happen sooner rather than later if it was felt necessary for the governor to explain in person to her superiors another murder within a mile of HMP Brackerley.

Tomorrow, Nell would find a moment to hand the information about the wills of her late fellow residents at the home to Susan. On one level, the findings were a shocking abuse of Dr Block's position. It could be totally innocent, with Dr Block putting the money into the running of the home which must cost a fortune to maintain. It was furnished like a hotel. But the legacies would inflame Susan's suspicions.

Nell wished she hadn't become involved. If Susan asked for something like that again, she would direct her to the McKenzies at the post office, or to Harrogate Library. Susan was fit enough to go out and about.

The business left Nell with an uneasy feeling, but what was taking up her thoughts was the prospect of saying goodbye to Lesley and Peter from California. Hearing news that Roland Herbert was alive and well had sparked that old rage and sense of abandonment.

Nell could not avoid church, but she might avoid seeing Lesley and Peter. The church would be packed because of the events of yesterday. Part of her wanted to say, 'Tell that lying idiot who let me down that he has a beautiful daughter.' But why should Roland Herbert know about Roxana when she would never know him?

If it was up to her, and only up to her, Nell would tell Roxana the truth. But there was Nell's sister and brother-in-law to consider. Their names were on Roxana's birth certificate, to avoid the shame of admitting that Nell brought an illegitimate child into the family and narrowly missed being sent to a home for unmarried mothers, with the likely consequence of losing that child to strangers.

That outcome would have been devastating – never to have known her own daughter. Her bright, beautiful, intelligent daughter had just supplied what might be explosive information about the esteemed Dr Block having benefited from his patients' legacies, on what might prove to be a grand scale. If not illegal, this must certainly be unethical. It gave a completely new slant on Susan, Victor and Emma's suspicions about Dr Block shortening the lives of his elderly residents. She hoped they were wrong.

Nell took out her fountain pen. Carefully, she copied the names of each of the deceased residents, their dates of death and the legacies to Dr Block. She wanted these out of her possession. She would return one copy to Susan and give the other to the police, to her old colleague and friend DCI Julian McHale, or one of his officers. They would know what to do with it. As she was writing, she hoped that there was some reasonable explanation, trust or some such thing, or—

She could not think of an 'or'.

It stank.

Forty

Sunday morning, 21 September 1969

The bells of St Michael and All Angels tolled. Nell led her officers and residents through the prison gates for their walk to the Sunday morning service. The mood was subdued. As they neared the manor house, there seemed to Nell to be an involuntary slowing down. Two police cars and a white van were parked inside the manor house gates.

A voice said, 'I'm getting the shivers.'

It was Diane, who had been let out of her cell for the service and was walking between the chief officer and Officer Kitteringham.

As Nell came level with the gates, her old colleague DCI Julian McHale stepped out to speak to her. 'Do you have time for a chat later?'

Nell nodded. 'Give me a ring?'

'See you later.'

As they entered the church, Nell tried to define the strange new atmosphere that seemed to permeate the ancient building. It felt to her that a haze of uncertainty hung over the congregation and the motes of dust in the air proclaimed bewilderment.

Nell, her officers, and residents took their usual places in the second pew, the first row normally being occupied by the Chapins. At first it looked as if they would not attend, but then they filed in: Penny, Amanda, Fred and his fellow band members, Bob and Tim. The chief constable was with them, sitting beside Fred. This took Nell by surprise. She knew that Lancelot Chapin was an important man in the county, just not how important. DCI Julian McHale sat next to the chief constable.

On the opposite aisle was Dr Block with some of his residents, including Susan Taylor, Emma the retired actress and Victor, looking smart in the suit he had worn for his ninetieth birthday party.

Nell had told the chief officer that she had a couple of old friends to speak to after the service and not to wait for her. She would follow on when they left the church.

To Nell, the vicar looked five years older than he had yesterday, and very tired. He managed a good sermon, asking for prayers for Lancelot Chapin, Norman Thwaite and for their families and friends. He added that a police officer would be by the church gate to take details from anyone who could give information, or who wanted to ask questions. The room at the top of the Co-operative Society would be open until seven o'clock that evening, with officers on duty, including the postmaster and special constable Mr McKenzie. 'Please speak to the police if you can help in their investigations. No matter how small or insignificant your awareness or knowledge may seem, if you have an inkling or a feeling that might be pertinent, do say.'

The silence then felt palpable, until a slight uncomfortable shuffling, a clearing of throats, and continuation of the service.

At the end of the service Dr Block's entourage walked up the central aisle to leave the church. Emma dropped one of her gloves and, at the same time, gave a rather theatrical and meaningful glance at Nell.

Nell dutifully picked up the glove and followed. 'You dropped this.'

'Oh, thank you.' She drew on her gloves, leaning towards Nell, whispering, 'Come to tea at three o'clock. Bring a plain-clothes police officer.' She walked on.

Susan said hello to Nell. Victor studiously ignored her until they were in the church porch. He was looking at a leaflet about the work of missionaries. Without moving his lips, he said, 'Three o'clock.'

Nell entered into the spirit of Emma and Victor's cloak-and-dagger performance. She picked up another leaflet and slid Susan's list of deceased elderly people's names and legacies between the folds and then she stepped outside.

Susan was on the church steps. She waved a walking stick at Nell. 'Had a fall, but you can't keep a good woman down!'

Nell moved to be beside Susan. 'Susan, you asked me for certain donations, legacies. Well, here is the answer.'

Susan, not quick off the mark, looked slightly puzzled. 'It was when we walked through the woods a little while ago.'

'Oh yes,' said Susan. 'So it was.'

Nell wanted to be sure. 'I've done what you asked. Can I now leave this for you to deal with?'

'This is exactly the right time. Thank you.'

Nell felt relieved to have passed on the information.

Yet when Dr Block came into view, pushing a frail old man in a wheelchair towards the gates, she felt a twinge of doubt. He seemed just the kind of man who would be appreciated by most of his residents.

He caught Nell's eye and with a mournful look reached out to shake her hand. 'Miss Lewis, such a tragic, heartbreaking death and so sad for all concerned. Now is perhaps not the time to say it, but your caterers did a magnificent job.'

'Thank you. I'll pass that on to them.'

Lesley and Peter were in the churchyard and came to join her as Dr Block went to shepherd his residents. 'We're so sorry about all this,' said Peter. 'We hoped we might have a chat and a cup of coffee, but we'll just jump straight to the heart of what we have to say. This may be our only opportunity.' He turned to Lesley. 'You tell her.'

'It's about Roland Herbert. Peter sees him at reunions. I told him we were coming to visit my parents. He asked about you, whether we kept in touch. I said no, we hadn't kept in touch. Is it okay if I give him news of you?'

'Don't bother,' said Nell. 'It's history.'

Lesley and Peter exchanged a look. Peter said, 'Lesley, let me tell this.'

Before Nell said that she didn't want to hear, Peter began.

'Nell, I know this might seem like a tall tale, and too late. Roland would've walked across coals to be with you. He hired a car for the two for you to drive to Gretna Green.'

Nell made no comment. Men would stick together. She'd never thought of Roland or Peter as liars, but she had been naïve back then. She had waited for that car, the car that did not arrive.

When she did not respond, Peter said, 'Roland was

confined to barracks, as one of a group chosen for a special operation that involved beach landings in Normandy. It was hush hush – no communication whatsoever – because it was the first attempt, the initial rehearsal for a landing on the French coast. Even now, it's kept quiet because it went very wrong. The authorities don't own up to mistakes that cost the lives of their own men, and that's what happened. You won't read about it, won't hear about it because we were sworn to silence.'

Nell said nothing. Whether this was true or not, it was all far too late. Roland could have got word to her somehow.

Lesley said quickly, 'Many men drowned. Roland was one of the few who were rescued, but he was badly injured. He spent almost a year in hospital. He's never forgotten you.'

Just forgotten his promises, thought Nell. She was surprised at Lesley taking Roland's part. It was naïve of her. Nell long ago decided that Roland was fickle, that there was a line of a song that summed him up. *'If I'm not near the girl I love, I love the girl I'm near.'*

'So he was in hospital almost a year?'

'Yes,' said Peter, 'leg on a hoist, covered in bandages. It was touch and go for a while.'

'And he kept on writing these imaginary letters to me, until he married his nurse?'

Nell saw from the look on Lesley's and Peter's faces that she was right.

'How did you know he married his nurse?' asked Lesley.

It was a good question. The answer was so simple. 'I had a subscription at W H Smiths lending library. Patient and nurse romances were almost as popular as doctors and nurses.'

Nell had overdosed on sentimentality and self-pity once,

but that was long ago. She became a police officer. She joined the prison service. Neither job was for cissies.

The chief officer was leading the walk back to the prison. Nell exchanged a peck on the cheek with Lesley and shook hands with Peter.

'I'm very glad to have met you both again,' she said, smiling. 'I wish you a safe journey home.'

'And you have a prison to run,' said Peter, catching her glance at the women heading back towards HMP Brackerley.

'I do.'

'We were meant to meet again. I'll write to you,' said Lesley.

'I'll write back,' said Nell.

Roland Herbert had once given Nell a practical gift, a powerful torch. 'For the blackouts,' he had said. The torch proved useful. Otherwise, Nell might have slung it long ago. Sentimentality helped no one. But she was glad to have had news of him. It would stop the wondering. Nell walked on, other things to think about. A lot to do.

She fell into step, today walking at the back of the crocodile that wove its way to the prison.

Nell turned her thoughts from the past to the here and now, thinking of Diane Redmond. Diane, who ought to be a success story. Nell thought she had allowed Diane too much freedom too soon.

Sunlight filtered through the trees, creating a dappled pattern on the path. Nell realised that she was walking very fast. She slowed down, hearing someone behind her.

'Nell! Is this a walking race!'

Nell turned to see Lesley pursuing her, out of breath. 'I'm

sorry. I didn't mean to stir up the past. Only I don't want to part without saying that Roland has always pined for you, if that's the right word. He felt ill when he didn't hear back from you.'

Nell remained calm. 'He married his nurse. I'm sure she helped him get over it.'

'It's a pure fluke that you and I have caught up with each other again. But Roland did say . . . '

'What?'

'That you would have married anyway, but it was Gretna Green because you were expecting.'

'Told the battalion, did he?'

'No! It's me wanting to know. Nell, you're my oldest friend.'

'My daughter was brought up by my sister as her own. If you ever tell anyone—'

'Oh, Nell, as if I would. But don't you think a child should know her parents? Even if it's only so that the parents can apologise for the bunions and the short sight?'

'Roxana doesn't need spectacles and her feet are just fine.'

Lesley smiled. 'I'm glad. Roland would love to know you're well. He'd love to hear about Roxana.'

'Lesley, it's all too late. He never wrote, not even to say how are you, do you need anything, do we have a girl or a boy?'

'Oh, but he did. When he couldn't hold a pen, he got some-one to write for him—'

'His nurse?'

'Perhaps he did. And perhaps she wouldn't have mailed his letter. But I wrote letters to you for him, one a month for four months. I sent them myself. Airmail. I also wrote to you, just once, with my address on the back. Your mother may have guessed what it was about.'

Nell came to a stop. So did Lesley. 'Roland never forgot you.'

They stepped off the path and stood by a tree, so quiet that Nell heard the leaves rustle in the breeze. Nell did not want to have her anger taken away. That might leave her feeling pathetic. She would not ask what Roland had said.

Officers and inmates had walked ahead. Even so, Lesley lowered her voice to a whisper. 'Do you think your mother intercepted Roland's letters, and mine? She didn't like you going with a Yank, did she?'

Nell thought of her mother, who did not really like Nell going out with anyone, but especially an American who might whisk her away. Nell worked, paid her way, did more than her share of housekeeping.

'My mother quite likely did throw Roland's letters on the fireback,' Nell added, as if this might be an explanation or mitigation.

'Can I tell Roland that I saw you, and you didn't receive his letters, but that you're well and—'

'I don't know. Just write to me, Lesley. I can't talk now. Have a safe journey back.'

'Look after yourself, Nell.'

'You too.'

Nell walked on, feeling slightly dazed. When someone whistled, as she rounded a bend in the path, Nell ignored the sound and carried on. When someone whistled again, she stopped.

Nell turned to look at the figure now standing by the oak tree. It was Susan, dressed in the same black coat and hat as she had worn at Monica Mason's funeral. She had a walking stick in each hand.

262

'I'm glad that woman kept you nattering,' she called. 'I'd never have caught up.'

Nell walked back to speak to her. 'Susan what are you thinking of? You were in a wheelchair yesterday with a damaged knee.'

'Tutankhamun would envy my bandages.'

'You should be resting.'

'Without these two walking sticks, I'd be resting flat on my back. Thank you for passing on information about the legacies to Dr Block. We will peruse with interest.'

'And?'

'And it didn't come from you, Nell. I appreciate that you have a position to keep up.'

'If it's about you, Emma and Victor wanting me to take a police officer to the home at three o'clock, I already have the message from Emma and from Victor.'

'It is too much to ask of you to bring a police officer to us.'

'Yes, it is.'

'We thought as much, and have a plan B.'

'Tell me,' said Nell, hoping that she would be excluded from plan B.

'Dr Block will be out this afternoon, but it would be just like him to delay departure. Come at three o'clock – not to the house. We will be by the first gate at the adjoining field. Our story is that you were going for a spin in that car of yours which doesn't get enough of an outing, and gave us a lift. Do this for me, Nell, and I will never ask another favour. Drive us to the Co-operative Society building. I'm not up to scratch today and I know that building. The room at the top is three floors up. I don't like the way that lift rattles. It has been known to stop between floors.'

'You could have spoken to the officers outside the church.'

'Weren't you once a policewoman, Nell?'

'Yes I was.'

'And now you deal with convicts. So, please take a guess at why I would not speak to those officers in public. I would have risked going to the post office to buy a stamp and speak privately to Special Constable McKenzie, but my information won't wait until Monday. No one with any sense will make a show of themselves in public.'

Forty-One

Brackerley main street was quiet on that bright Sunday morning when Sergeant Ambrose arrived at the Co-operative Society building to prepare for the meeting. She had arrived at 7.30, having no wish for an audience while writing on a blackboard.

She was let in by a caretaker who wore a brown overall. 'Shocking do,' he said. 'I hope you catch whoever done it.'

'We will,' said Angela.

The caretaker looked oddly pleased with himself, perhaps glad of the overtime. Double pay on Sundays.

'Special Constable McKenzie was here,' said the caretaker, as he led Angela up the stairs. 'He set up a blackboard. He's gone home for his breakfast and will be back.'

There were two top rooms at Brackerley Co-operative Society. The smaller one, where Co-op staff took their breaks, would be used for taking witness statements. In the larger space, stored groceries had been moved to one end of the room to allow for a single table and half a dozen chairs ready for the briefing. Joining Angela would be DCI

Julian McHale, DI Ian Dennis, PC Mudie, and Special Constable McKenzie.

Angela used the left side of the board for times, from the moment the caterers and then the bar staff arrived to set up, until after the body was discovered. She had her notes of names and facts. As a rehearsal for her briefing, she told the story to herself in her head. The caterers arrived at nine, bar staff at ten.

What Angela could tell her colleagues was that Norman Thwaite was in the clear, that he listened to the father of the bride's speech. He spoke briefly to his wife. He drove from the premises at 1.15. The gateman noted the time of Norman's departure. Only a certain number of guests parked in the grounds. Norman was one of them. Others were directed to park in the nearby field. Norman and his son Paul had dropped off Gloria at the manor house that morning. Gloria went in a car to the church. Norman and Paul walked. Angela had made further enquiries. Paul was seen congratulating the bride and groom outside the church, waving to his parents, and walking off through the church gate. That was the last sighting anyone had of him. He was in just one photograph after the wedding.

The next-door neighbour, Ted Platt, saw Norman return and park outside his house, without Mrs Thwaite. Mr Platt gives the time as 1.30, saying he had just turned off the one o'clock news. Mr Platt was not entirely sure what time he knocked on the back door, let himself in and smelled gas. At that time, Mr Chapin was mingling with guests and had photographs taken. Mr Platt made the 999 call reporting the suicide at 2.22 pm.

Diane Redmond took what should have been a

fifteen-minute break at 2.00 pm. She sat on the bench behind the marquee, and had a smoke – half a Senior Service. She mentioned hearing three records. According to the DJ, two of these three records were played before she went on her break. The record she claimed was the spur for her to abscond had been on the DJ's playlist at 2.15. She saw no one else behind, on or near the bench, or behind the marquee while she was there or as she left. When Diane wasn't back by 2.30, Linda was sent to look for her and found the body of Lancelot Chapin with a knife through his heart.

Norman Thwaite was not on the premises when Mr Chapin was murdered.

It had taken Angela over an hour to go over notes and chalk on the board and ten minutes to pass on the information. A WPC had been drafted in to take notes and write up a report.

Angela was so caught up with her blackboard timings that she left until last Cherry Davenport's statement about seeing Penny Chapin and Bob, the best man, in a boutique on London's King's Road where Penny bought a kaftan for herself and a shirt for Bob.

Ian had checked his notes and gave the dates when Penny was in London, and the name of the hotel she stayed in. He reported that Lancelot Chapin had noted the dates of Penny's visit on his calendar, along with the hotel telephone number, and that it was the same hotel at which Lance and Penny had stayed when they had gone to visit Amanda and to meet Fred. The invoice for that and a subsequent visit were in Lance's accounts file, but nothing for Penny's later visit. Penny had her own bank account. Ian had not seen Penny's cheque stubs or statements.

'Let's see what else we hear about Penny and Bob,' said

Ian. It could be simply that Penny might be backing the band's hopes for a rock festival in the grounds of Brackerley Manor House. If so, the Northern Knights could all be kitted out in gold-plated suits of armour, and the good folk of Brackerley be complaining about motorbikes, coach trips, hippies, and tents.

Ian gave an account of Mr Chapin's business contacts, adding, 'He had an appointment with the coroner for next Wednesday. We need to know the purpose of that appointment, also who else Mr Chapin was talking to yesterday. Had he gone to the bench to meet someone privately? We're waiting on forensics. In the Chapin kitchen there are four knives from a set of five.'

At that moment, the door opened. DCI Julian McHale came in. 'Morning everyone. I've just spoken to Mrs Chapin and the chief constable. They know each other socially. He'll call on her tomorrow morning at ten. I'll be there to give a progress report.'

Julian looked at Angela's notes on the board. 'I see you've made a start.'

'A good start,' said Angela. But a progress report might contain very little that would be of interest to the widow who wants to know who killed her husband.

'Let's look at motives,' said Julian. 'There may be something that will ring a bell for Penny – a falling out, a debt, someone incensed about the sale of land.'

'This may not be something Mrs Chapin wants to hear,' said Ian, 'but the motive I start with is financial gain.' When Ian cleared his throat, Angela knew that his thought processes had led him to an idea that would transform itself into an order, to be issued in the form of a request, and addressed to her. She also knew that he was testing a loose tooth with his tongue, and that he was afraid of the dentist.

Ian said to Julian, 'Sir, would it be a good idea to list motives on the board?'

'Yes it would,' said Julian.

Angela had left the chalk on the ledge of the blackboard, but it had found its way onto the table. Perhaps Ian intended to be sure to take his chalk home, but he now pushed it towards Angela, giving her an encouraging look and saying, 'So, the first motive is gain. Chapin wealth comes from the land and property. Property brings in an income. The land could bring in more than it does. It's not farmed. It's not utilised. Lancelot Chapin has three overseas investments that are allowed to grow, and two from which he takes an income. He has two local investments, involving director-ships that provide steady returns. He is a director of the Brackerley Maternity Home and the Brackerley Home for the Elderly. He has an income from the village houses built by his grandfather. Families that have stayed put are on a controlled rent, according to the stipulation the grandfather made, and that rent is less than the market value. The Chapins own the leasehold on the land so draw an income from that. When families move out, he can increase the rent to current values. The estate office combined with rent office is a few doors away, above the bank.'

Angela rose to the occasion. Now a dab hand at chalking, she wrote, and underlined, the word MOTIVES.

On the line below, she wrote *Gain.*

I should have been a teacher, she thought as she looked round the room.

Julian said, 'Second, I'd look at conviction, the strong

belief that the meadowlands must remain untouched. The protestors started with petitions, went on to wire cutting and damaging property. They infiltrated the reception and walked out when they heard something that didn't suit them. That's a peaceful protest, but it only takes one bad apple to turn something nasty. Were there gate crashers?'

Under *Gain*, Angela wrote *Conviction*.

She decided against telling Ian that there was an open invitation to many of the villagers, among whom were protestors against Chapin's plans. Ian could find that out for himself.

Ian returned to *Gain*. 'The chief beneficiaries under Mr Chapin's will are his wife and daughter Amanda, and by extension Amanda's husband, Fred Harding.'

Julian said, 'Amanda didn't appear when I was at the house this morning. From what Mrs Chapin said, I got the impression that she was still upstairs.'

'She went to her aunt's house last night,' said Ian, leaving it to Angela to explain to Julian's raised eyebrows the closeness between the families.

Julian was surprised. 'It was Amanda's wedding day. Her father has been murdered, and she leaves her husband and stepmother and goes to see her aunt and stays the night?'

'Her widowed aunt, sir,' said Ian. 'Mr Chapin was generous to Mr Thwaite. In 1958, he bought a Morris Minor for Norman's use. There's no sign of any payments being made for that car. I compared the number plate of the original Morris Minor with the car that is parked outside the Thwaites's Willow Lane address. Mr Thwaite has kept the same car. Mr Thwaite serviced Mr Chapin's Bentley, but no payment is made for that service. So, mutual aid, but somewhat one-sided.

'Gloria Thwaite is employed as housekeeper and receives a weekly wage. That is as much as I have gleaned from the documents in filing cabinets and in the safe.'

'Thank you, Ian,' said the DCI.

'Also – this may not be significant – Amanda and Fred have been cohabiting in a squat. When I interviewed Amanda, Fred was over attentive, interrupting the interview bringing in a pair of socks, offering to sit in. There was a full house last night. Band members, guests staying the night. I got the impression Amanda wanted peace and quiet with her auntie.'

Ian wondered whether he ought to have done more than send a constable to follow Amanda to Willow Lane. Was he missing something? Gloria was a minor beneficiary under Chapin's will, but the legacy would mean a great deal to her.

Gloria's husband must have suffered from depression. Had there been some request from the Thwaites for help that was refused by Lance Chapin? Might Gloria be a person of interest?

Special Constable McKenzie was shuffling in his seat, and frowning. Julian gave him the nod to speak. 'You've thought of something, Mr McKenzie?'

McKenzie leaned forward. He knew himself to be the one with the greatest local knowledge. He humbly took pride that he and his wife were well-informed about going-ons in Brackerley. They were the founts of knowledge, the keepers of secrets. Like all postmasters and postmistresses across the land, they were the most respected pillars of the community. 'Ask at the post office' had not become the village mantra without good reason.

'Mr Chapin was an honourable man, but we all have flaws.' Mr McKenzie picked up his fountain pen and clung onto it. 'I wonder if the relaxed setting of a wedding might have given an opportunity to a villager who held a powerful grudge against him, someone who wanted to take revenge. Rightly or wrongly, it was believed that Mr Chapin delayed the gas switchover. Two lives were lost by suicide, one of them a girl of seventeen.'

'Indeed,' said Ian, in a manner that suggested he had thought of little else but revenge all day. 'Something Mrs Chapin said hinted as much when she spoke about the trip wire that caused her injury when her horse stumbled. She believed the sabotage was intended to unseat her husband. Revenge is a powerful motive.'

Under the motives *Gain* and *Conviction,* Angela wrote *Revenge.*

Special Constable McKenzie raised his hand. 'There's a lad called Brendan whose name comes up whenever there's trouble.'

'We all know about him,' said local constable Mudie. 'Brendan was there on Saturday, filling his face.'

'And that's all he was doing, that and showing off,' said McKenzie. 'PC Mudie and I kept an eye on him and so did our wives, didn't we, Mr Mudie?'

'We did,' said Mudie. 'And under the topic of revenge, I'm wracking my brains as to a person likely to want rid of Mr Chapin, and I have come up with several, but am reluctant to name names too soon. I have spoken to those villagers on more than one occasion. It is a law of nature for landlords to be resented, but I say to those who complain, "Better the devil you know." Despite that, there are those who occupy Chapin houses who have wished their landlord to the devil.'

'Then may he rest in peace,' said Special Constable McKenzie.

'Amen to that,' said PC Mudie, before deciding he had said too much.

Angela glanced at Ian for confirmation that wishing a landlord to the devil was a motive. Ian gave a nod. Below *Gain, Conviction, Revenge,* Angela wrote *Elimination.*

As he saw his suggestion written on the board and given a name, PC Mudie felt a surge of pride. Indeed, he felt slightly drunk with it.

He waited for someone to come up with what to him seemed the blindingly obvious. When no one spoke, PC Mudie said quietly, 'Ought we to look at the prisoner at HMP Brackerley who is in for murder?' Mudie scratched his ear. 'Linda Rogers is serving a sentence for killing a man for no apparent reason – or none that she would give. Yesterday, she could have got her hands on any number of knives, while wearing white gloves and leaving no prints. She knows enough about investigations to attempt to guard against blood splatter.'

'What would her motive be?' Angela asked, as she returned the chalk to the blackboard ledge and flicked chalk dust from her fingers. 'I interviewed her. The prisoners' shoes and clothing have been sent for examination. If there is any evidence against Linda Rogers or any other prisoner, that will be considered. She had no motive for wanting Mr Chapin dead.'

Mudie, suddenly free from his shell, said, 'But there was no motive when she killed that man in the university halls of residence. There is such a thing as lust for killing. It has been written about.'

Mudie knew this for sure. Whenever he had asked his grandmother to tell him a bedtime story, she had always read from what his mother called one of her bloodthirsty penny dreadfuls. These readings had encouraged young Phil Mudie to join the police force.

Ian looked at Angela, giving her the nod to write. She picked up the chalk, and wrote *Lust for Killing*, before slamming down the chalk.

'I think you have something to say about Miss Rogers' previous conviction,' said Ian.

Angela had thought he would never ask. 'There is a group formed in Camden called Justice for Linda. They are convinced there was a miscarriage of justice in her case. They say because she would not speak in her own defence, that does not mean she was guilty of an unprovoked attack. They claim to know that Linda's victim had assaulted and traumatised not only Linda but others, and that Linda could not bear the humiliation of recounting why she reacted as she did. This group do seem to have information from somewhere, though we don't know where. I understand that Linda is a model prisoner. We have her clothing and her shoes bagged. We can safely wait and see whether forensic evidence gives us reason to believe that Linda Rogers would have taken a knife with her when she went to see whether Diane was still powdering her nose or having a smoke.'

There was a moment's silence in the room. Everyone had been encouraged to speak. PC Mudie had no aspirations to be a detective, his strength was his local knowledge. There was a certain amount of appreciation and sympathy for him.

Mudie was conscious of this feeling as he looked at the words on the board. He was satisfied to read *Lust for Killing*.

Angela wrote one more word. *Jealousy*.

She looked at Julian. 'Sir, before you came in, I reported information that may suggest a romantic triangle, with Mrs Chapin and Bob the best man being more than friends.'

'Ah,' said Julian. 'There's always talk. Keep looking.'

274

From the look on Julian's face, Angela guessed that the DCI hoped they wouldn't find anything in that direction. So would I feel that way if I were meeting Mrs Chapin and the chief constable tomorrow, she thought. Of course, it could have been purely a spur of the moment burst of generosity that, having bought herself a kaftan, Penny splashed out on a shirt for her future son-in-law's best man.

Ian cleared his throat. 'There is something that Tim the guitarist believes we should know, and Bob wants to keep quiet about. We'll interview them at the station.'

Special Constable McKenzie frowned, and then chipped in. 'Some people might think Mrs Chapin flighty, with her long hair and long dresses, but there's more to her. She's friends with my sister who teaches at a college. Penny went to night school for several years, qualifying in basic accountancy and office work and typing. She plays a big part in keeping up the business side in the Chapin household. Let's just say, she'll keep things running. As to anything outside that, I've no knowledge. She may or may not be on good terms with a man nearer her own age.'

Gain
Conviction
Revenge
Elimination
Lust for Killing
Jealousy

Julian, Ian, Angela, PC Mudie and Special Constable McKenzie looked carefully at these six motives.

'Okay,' said Julian. 'We have motives, we have statements.'

We're relying on timings from the accounts of the prisoners' breaks, between the time Diane Redmond went on her break and Linda was sent to look for her. Is Diane Redmond lying? Did she do a runner because she saw the body, took fright, didn't want to be involved? She'd know how serious it would be to have walked past a murder victim, or to be the last person to have seen him alive.' Julian looked at Angela. 'You interviewed her?'

Angela, still standing by the board, wished she had gone back to her seat. 'Yes sir, I interviewed Diane. Her account rang true.'

'She'd had time to think about it.'

Angela liked the DCI. He was smart and approachable. But to be chalk monitor *and* have your interviewing skills questioned in front of colleagues, the local PC and a special constable was a bit much.

Angela went back to her chair. 'Sir, Diane and the other caterers saw Mr Chapin in the marquee that morning. He came to say hello. If he had been on the bench, alive, Diane would have spoken to him. I believe she would have said so in her interview.' Angela did not state the obvious and say that helping police with enquiries would look good on a prisoner's report and count towards parole. 'Had Diane seen Mr Chapin with a knife in him, would she, with her head full of love songs and thoughts of her kids, have walked past him? No. Would she have finished her smoke and dropped her tab end under the bench? No. But she did flick her tab under the bench. During examination of the scene, her tab end, with her lipstick on it, was found.'

Without missing a beat, Julian said, 'That brings me to my next point. Either Lancelot Chapin was on that bench to have five minutes away from the madness of a wedding, or he was there because it was a private place to talk to someone he knew. Someone he trusted.'

The telephone rang.

Forty-Two

DI Ian Dennis, who was nearest the phone, picked it up. He listened. 'Yes, sir, and he is here.' He paused, raising his eyebrows. 'Just a moment please.' Ian put his hand over the mouthpiece and passed the phone to Julian. 'Sir, the chief constable's office. He's left his office but had one more question.' Everyone went quiet while Julian took the phone.

'DCI McHale speaking.'

After a moment, Julian said, 'Yes, I was there this morning. We've done everything necessary. I'm at the local incident room now.' He listened for a moment, put his hand over the mouthpiece and said to Ian, 'How many people have we seen this morning?'

Ian held up four fingers, knowing that this included a couple with suspicions about their next-door neighbour's comings and goings; the Co-op carctaker who had a neighbour dispute with one of the meadowland protesters; and a fourth who complained about speeding traffic, saying that if it got any worse, Brackerley would need a lollipop man to see children across the road to school.

Julian said, 'We're not into double figures yet but we're expecting people later, as they leave the eleven o'clock church service.' He paused. 'Yes. I'll be at the manor house tomorrow morning.' He replaced the telephone receiver, moved his hand across his chin in a checking-for-stubble fashion and looked at Ian.

Ian said, 'We won't have anything from forensics before Tuesday. We're hurrying up developing and printing photographs. Of the photographs we have so far, we've put names to faces. From the brief initial interviews, we know who people were talking to and are working to see if it stacks up. We'll look out for interlopers, anyone who wasn't on the guest list, or didn't account for their movements.'

Julian knew that their job was not just about *doing* something, it was about being *seen* to do something. He spoke to them all. 'We need someone knocking on doors in the village. What about the people who walked out when Chapin admitted that the sale of land was still likely to happen? Where did they go?'

'We don't know,' said Angela. 'They could have gone home, or to the pub, or wherever they meet to work out their petitions and so on. Probably one of their houses. I have names and addresses.'

'We need to talk to them,' said Julian. 'Who are these people? How committed are they to opposing the developments? Do we have any fanatics out there?'

PC Mudie, seated directly opposite Angela, raised his hand. Mudie had deliberately avoided promotion, being happy to let others do the brain work. He worried slightly that he had attracted too much attention to himself this morning. He ought to be careful or there might be a suggestion that he take the sergeants' exam.

'Permission to knock on the early leavers' doors? Permission to go now and be back by half past two, sir?'

'Granted,' said the DCI. 'I want times people arrived, where they were, who they were with, who they saw or talked to, did they take photographs and if so, let us have their rolls of film, which we will return intact. Give them a signature. Find out if for any reason they came back to the manor house later. If they came by car, get registration numbers. Find out about these petitions and protests, and any wild cards. Any threats, or damage to property.'

'Yes, sir.'

In this respect, PC Mudie was on his toes. He had asked the gateman for a list of names and car number plates. During the reception, he had walked the manor house grounds, called in at the refreshment tent and availed himself of a good lunch.

Mudie left the room, trying to hide his smile. Too much talking and listening gave him a headache. He liked knocking on doors and asking questions to which there would be definite answers or a don't know. He liked the interested way people looked at him when he gave his rank and name. He liked the glimpses into houses. He had told his wife that parquet flooring seemed to be popular, especially with people who had an expensive car on the drive.

Mudie closed the door gently behind him. But for the clatter of his boots, he would have skipped down the stairs.

Julian continued. He looked at Ian. 'Any note to himself in Mr Chapin's diary or on the calendar about someone he might have wanted to speak to at the reception?'

Ian shook his head. 'No. Nothing in his diary for yesterday except the word "Wedding". His first appointment was Tuesday, with Tom Jackson the surveyor and on Wednesday with the new coroner, Mr Kempster. The duty officer at the station tried to contact Mr Kempster on his home number today but there's no reply. There are more photographs being gathered. We'll identify every person, starting with anyone who was with or near Mr Chapin, and anyone among his acquaintances with whom he had unfinished business. There are other ways in and out of the manor house than the main gates, but being relaxed enough to sit on a bench and talk to someone indicates that person was there by invitation.'

The DCI looked round the table, taking in everyone. 'What about the Northern Knights band? Check their backgrounds. Do they really have a tour lined up or is that a load of baloney? They're of no fixed abode. Are they looking for a more luxurious squat?'

Ian said, 'Sir, I have their agent's telephone number. Sunday, no one's answering. We'll call tomorrow. The manor house will be searched today, with the explanation that the perpetrator may have entered the premises.'

The DCI nodded. 'Make sure they go about their search in a way that won't involve complaints to the chief constable.'

Forty-Three

The curtains at 33 Willow Lane stayed closed. Paul took cups of tea and slices of toast upstairs to his mother and Amanda. They were in the twin beds that had been his and Steven's.

Paul had slept in the chair downstairs, or sat there all night, dozing, waking, going out to walk round the garden. He sat on the bench by the cherry tree, watching the sun come up. Who would look after the garden now, who would wage war on the dandelions? His mother only ever topped up the bird bath and put out crumbs. Look after your mam, Dad had said in his note. Paul would have to come home. He couldn't leave her alone. He would drive to work each day in his dad's car.

It had taken him by surprise when at mid-morning someone came to the back door. It was Mr Grieves, the vicar. Paul asked him to come into the garden and sit on the bench, thinking that his mother and Amanda may not be sleeping, but he didn't want them disturbed. Whatever the vicar had to say, Paul did not want to hear. He remembered the religion classes at school. He remembered what was said about suicide.

The vicar sat on the bench and praised the garden. He told Paul that prayers were said for 'them' at the early service and would be again at eleven o'clock. Paul guessed that the 'them' was his mother, himself, and Steven.

'And for Mr Chapin?' Paul said, knowing who would take precedence, who would be allowed to be buried in the churchyard, who would be allowed into heaven.

The vicar circled round this, saying often there was a last-minute regret, a last-minute changing of mind.

Paul did not say, 'Much good that does us.' He looked at the long shadow of the poplar tree.

'I saw Mrs Chapin,' said Mr Grieves. 'Fred will call soon for Amanda.'

A little later, after the vicar had left, the kitchen door opened. Amanda came into the garden. Paul gave her the message about the service, and about Fred. 'He'll call soon.'

'Okay.'

'Did I do the right thing not telling Mam the vicar was here?'

'Yes.' Amanda looked at the apple tree. Some apples had fallen. Auntie Gloria ought to be baking a pie, making chutney. 'Your mam wonders at the notes. She says the little note saying sorry was in Uncle Norman's jacket the last time he tried to take his life and she stopped him.'

'What?!'

'She thinks the other note in your wellington boot might be the same. You haven't been home for a while. When did you last wear your wellies?'

'I don't know, maybe digging the garden over, could have been March.'

'I thought you should know. She's surprised that Uncle

Norman used a whole page of Basildon Bond to write so few words to you, and not a word for Steven.'

Paul did not have an answer for that. Amanda said, 'I'm going to stay in the garden for a while. Will you make me another cup?'

'Yeah.'

Usually, he would have said, 'What did your last servant die of?' But this time he simply said, 'Anything else?'

'Soft boiled egg for your mam, two-and-a-half minutes, half a slice of bread and butter cut in soldiers. She hasn't eaten.'

'Do you want an egg?'

'Yes please. Hard boiled, five minutes, bread and butter.'

'Stop here if you want.'

'Better not. There are people I want to see the back of. Last night, the house was full. Penny's best friend came to the wedding and brought her sister. They're in the top room. There's Bob and Tim and two old friends of Dad's who came a long way. I'd never met them, they were just names to me, names he mentioned once or twice. And that stupid thing we did yesterday, going to talk to people in the marquee. Penny's idea, and all the time, I'm thinking, Dad's dead. And now I'm thinking the same about Uncle Norman.'

'It's mad,' said Paul. 'It's not real. We're with our parents all our lives and think we know everything about them. We know nothing.'

'Don't think about it yet. Just boil the eggs.'

It was a revelation to Amanda that they could speak of ordinary things, of tea and bread and eggs. But neither of them could bear much else.

The memory had been in Amanda's thoughts most of

the night, since Auntie Gloria told her about the previous occasions when Uncle Norman had tried to end his life, and how she blamed herself, how she could have done more and especially on Amanda's wedding day, the day when by rights Norman should have walked Amanda down the aisle. And she told Amanda about that night in 1947, the deep snow, and the next morning her baby gone from the cot in the nursery.

'Died in the night.'

Amanda went to the tree that she, Steven and Paul had used as their dead letter box. They thought it was entirely secret, but there was one day, much later, when they had long ago stopped playing spies. She had called and no one was in. There was no note in the dead letter box but there was a bag of Liquorice Allsorts, with the blue ones gone. Uncle Norman always ate the blue ones, because no one else would. He had cut out the empty stop press column of the evening paper and wrote, 'to our little lass, back in an hour or so'. It turned out that Steven had fallen from a tree and broken his arm, and they'd all four of them gone to the hospital in Harrogate.

Remembering that incident told Amanda that Uncle Norman knew about the dead letter box. He must have seen them leaving and collecting messages, passing on clues about 'the-enemy-without', Herr von Strickenfoot, and 'the-enemy-within', Lord Dastardly Rich, and his wife, Lady Furcoat.

Patriots and spies, cowboys and Indians, Roundheads and Royalists no longer left messages in the dead letter box.

Amanda went to look, just in case.

There were four envelopes there, each in Uncle Norman's best writing. One was addressed to 'My Dearest Wife'.

There was a letter each for Steven and Paul. And one for 'Our Little Lass'. Those three words said what Auntie Gloria had taken a much longer time to tell Amanda last night as they lay in the beds that had been Steven's and Paul's.

Amanda looked across the neat garden. She spoke to the solitary dandelion that had appeared overnight.

'It wouldn't have mattered,' she told the flower. 'I could have walked myself down the aisle, or all four of them could've. Dad and Uncle Norman on one side and Auntie Gloria and the ghost of my dead mother.' It chilled Amanda to think that the mother who died when Amanda was six had also been deceived, but perhaps that was for the best. She died believing she gave birth to a healthy baby girl. She died knowing that baby was in good hands.

Amanda decided that if she ever had a child with a wish for wedlock, she would urge that child to marry secretly. They might avoid difficult situations. Their nearest and dearest might survive.

The dandelion appeared to nod. As she heard her own thoughts, Uncle Norman's voice came from the dandelion. He said, 'I've never known a child prefer hard boiled eggs to soft.' He said, 'I don't mind eating the blue Liquorice Allsorts. You get used to anything.'

Just as Amanda thought she may be going mad, Auntie Gloria came into the garden wearing her dressing gown. She sat on the bench and Amanda went to join her and gave her the letter addressed to 'My Dearest Wife'.

'Here's what I would have liked to know a long time ago,' said Auntie Gloria.

She read the letter but could not bring herself to read the words aloud. She passed the letter to Amanda.

Dearest Gloria,

*I should have believed you when you claimed our child
had been taken. I thought you were delirious with sorrow.
My folly was to believe what I was told by the doctor. He
said a tragic infant death could happen, even when a woman
had healthy babies before. He said your brain and your body
could not take in that your baby died. He said he could
arrange for you to have a place in a special hospital where
they would treat you for what was happening in your mind
and because you were under his care, although he had no
responsibility, he would arrange a place for you without
charge. Do you remember that I told you? You went quiet.
You said, 'He is talking about a madhouse for a woman who
won't believe lies. Who will look after Steven and Paul if you
have me committed because I recognise a lie? Who will look
after you?'*

*Do you remember, Gloria, that for a long time, you
would not speak to me? You went to see Mrs Chapin. I feared
in case you would take the baby and be in trouble, and I
thought you might be sent away. You began to look after
Amanda. It was long afterwards that I knew you was right,
that Amanda was ours. Even then, it was not until Lance
Chapin said something, when he had a skinful on him, that
the penny dropped. He was good to me when times were
hard, letting me build the garage business for a peppercorn
rent, until I got on my feet. One day him, me and Governor
Harding from the borstal had too much to drink. Lance
put his arm around me. He said, 'Norman, Amanda has
brightened my life. I am so very grateful.'*

*I thought he meant grateful to his late wife, or to God,
but then it dawned on me. It dawned on me so slowly that*

it was the next day when I woke early and got up, couldn't sleep. It was me. Lance was grateful to me.

I had been dense. I am writing this to you when we heard from Amanda that she was engaged to be married. I should be walking our daughter down the aisle. You asked me time and time again what ailed me. I didn't have the words to tell you, but I think you knew,

Your loving husband Norman

When Gloria had stopped crying, she said, 'Norman was always slow on the uptake. He believed in people's good nature. But when the penny dropped, why didn't he tell me, why didn't he speak?'

It took Amanda a long time to find words. She looked at her Auntie Gloria. 'Uncle Norman didn't have to take his life. We wouldn't have blamed him. He didn't know any better.'

Gloria's face was like a mask. 'Oh, I blamed him. He should have believed me.'

Amanda put her arm around her Auntie Gloria. 'Did my mother know, at the end I mean?'

'No. Your mother was a lovely person. The day I went to her, and held you, I saw that she may never be properly well. I couldn't say what I meant to say, I just knew that I must take care of you.'

'And Dad?'

'Lance understood that no one would take care of you as I would. Penny came later, as a childminder.'

Fred had walked to meet Amanda, not sure of the house number, looking for the neatest garden with the green gate, green door and floral curtains.

As they walked back to the manor house, Amanda said to Fred, 'I should tell the police that Penny and Bob have been having it off for ages.'

'I wouldn't,' said Fred. 'Neither of them would have harmed your dad. Penny loved Lance, in her fashion, just as he loved her, in his fashion. Bob thinks your dad was cool.'

'Spare me Bob's opinions.'

'I'm sure the police will find out who killed your dad, my father-in-law.' Fred took Amanda's hand. 'I had looked forward to having a father-in-law.'

'Oh for heaven's sake, Fred. Does it always have to be you, you, you.'

'No of course not. Not when there's you, you, you. You're just so hard to get near sometimes.'

Several neighbours smiled and raised a hand in greeting as Amanda and Fred walked by.

'Did your dad know about Bob and Penny?' Fred asked.

'I don't know.'

'We know nothing, do we?'

'That's what Paul said.' She squeezed Fred's hand. 'We're in the dark.'

'Who's Paul?'

'My brother. He shook your hand at the wedding.'

'Probably against his better judgement.'

'Almost certainly against his better judgement.'

'Hang on. What brother is this? You had one brother you barely remember. You told me about him, his accident on a boat.'

'I'll tell you another day.'

'So, Amanda, we'll have another day then?' he said.

'Oh at least another day, Fred, perhaps a thousand, perhaps ten thousand.'

Amanda couldn't cry yet. There were people she had to send packing from the house before they got the idea that it was a free for all. That would have to wait until the police had finished with the hangers-on.

Before Amanda could rise from the dizziness of such losses, she needed answers.

Forty-Four

Nell drove along the lane towards Brackerley Home for the Elderly. It was a bright sunny day. Wildflowers bloomed by the hedgerow and, as she slowed for a rabbit making a dash across the road, she could understand why people were so set on keeping the meadows.

By the time she drew in by the first gate, as directed, the windscreen was covered with insects. She squirted water, got out and cleared the windscreen with a sense of regret. Why did insects gravitate to windscreens? Or were they simply hovering in the air, waiting for their end?

The three delighters in mystery were not waiting. There was no sign of Victor, Susan or Emma. Nell turned the car around, so as to be pointing in the right direction for the village. She sat for another ten minutes before the trio appeared. They walked in single file, staying close to the hedgerows, Victor with one walking stick, Susan, wearing a straw sunhat, with two sticks. Emma, with the grace of a ballet dancer, walked unaided. She carried a bag.

Nell got out and opened the doors for them. The number

of her walking sticks being greater, Susan took the front passenger seat. Emma and Victor climbed into the back.

As they set off, Emma said, 'Nell, you are about to save Dr Block's life. We won't have to kill him before he kills us. We shall make our statements and the law will take its course.'

'Yes,' said Susan. 'I shall pass on the information that you uncovered for me regarding the legacies. I'll explain that Monica visited her family solicitor and changed her will to what it was before Block leaned on her with his overwhelming reasonableness and charm.'

'We were already onto him,' said Emma, 'and did not want to arouse his suspicions.'

'Say no more!' said Victor. 'Miss Lewis does not need to know and does not want to.'

At that moment, Nell would have liked to know, but already felt she knew more than she needed. She thought it best to remain in ignorance of whatever she was in ignorance of. For now.

When Nell drew up outside the Co-operative Society building, DCI Julian McHale was waiting at the door, along with the caretaker and Angela. Nell helped Susan out of the car. The caretaker opened the other door for Emma, who graciously took his arm. Julian acknowledged Nell with a nod as he opened a rear door. 'Sir Victor,' he said, as he offered his arm, and took Victor's walking stick to allow a more dignified exit.

'Thank you, dear boy,' said Victor. 'And thank you, Miss Lewis.' As he entered the building, Victor said to Julian, 'I am out of practice at elimination and much prefer the sort of simple British justice that rejoices in a humiliating downfall and a prison sentence.' Nell had lowered the window. Emma turned back and stage-whispered, 'The magic words, you know. Victor knows all the magic words.'

What are they up to, Nell asked herself. *Sir* Victor? No one had hinted that Victor had a knighthood. For what? They are all mad, she thought. Perhaps Dr Block benefits from legacies, and there are always suspicions of how a modestly placed man turned his fortunes around. What if we are wrong? But if that were the case, Block would not have failed to inform Monica's family solicitor of her death. Nell stepped out of the car, leaning in to reach a bag from the back seat which she passed to Emma.

'Thank you, Nell. It made it look so normal to any of our friends at the home that the three of us trotted up the lane together and happened to be given a lift by you. You are politely withholding curiosity. Victor and I go back a long way. We were both honoured at the palace on the same day. He gained his knighthood, me my damehood. We decided to come north. I avoid my luvvie friends and gossip of glories past. Victor avoids the boredom of gentlemen's clubs and the risk of assassination. Revenge and professional jealousy have equally long arms.'

Not knowing what to say, Nell said nothing. It was sometimes a marvel to have a glimpse into another person's past life.

DI Ian Dennis came to speak to Nell, being formal. 'Thank you, ma'am. We'll see the ladies and Sir Victor return safely.'

Nell, chauffeuse of the hour, gave the DI her note explaining that it was she, not Dr Block, who had informed Monica Mason's family solicitor of her death.

Nell hoped to have no further involvement in the investigation.

Forty-Five

In the rooms on the top floor of the Co-operative Society building, officers continued taking statements from latecomers who had waited until after their Sunday dinner to report to the police.

Angela, with temporary possession of the manager's office, asked her witnesses to sit down.

'I'm Sergeant Ambrose. May I take your names and addresses.'

'Miss Susan Taylor, resident at Brackerley Home for the Elderly.'

Susan appeared relieved to be sitting down. She balanced a walking stick against the chair.

'Thank you for coming in, Miss Taylor and—'

'Dame Emma Whitaker, of the same address as Susan. Do call me Emma.'

'Thank you, Emma.'

'And I'm Susan.'

Emma held a black leather bag. She sat back, motioning Susan to take the lead.

Susan seemed nervous. When she hesitated, Angela prompted. 'I take it you are here because you may have information regarding the police investigation into Mr Chapin's death.'

'Yes,' said Susan. 'We are here to tell you about Dr Block and our suspicions that residents of our home die before their time, once they have left a legacy to Dr Block in their will. We also have a question.' Susan turned to Emma.

Emma took the list of deceased residents' names and handed it to the sergeant. 'This is the list without the amounts. Susan has the other list given to her this morning.' Susan handed a second list to the sergeant. 'We believe our friends died too soon, so that Dr Block could benefit from their wills. Mr Chapin was also a director of the Brackerley Home for the Elderly. I made him aware of these untimely deaths.'

Angela took the list. She began writing, and then said, 'And what is your question, Emma?'

'We asked Mr Chapin to contact the coroner about deaths at the home. We don't know whether he did contact the coroner.'

Angela suddenly felt that here was an important link. Mr Chapin's Wednesday appointment was with the coroner.

Angela's pen was running out of ink. Fortunately, the Co-op manager had a jam jar on his desk, containing two biros and three pencils. Picking up a biro gave her time to think. 'You have suspicions about Dr Block?'

There was a hesitation while the women appeared to decide who ought to speak. Emma said, 'You have known Dr Block longest, Susan.'

'Yes, a long time. Shall I start at the beginning?'

'Please do,' said Angela, hoping she would not regret these words.

'I am a trained nurse. After the last war, I worked for Dr Block at his maternity home. When of retiring age, I moved to live in the Home for the Elderly, and am still there. The accumulation of money was always at the top of his list. Dr Block made money from babies, from babies born out of wedlock, babies of girls who would otherwise have been sent to an institution. Now he's making money by other means. How do you think someone who came in as a penniless doctor ended up as director and main shareholder of the maternity home and the Home for the Elderly? There isn't the same amount of money to be made from babies as there was once was. Old people are easier targets. Old people who leave a legacy to the good doctor. He wants me gone. My legacy would be silence.'

'Silence about what?' Angela asked.

'About the way he ran the maternity home. I know too much.'

Angela was saddened and intrigued by what Susan had to tell her about Dr Block's early days in Brackerley, when Susan was pleased to have the job in the maternity unit at the mother and baby home. It had taken her a long time to realise that Dr Block dealt with mothers and babies in a way that lined his pockets, preying on women and girls for whom giving birth would have been a calamity. A woman whose husband was away at war when she became pregnant, or a girl who would have been sent to an institution. The doctor was able to oblige a childless woman who preferred to adopt a baby rather than take in an older child who may have an unfortunate history.

'How long did you work there?' Angela asked.

Susan hesitated. 'Seventeen years. When I retired, I took a reduced hours post at Brackerley Home for the Elderly. I was still fit, had always walked everywhere. I had free lodging at the home, and the promise that my stay would be permanent.'

Angela paused in her notetaking. 'Susan, in spite of your accusations about Dr Block's practices, you went on working for him?'

Susan nodded. 'Some of the things he did for women in trouble saved their marriages, let them go on leading their lives. That was what I thought. By the time I realised he went too far, I was in too deep myself, and I had nowhere else to go.'

'What do you mean by too far, too deep?'

Susan shook her head.

Emma said gently, 'Susan, you must say. You told me. Tell the sergeant.'

'I was there the night that Gloria Thwaite's healthy baby girl was taken from her and given – not sold but given – to the first Mrs Chapin. Both mothers were sleeping. Baby Chapin died in the night. Mr Chapin was influential, a board member of the maternity home. He bought more shares. He used his influence with the great and good of surrounding town corporations to pay for a certain number of places at the Brackerley Home for the Elderly, for hardship cases.'

Susan's words set Angela itching to write a note. She wanted to write 'Thwaite' and a question mark. If this improbable story about the Thwaites' baby was true, they would need to look again at whether Norman Thwaite could have somehow found his way back to kill Chapin, and then committed suicide. Or what about Gloria, and her statement that she never left the wedding, or Paul, who went only to the church service?

Angela said quietly, 'Would you be prepared to sign a statement about what happened that night?'

'I'm not sure. I have to go on living in Brackerley. There's nowhere else for me. Besides that, I don't want to say anything bad about Mr Chapin. I think Block arranged for the Chapins to go home with a baby because they were important. Mr Chapin was wealthy. Mrs Chapin had a private room. She didn't know about the switch of babies because she had chloroform and was then anaesthetised. It was Mrs Thwaite who knew, and who was ignored, and sent home.'

Emma dipped into her capacious bag. She took out foolscap sheets of ruled paper, covered in neat writing. The document had been hole-punched and threaded with red ribbon. 'It's all here, dated, signed and witnessed,' said Emma. 'You wanted to do it, Susan.'

'For after I'm dead. Who'll take my word against Block's?'

'What is this?' asked Angela.

'Susan's account of Block's running of the maternity home.' Emma turned to Susan. 'Have courage. If you hand this document over to the sergeant, you may not be dead quite so soon.' Emma put her hand on Susan's arm. 'Victor and I will take care of you.'

Angela began to read. She turned the pages quickly and eventually looked up from the closely written document. 'This was a long time ago. These are serious allegations.'

'Then regard it as a character study,' said Emma. 'Dr Block is a man from a middling background who has done well for himself and is still at it. Everyone trusts the good doctor. He would have made a reasonable actor in certain roles, typecast as a confident gentleman, or a con man. Of course, he could have widened his character range if willing to reveal his slimy side. He now brings his practised confidence into bumping off his elderly residents after they change their wills in his favour.'

'Are you both suggesting that Dr Block has, as you say, bumped off some of your fellow residents?'

'Yes,' said Susan.

'No,' said Emma. 'This is not a suggestion. It is a certainty.'

Angela made a note, giving herself time to think. If true, this would turn into a long and complex investigation, beginning with a coroner. The coroner Mr Chapin was to have met on Wednesday. Angela needed to know about yesterday. Angela was not panicking. She never did. It was simply a sudden urge to hurry along the corridor to where the DCI was interviewing a third resident, Sir Victor, and push a note under the door saying 'Help!'

Was she being led down a blind alley or taking the first step into a major investigation into multiple murders? Angela felt unprepared for this extraordinary turn of events.

She needed to report on the investigation into Lancelot Chapin's murder. On that, so far, she had little detail.

'Susan, Emma, I'm noting your very serious accusation against Dr Block. I will speak to my detective inspector and chief inspector. Let us for now think about the events of yesterday, when Mr Chapin was murdered. Did either of you see or hear anything suspicious?'

Susan and Emma answered together. 'No.'

Angela thought back to her arrival at the manor house on Saturday, when two cars had left the premises. One with four children on the back seat, and the other driven by Dr Block, with elderly residents in the back, a man and woman. She recalled her glimpse of them. Victor and Emma?

She would start with Susan. 'Susan, after the wedding, what time did you leave the manor house?'

'I'm not sure. I was upset that day.' Susan took out her

hanky and wiped her nose. Tears came to her eyes. 'That was such a horrible, horrible day, and poor Lancelot Chapin. And Mrs Chapin, and Amanda.'

Angela gave Susan a sympathetic look, and then asked, 'Who drove you?'

'I can't remember.' Susan looked aghast. 'I can always remember, but I can't remember. I know the big gates had been locked. I was wheeled through a side gate.' She turned to Emma. 'Emma, I am not going gaga, but I can't remember who drove me back, and I have a good memory.'

'You do and you don't,' said Emma. 'You can never remember where you put your gloves.' She sighed and spoke in a scolding tone. 'You are worse when you let yourself get into a tiz-woz. Victor and I were taken back the way we had come. You told me you were given a lift by a young man in a white van.'

'That's right,' said Susan, suddenly relieved. 'So I was.'

Emma turned to Angela. 'Victor and I were driven away by Dr Block. We were let through the manor house gates after the word was spread that no one should leave the premises. Perhaps you can put a time to that, Sergeant. I can't.'

'Had you expressed a wish to leave, and to go back home?'

'Absolutely not. We had expected to make a day of the wedding, looked forward to it for weeks. Obviously, everything changed after the announcement, but we knew we were meant to stay and we would have stayed, if not for Dr Block insisting that he was taking responsibility for us going back.'

Angela pictured Dr Block when he had returned to the marquee, sitting opposite her, being helpful. Emma and Susan knew him well enough to bear a grudge, to make criminal

300

accusations against him. Angela needed to think, she must stick to investigating the murder.

She picked a group photograph, with Dr Hampshire, Mrs Chapin and Dr Block, and a second photograph with several other guests.

'Is Dr Block in either of these photographs?' Angela asked.

'There he is,' Susan said. She seemed glad of an easy question that did not involve remembering yesterday.

Emma put on her glasses and pointed out the same figure. In the photograph Dr Block was wearing a white carnation buttonhole.

Being in the unusual situation of taking two statements at once, Angela quickly drew a line down the centre of the next two pages in her notebook.

'We should have asked Mr or Mrs Chapin ourselves whether the coroner was notified,' said Susan. 'We missed an opportunity.'

'We couldn't have,' said Emma. 'Mrs Chapin was never alone, outside the church or at the reception. I tried three times to steer her away for a private word, and it was just not possible, even for me.'

'What was your question?' asked Angela. 'Whatever you have thought of, it doesn't matter how insignificant, please say.'

Emma and Susan looked at each other. 'You,' said Emma, clasping her hands. 'You're dealing with the evidence, and we haven't had an answer on that point.'

Susan said, 'I'm on the verge of tears as it is.'

Emma said, 'Tell, cry, and have done with it.'

Susan took a hanky from her sleeve. 'Our friend Monica Mason left two final requests, to trusted persons, passed to them at the graveside. One was to ensure that in the event of her death Monica's family solicitor in Blackpool would be notified so that her last will and testament would be executed, and not the will in which Dr Block was a beneficiary. That request was carried out.'

'Carried out by?' queried Angela.

'Miss Lewis, who attended Monica's funeral. She preferred not to know any details but carried out Monica's wish that she notify the Blackpool solicitor,' said Emma. 'One risks being overheard on the telephone in the home.'

Angela prompted. 'And the second request?'

Susan wiped her nose. 'Monica wanted Mrs Chapin to remind her husband of our request that he contact the coroner and ask for an investigation into premature deaths at the home.'

'This may be helpful.' Emma dipped into her bag and handed Susan a missionary leaflet. 'You dealt with this, Susan.'

Susan gave Angela the missionary leaflet.

'Christian missionary?' said Angela, thinking that a woman who could not remember how she got home yesterday, remembered seventeen years of the doctor's misdeeds and now seemed to be promoting missions, may not be the most reliable of witnesses.

'What's inside,' said Susan. 'My list, my completed list of deceased residents and the legacies to Dr Block.'

'All verified,' Emma added.

Angela looked at the list, not jumping to either conclusion that occurred to her. Dr Block was appreciated by the people he cared for. Or he was taking advantage of the elderly in his care.

Susan waited until Angela had looked at the list. 'I still

keep a set of keys to the office. Some medical records are Dr Block's invention. On the evening of the day when the doctor drove to London, a Sunday, and Victor's birthday, Victor, Emma, Monica and I went into the garden. We were planning our outing to Blackpool the following day. Would Monica's appointment with her family solicitor clash with the tea dance in the tower ballroom, that sort of consideration. According to Block's notes in Monica's medical records for that Sunday, Monica was poorly, required additional medication, and complained that the light hurt her eyes. Block returned from London late that Monday, just half an hour after we were back from Blackpool. That did not stop him continuing with a fictional account in Monica's notes. She was unwell. He prescribed medication. He considered calling in Dr Hampshire to give a second opinion but noted that Monica was too tired to talk.'

Emma shook her head. 'I told you. Block could have taken to the stage. Of course Monica was tired!. Tired from wearing out her shoes in the Tower Ballroom dancing and screaming her head off on the Big Wheel.'

It occurred to Angela that Monica may not have wanted to put a damper on the outing by complaining about feeling unwell afterwards. She put this possibility to Susan.

Susan sighed. 'We all do that. It's tedious to hear about ailments. But Monica kept a diary, which she hid behind the encyclopaedias. She wouldn't have missed an entry, and she wouldn't have minded you reading her entry for the day before her death, if it brings her killer to justice.'

Emma produced a page-a-day diary from her bag and handed it to Angela, saying, 'Witnesses would tell you how well Monica was on the day when, according to Dr Block, she was supposedly at death's door. Monica was applauded in the Tower Ballroom.'

'There were dancers who remembered Monica's bakery,' said Susan.

Dame Emma preferred to have the last word. She explained to Angela that she felt responsible for Mr Chapin's death. 'Lance Chapin had a soft spot for me, having been a fan of the theatre and particularly Noel Coward. Lance saw my Elvira in *Blithe Spirit*. It was a delight to him that I support village doings. He asked if I would cut the ribbon for some event he had planned.' She sighed deeply. 'It was I who persuaded Lance – Mr Chapin – to make an appointment to speak to the coroner about the number of deaths at the home. Lance was kind, but reluctant. He was too tactful to say, "What other than death do you oldies expect?" but he did agree to make an appointment with the new coroner on the matter. "To put your mind at rest," he said.'

Emma gave a heartfelt sigh. 'Officer, do you know whether Lance had the opportunity to speak to the coroner? I am thinking perhaps he did not, what with the wedding and all.'

'We're still gathering information.' Angela felt her heart begin to race. She hoped she would be able to do something about this speed up of heartbeats or she might be dead before she reached her next big birthday.

Angela was considering possibilities. Might someone not know Mr Chapin made the arrangement to meet the coroner, and intend to stop him doing so? Or did the murderer know about the arrangement, and kill Mr Chapin to prevent the meeting?

When Angela asked her question, she did so as if it were an afterthought. 'Did Dr Block know, or suspect, that you intended to confide your suspicions to Mr Chapin?'

It was Susan's opinion that he did not.

Emma was silent, for too long, and then said, 'I suspect he did know, that he overheard something that put him on guard. He wears soft shoes. He eavesdrops. He slides into the room. He did so one day when Susan and I were talking quietly.'

Susan put her hand to her mouth. 'Oh! So he did. Did I give us away, and did I put Mr Chapin's life in danger?'

'No,' said Emma, 'I don't think so, at least not entirely.' Emma turned to the sergeant. 'I believe Block has suspected for a while. He has a sixth sense when it comes to guarding himself. A recent inmate sports inefficient hearing aids but hates to miss anything. Block showers her with kindness. He walked in on us one day when she was asking questions about Monica's funeral and what were Monica's last wishes. I daresay that Block charmed from her whatever she knew, or thought she knew, and put the pieces together. He may even have talked to Mrs Chapin, who would be unsuspecting.'

'You've both been very helpful,' Angela said. 'You told me that your friend Monica left instructions regarding a reminder to Mrs Chapin to speak to her husband about involving the coroner.'

'Yes.'

'Do you have that instruction?'

Emma shook her head. 'It was written on the inside rim of a "Kiss Me Quick" hat. I passed it to Mrs Chapin. She may have kept it. Last wishes and all that.'

'And your information regarding residents' last wills and testaments showing residents' legacies to Dr Block?'

'Public knowledge,' said Emma, before Susan had time to reply.

The police could check that for themselves. Miss Lewis had enough to deal with.

'Ladies, would you mind waiting while I type your statements?'

Angela appreciated that Susan and Emma were prepared, in exchange for cups of tea and half-coated chocolate biscuits, to wait for their statements to be typed. Angela had already had signatures for the statements of the prison caterers. She sometimes thought that her Elementary RSA evening class in touch-typing was her most useful qualification. She left her latest witnesses to their tea and biscuits and went to the office next door, relieved to see that this Co-op had not upgraded to electric typewriters.

Forty-Six

DCI Julian McHale studied the man on the other side of the square Formica table in the room where, during breaks in working hours, Co-operative Society shop assistants drank tea and ate sandwiches.

Victor's pale blue eyes showed no signs of dimming. He seemed wearily detached as he gave his name, omitting his title, and his address as Brackerley Home for the Elderly. Victor's credentials had been revealed to Detective Chief Inspector Julian McHale that morning, by the chief constable, on a need-to-know basis. Retired agents remained a special group. Whitehall's interest in their security never wavered.

Victor gave his statement and came straight to his conclusion.

'Chief Inspector, I believe the person to interview in connection with the murder of Mr Chapin is Dr Block.'

'On what grounds do you suspect the doctor?'

'My friends Emma and Susan spotted that our fellow residents were meeting the grim reaper sooner than expected and that in each case had left a legacy to Dr Block. They are far more knowledgeable about him than I.'

'You were close enough to Miss Lewis to work out that there had been a serious incident. Did you see Dr Block approach the marquee?'

'No, but that would have been earlier. I asked myself who has most to lose if there is an investigation into premature deaths? The answer was glaringly obvious. The beneficiary. Dr Block has a strong sense of self-preservation. At present, he may be with his mistress, Mrs Philips, a widow. Block sees her most Sundays and one weekday. She owns a house on St Gregory's Road in Harrogate, close to the golf course. I suspect that Block may have taken his clothing and shoes to St Gregory's Road, in case of contamination, perhaps for eventual delivery to some charity. He would not risk a dustbin or a garden fire.

'Mrs Philips is a charming lady of means who does charitable work and has the misfortune to be smitten by the murderous doctor. I spoke to her when she gate-crashed the summer fête. Block appears genuinely fond of her but tries to keep that side of his life separate. I should think she is safe until she marries him.'

'Let me get this right,' Julian said. 'You are convinced that Dr Block killed Mr Chapin. You are not saying why or how and yet you assume contamination.'

'Blood spatter.'

'I was close by when a smart young prisoner waitress came to give the news to Miss Lewis. One simply needed to pay attention to what had gone before and what followed. It was not difficult to deduce. It is a terrible burden, to feel in part responsible for the death of a man, whatever his shortcomings.'

'Why responsible?'

'Because of my complicity in asking Mr Chapin to contact the coroner regarding the link between the demise of my fellow residents and their legacies to the doctor. We were a little slow in making the connection. Except for Susan, who knew his ways and that he was capable of killing in a subtle manner.'

'Sir, why would a man who, if you are to be believed, eliminates his patients in a subtle manner—'

'Sleeping pill in the cocoa, lethal untraceable injection during sleep—'

'Why would that man be so crude as to put a knife in another man's heart?'

'Block lacks imagination and empathy. He considers his own survival. He wanted it to appear that the murderer of Mr Chapin was someone with a grievance, a careless person, a protester, or the parent whose child committed suicide by gas and who blamed Lancelot Chapin for the death. But who would know precisely where the knife should enter, swiftly and without warning? Not an anti-hunting person who abhors blood sports. Not a tenant with a leaking roof. This was something more serious – the threat of Block's exposure. A man known as a pillar of the community could not bear to be toppled by Mr Chapin asking the coroner awkward questions.'

'You got in the car with Dr Block on leaving the wedding reception.'

'After watching him take off his jacket. As he did so, I spotted a couple of tiny dark stains, and caught the scent of blood. He folded the jacket quickly, laying it front side down on the floor of the boot.'

'What about fingerprints on the knife?'

'I doubt you will find any. He will have worn a glove, unless he used his handkerchief. If he did, perhaps there will have been a slip, half a fingerprint, half a thumb print. He isn't a professional killer, simply well-practised.

'Dr Block made a trip to London for a reason – to visit his tailor and collect a new suit, previously ordered to the exact specifications, to be identical in detail to his existing suit. He brought the suit back with him, in a box boasting his tailor's name. His tailor would have had the tact not to ask why his valued customer wanted two identical suits. I dare say Block will have worn the new suit on several occasions so as not to arouse forensic suspicion. He was let down on the shoe front. Perhaps it was much to the mortification of his excellent shoemaker that they were not able to provide new footwear in the time demanded. Or perhaps he was being economical. He wore shop-bought shoes on the day of the wedding.'

'What motive would Dr Block have had for murder, for the murder of his business partner?'

'Mr Chapin was an obliging man, with a soft spot for my friend Emma. Emma asked Mr Chapin to set her mind at rest and speak to the coroner about residents' deaths and bequests. Mr Chapin had no idea that Block was being "remembered" in the will of his residents until Emma told him.'

Julian asked, 'Sir Victor, are you willing to make a formal statement?'

'No title, please, Chief Inspector.' Victor produced a long envelope from his inside pocket. 'I have already done so, signed, dated, and witnessed. At my age one must take precautions.'

Julian read the succinct account handed to him by Victor. Had this account come from anyone else, Julian may have paused before making the call. He saw Victor back to the car, and then went to the incident room.

Angela had turned the chalked side of the blackboard to the wall. 'We don't have a key to this room, sir. I have notes of all that's on here.' She picked up the blackboard duster and began to wipe the board.

Julian watched her. She was smart. She missed nothing. 'What do you know about Dr Block?' he asked.

'Just the facts?'

'Start with the facts.'

'Sir, he left the scene of the crime after the announcement not to leave the premises. He was allowed through the gates because he was returning two elderly residents to the home, Victor and Emma. He hadn't sought police permission to leave.'

Angela slowed down her cleaning of the blackboard. It was Ian's board. He hadn't turned it round. He hadn't asked a PC to clear the board. It may not be 'important', but which of the men would be appointed blackboard monitor? She would have preferred not to be talking about Block, because she had disliked the man instantly, and she ought to be able to separate that sort of gut response from a cool analysis. The DCI was waiting for her to continue.

'I was at a table in the marquee when Block came back.' Angela went on wiping chalk as she gave her account. 'He asked to share my table in the marquee, he had come back to give his statement. He identified himself.

'I asked to see his invitation to the wedding. He checked his inside pocket for his wedding invitation and then his top pocket for a business card but had neither. I think he was trying to show me how important he was, that, like royalty, he had no need to carry things with him.'

Or, thought Julian, because he had changed his suit. 'Anything else?'

'In his photographs at the reception, he was wearing a carnation buttonhole, but that was gone. I assumed he'd gone home, emptied his pockets, and took his time coming back to be interviewed.'

'What did he have to say for himself?'

'He was vague on detail. He spoke to so many people. The photographs we've managed to get hold of so far appear to corroborate that.'

'And?'

'He said that he was with other guests or his elderly residents the whole time.'

'What was he wearing?'

'Same suit, as earlier, but as I said he'd lost his carnation and either forgotten or ditched his invitation.' Angela went to the photographs that were set out on the table. 'Here he is, with others, outside the church, and here by the manor house, drinking champagne with Mr Chapin. In both he is wearing a white carnation.'

There was a brief silence. Angela wondered whether Mr Chapin's carnation had turned red with blood.

The time on the polaroid picture of Lancelot Chapin and Dr Block standing near the manor house drinking champagne was 2.15 pm.

Angela pointed to the timings on the board. 'Mr Chapin and Dr Block were in conversation fifteen minutes before Linda was sent to look for Diane and discovered Mr Chapin's body.'

'What are you thinking?' Julian asked.

'I'm wondering who wanted a private word, behind the marquee, with Mr Chapin. Was it Dr Block?'

'Possible,' said Julian as he went to the telephone.

'I'm also thinking, that's not a private line, sir. Special Constable McKenzie is still in the interview room. Shall he and I check the phones?'

'Do that.'

'And since you ask, sir, I'm also thinking that I took a dislike to Dr Block. He turned on the charm and gave me the creeps. But that doesn't mean he's a killer.'

'It doesn't mean he's not,' said Julian.

Angela finished cleaning the blackboard. 'Sir, while I'm checking the phones, you might like to take a look at the statements I've taken from residents of the home, Emma Whitaker and Susan Taylor. Susan worked for Dr Block in the maternity ward in the 1940s. They claim that Dr Block had residents re-write their wills and leave him a legacy. He would not have wanted Mr Chapin to talk to the coroner. I think we have a suspect for the murder of Lancelot Chapin.'

'We'll bring him in for questioning at the station. You spoke to him. You can explain that there are one or two points that need clarification. We'll take him to the station and search the Brackerley Home for the Elderly and his lady friend Mrs Philips' house on Gregory Street. What's his full name?'

'Rupert Everard Block.'

The waiting seemed endless to Angela. She sent to the Hare and Hounds for food. Special Constable McKenzie brought in the newspapers. At four o'clock, they had word that officers from Harrogate would be parked on a side street off Leeds Road at 5.30 pm.

Angela felt suddenly uneasy. This all felt a bit too quick. Block was confident. He must believe that he had covered his tracks every step of the way, and perhaps he had.

As they left the premises, Angela thought she could read what was in Julian's mind, but it was her own thought: we will have such red faces if there is nothing to find but Block and his friend sitting in the front room reading the Sunday papers.

A car and driver were waiting.

Julian checked his watch. He looked confident. Angela wished she felt as confident as Julian looked. Julian hadn't met the slippery Dr Block.

Forty-Seven

Angela drove. She knew Gregory Street. It was off the Leeds Road. The houses had front gardens and a path leading to a larger back garden. There were a few cars parked along the street, but no sign of Dr Block's Humber Hawk. Their driver parked on the opposite side of the street, and beyond Mrs Philips' house. Angela could see the gate through the rear-view mirror. A second unmarked car came to a stop in the turn-off that led to the golf course. Julian got out and went to talk to the search team. Angela and a constable walked to the house.

Angela hoped that she hadn't let her dislike and distrust of Dr Block and his stethoscope manners lead her to be unnecessarily suspicious of him. What if he hadn't changed his clothes, as she suspected from the invitation and business card missing from his pockets and the lack of a carnation in his lapel? It wouldn't be difficult to lose a carnation over the course of a day. And no one would have identical expensive suits, would they?

Was there such a thing as mind-reading, she asked herself.

Because the DCI said, 'I had Dr Block put under observation – a courting couple near the boundary of the Home for the Elderly, and a young chap walking his dog from the woods.'

'Was that because of my suspicions?' Angela asked.

'That and the statement from Victor.'

The DCI was waiting for a prompt for him to say more about the observation. Angela obliged. 'What did they see, sir?'

'The doctor put a large hold-all in the boot of his Humber Hawk. He may have got here before us, taken his bag in the house and gone to park his car elsewhere.'

Angela still felt uncertain. 'Sir, I hope he hasn't just brought his shirts to Mrs Philips for washing.'

'No. He'll have that done on works premises, at the home. He'll keep Mrs Philips sweet and cherished.'

'I'll knock on the door.' Angela got out of the car.

They're not married, she told herself. If he's gone to a pub, she's gone with him. She walked across to number 75, taking a closer look at the house as the garden gate clicked open. There was a skylight window. That meant there would be an attic or loft – a hiding place for a novice but perhaps not for Dr Block.

Angela took the couple of steps to the front door and rang the bell.

Heels clicked on a tiled floor. The door opened. There was a smell of Sunday roast. Mrs Philips was in her forties. She wore a summer dress, and a Betterware apron. Angela had a soft spot for someone who bought from a Betterware saleswoman who knocked on the door. She's normal, thought Angela. Poor woman. What does she see in Block?

'Mrs Philips?'

'Yes.'

Angela showed her badge. 'I'm Sergeant Ambrose of CID. I spoke to Dr Block earlier. There's something I need to ask him. I believe he may be here?'

'He will be, but he's gone to the golf club. Would you like to come in and wait? He won't be long. He doesn't usually stay this long.'

'Thank you but I have a colleague with me. I'll wait in the car.'

Angela went back and spoke to the DCI. 'He's at the golf club. Why would he drive the short walk to the golf club?'

'Go see.'

'Yes, sir.'

'And take Andy Jenkins, just in case.'

As Angela and DC Jenkins drove to the golf club, a call came on the radio – a sighting of Block's Humber Hawk leaving Harrogate along the Leeds road.

'He's gone out of the other golf club exit,' said Angela. 'Let the DCI know.'

It was two miles before the car came into view.

'Do we put the siren on, flag him down?' asked Andy.

'No. Let's see where he's going.' Angela reached in the glove compartment, took out a hat and put it on, and did the same with her sunglasses. 'I'm not going to get too close in case he looks in his rear-view mirror and recognises me. He'll notice a woman driving and a male passenger.'

'Do you reckon he's heading for Leeds, Sarge?'

'Yes. He's being crafty. It would be risky to leave anything incriminating with Mrs Philips. He'd know we would look there. Do you know Leeds, Andy?'

'I was there for three years.'

'Keep your fingers crossed that that's where he's taking his bag.'

'Any ideas where, Sarge?'

'Doorway in the centre, near the railway station?'

'Could be. There's the dark arches, and St George's Crypt, a shelter for homeless men, the Salvation Army Hall, and a hostel near Leeds Bridge.'

The number of cars increased as they came closer to Leeds. If Block knew exactly where he was heading, he could be there, and then on his way elsewhere before they caught up with him.

'We can't cover them all, Andy. How about seeing whether we could have back-up from your old mates in Leeds.'

'I'll try.'

Andy put in the call, gave their details and details of Block and his car.

The Leeds police would keep a lookout for the Humber Hawk entering the city. It was a quiet night in Leeds, a few hours before pub chucking-out time. Angela and Andy would be met as they came to the town centre. There were look-outs on the likely places for a drop off and, just for interest, what was in this bag?

Andy told them. Clothes. A pair of shoes.

'That's a shame,' came the answer. 'If some poor homeless fellow grabs the bag, he'll think it's Christmas.'

Angela signed off. She could breathe again. She slowed down, not able to overtake a group of over-fit cyclists without colliding with a van. She felt a sliver of envy of the cyclists' speed.

Whether Block knew he was being followed, there was no knowing, but he did a sudden turn-off.

'He knows a shortcut,' said Andy. 'So do I.'

Angela pulled in by a gate. She kept the engine running. 'Take over.'

It would be quicker than Andy giving her directions.

After another couple of miles, Angela took the call back.

'Sergeant Ambrose here. PC Jenkinson is driving.'

Angela thanked her lucky stars that she had the right partner with her.

Block was heading towards St George's Crypt.

'Thanks,' said Angela.

'Gotcha!' said Andy, and to Angela, 'It's along behind the Town Hall.'

When they arrived at St George's Crypt, a police van was parked across the gates. Block's Humber Hawk was in the yard. He was standing beside it, his bag on the ground.

Angela exchanged a word with the officer in charge.

She then approached Block.

'Dr Block, would you please open the bag.'

'No! I am not under arrest.'

'It will be easier for you if you open the bag. If there is nothing to hide, please do so now.'

Block looked from Angela to the police who surrounded him. For a moment, Angela thought Block would go on objecting or, worse still, one of the male officers would become the heavy and try to take over.

Block may have thought the same. He looked at her, at PC Andrew Jenkinson, at a burly Leeds constable, a Leeds detective sergeant and a constable.

Block stopped and unzipped the bag.

He had not packed well. On top of a suit and crumpled shirt was a pair of shoes. 'This is my donation to the crypt.'

He now blanked Angela and spoke to the detective sergeant. 'Since when did a charitable act attract police attention?'

The DS ignored him.

Angela said quietly, 'This bag and its contents are required by Harrogate police as evidence. You may zip up the bag.'

His face turned red.

Don't you dare have a heart attack, thought Angela.

Block suddenly launched himself at her and lashed out. How she did it, Angela was never quite sure, except that she stuck out her foot, caught Block off balance and did some sort of throwing movement as she launched herself against his side.

There he was. Flat on the ground.

Andy put the cuffs on. He and the constable brought Block to his feet.

Angela said, 'Rupert Everard Block, I am arresting you for obstructing a police investigation. Do you wish to say anything in answer to the charge? You are not obliged to say anything unless you wish to do so, but whatever you do say will be taken down in writing and may be used for evidence.'

On the journey back, Angela was happy for DC Andy Jenkinson to drive, and for Dr Block to be returned to Harrogate in a police van, with security. She hoped that Rupert Everard would have the courtesy to telephone Mrs Philips and say that he would not be back for dinner. Hold the Yorkshire pudding.

Forty-Eight

Monday, 22 September

After the early morning staff meeting, Nell sent for Diane. Looking as if she hadn't slept, Diane was brought in by the chief officer.

'Take a seat, Diane.'

'Thank you, ma'am.'

'Diane, you know why you're here?'

Diane nodded. 'Because I was going to go home without permission.'

'You were attempting to abscond and caused a great deal of upset in the process.'

'Where are you going to send me?'

Nell had no intention of sending Diane anywhere. Too much effort had gone into Diane's rehabilitation to send her away. It would be like snakes and ladders. Climb so far, make a wrong shake of the dice and slither down a snake. Nell had not given up on Diane and nor had Kit.

'Diane, you let yourself down and you let me and my officers down.'

'I wasn't thinking straight.'

'You explained your state of mind.'

Diane had probably had difficulty thinking straight for years, since her husband was lost at sea. In her own way, Diane was also lost at sea. It would be no great consolation to her that the now disgraced prison officer who drew Diane into storing contraband goods was serving a long sentence in HMP Durham.

'What's going to happen to me?'

'My officers, particularly Officer Kitteringham, have worked hard to do their best for you.'

'I know that, ma'am.'

'And you've done well yourself, at the gas board. They would be sorry to lose you.'

'I like it there, if only I could be in Hull—'

'Perhaps you will one day. There is a gas board in Hull?'

'Oh yes.'

'Then hold on. Hang in there. I'm not sending you any-where, even though you've had one chance. I'm giving you another. Your punishment is twenty-eight days without association time. You will stay in the room you are in now for those twenty-eight days. You will continue your work for the gas board and continue catering classes with officer Kitteringham. You will do extra work after normal hours, cleaning a classroom each evening. Chief Officer Markham will direct that work.'

'What about seeing my kids?'

'You are not being deprived of visiting rights. You will see your family next Saturday.'

'Thank you.'

'Diane, we hold out great hopes for your future. Keep your nose clean and your eye on the finishing line. When the time comes, Resettlement will do their best to help you find a job in Hull, so you can pay your way in the world and do things for your kids. Be strong.'

Diane was crying. 'Thank you, ma'am. I thought you might add to my sentence. I thought I might be sent far away.' She searched her pocket and sleeve, produced a hanky and blew her nose. 'It's like you switched on a light at the end of a dark tunnel.'

'Don't let me down.'

Diane said, 'I feel that relieved.' She started to sob.

Nell went to the other side of the desk. She put a hand on Diane's shoulder. 'Attempting to abscond a second time will go on your report, but you gave helpful information to the police on Saturday. That counts.'

Nell would have liked to add that when Diane did leave prison, the bad apple prison officer who put her there would still be serving a life stretch in HMP Durham.

Forty-Nine

On Monday morning, Amanda lay awake, looking at the ceiling. For once, Fred was up before her. He brought cups of tea. 'I've waved off all the stopover guests.'

'Good.' Amanda sat up and took the tea.

'I rang Paul. I told him that he and Gloria are the only ones you won't mind having here, and to come over as soon as they like, and stay if they want to.'

'What made you think of that?'

'Does it matter? It just came to me.'

'What made you think of it. It's not like you.'

'I'll never get away with anything, will I?'

'No.'

'I went to the door earlier. A Mrs McKenzie—'

'The postmistress.'

'She handed me a casserole. I said thank you and then I thought, what if people do the same for Gloria and Paul. They might be better off out of that house for a while.'

'You're right. What did Paul say?'

'He'll speak to his mam. Oh, and there was a call from the

police. The detective chief inspector will call at half past ten to talk to you and Penny.'

'Oh, that's why you brought me a cup of tea.'

'Do you want me to come in with you when the police arrive?'

'No. I want you to make all those awful phone calls.'

DCI Julian McHale and Sergeant Angela Ambrose sat with Penny and Amanda in the room that looked out on the garden. They formed a circle, Penny and Amanda seated on the sofa, Julian and Angela on armchairs.

Julian said, 'You may not have been expecting us so soon, but I know you want to be kept informed of the investigation.'

'Do you have news for us?' Penny asked.

Amanda said nothing. She did not want to know. She wanted to wake from a bad dream.

'We have a suspect in custody. He has not yet been charged with the murder of your husband, of your father. We are building a watertight case and that requires forensic evidence. We have the suspect on a holding charge and are continuing to question him.'

'Who is it?' Penny asked.

Julian answered, 'Dr Block.'

There was a long silence, broken by Penny. 'It can't be. Surely not.'

Amanda clenched her hands. She leaned forward. 'Dr Block stabbed my dad to death? Why? Why would he, how could he?'

Julian left this question for Angela. 'We can't go into details, and we are not releasing his name to the press, though no doubt they will soon be aware. Block had motive and opportunity. We have reason to believe that forensic evidence will link him to the death of Mr Chapin.'

Angela would have liked to give chapter and verse of Block's evasion and resistance, but that would help no one.

Julian said, 'I contacted Dr Hampshire. He will call on you later. He says not to be concerned about the residents in the home. With your permission, he will speak to the manager at the home and make any necessary arrangements.'

When the police had gone, Penny and Amanda stayed where they were, sitting in the sun. Penny got up and closed the curtains. 'It's too bright.'

They sat there for a long time, sometimes saying a few words, sometimes not.

Gloria's arrival broke the spell. She came into the room and went straight to Amanda and gave her a kiss. Penny stood. She and Gloria gave each other a squeeze. Gloria sat down in the chair Angela had vacated.

Amanda looked at Gloria – her aunt, her mother, who looked stricken and forlorn, but said, 'We've all had such a loss, such losses. It's a good thing none of us is helpless and hopeless.'

It took a few moments for Penny to tell Gloria who killed Lance. 'It was the esteemed Dr Block, God's gift to Brackerley, to medicine and to women, or so he thought. He killed Lance. I'd like to get hold of him and have that poker in my hand.'

Fifty

One item of Monday morning's mail struck Nell as being an opportunity for Linda. It was from Mrs Newman, a Harrogate Women's Institute member and librarian. There was a vacancy for a part-time library assistant. Mrs Newman had met Linda, knew that she would qualify, and enquired whether she would be interested in making an application.

Chief Officer Jean Markham was Linda's personal officer. She was supervising in the workroom where inmates undertook various tasks from putting wooden spoons into ice-cream tubs to adding decorative trimmings to greetings cards, or operating a fly press for an engineering company.

Nell went over to the classroom block to speak to her chief officer, who came out into the corridor.

'Chief, how is Linda, after Saturday?'

'She spent Sunday not wanting to socialise, or talk to anyone, ma'am. She was in the walled garden, and then walking to the farm to see the pigs. She was up there with them this morning. I do believe they talk to her in pig-grunt.

Oh, and she won the toss to watch a book programme on television yesterday.'

'And now?'

'Hard to tell. She turns into a zombie when she comes into the classroom.'

'I'll be arranging counselling sessions.'

'Make it compulsory, ma'am. Linda won't willingly talk to a stranger.'

'This came.' Nell handed the chief the librarian's letter.

The chief looked up from reading the letter. 'This is up Linda's street, especially if she could do it as a volunteer first, without a big commitment, ease herself in.'

'Will you follow it up?'

The chief nodded. I'll call the library during the break. Kit will be taking over the class this afternoon. 'If Mrs Newman is free, I'll put my civvies on and take Linda out. I know this library. It's a bus ride and a ten-minute walk away.'

'Should we be raising Linda's hopes?'

'She doesn't have any hopes outside of her studies, ma'am. It's time she did.' Nell picked up the phone and dialled the number for Mrs Newman to tell her that Chief Officer Markham and Linda would visit the library this afternoon.

'Excellent,' said the chief. 'We must put a boot up Linda one way or another. You'll never guess what she said this morning?'

'Go on.'

'I took her aside and said how well she'd done on Saturday, and that it would count on her report. Linda said that she knows every resident wants a good report for when parole comes up, but she doesn't want to reduce her sentence. She'd just as soon stay here, and she worried that one of the guests might have heard her being called Linda and made a guess at her identity.'

Nell sighed. 'We'll get there. I think Linda and Cherry have palled up. Some of Cherry's confidence might rub off on Linda.'

The chief took a call from the gatehouse. 'Ma'am, Detective Chief Inspector Julian McHale has just been let through the gates. Wants to know if it's convenient to talk.'

'Yes, I'll let him in myself.'

Nell went into the hall. As the chief officer left, Julian came in.

'Come through.' Nell took one look at his eyes, and the way he allowed himself a smile.

She said, 'You have news?'

'Is it that obvious?'

'It is to me.'

Nell and Julian went back a long way, having started at the same police station on the same day, two rookies with very different plans. Julian had always intended to be in criminal investigations. The CID was too much of a boys' club to attract Nell.

Nell had two comfy seats by the window. 'Do you want a cup of tea?'

'No thanks. I had enough tea at the manor house.'

'How are they?'

'Take a guess, but it looks as if Penny and Amanda are pulling together. There'll be a lot to deal with.' Julian took some papers from a briefcase. 'Statements from your residents for checking and signatures. But first, I have some news. We've made an arrest.'

'Really? That's so soon. Well done! Have you charged someone?'

'Not yet, but not far off. Dr Block was attempting to dispose of the suit he wore on Saturday. It's with forensics now, along with his footwear. Angela gave chase and caught him in the act of attempting to dispose of clothing and shoes. Without forensic evidence, he might have been able to put up a defence, claim evidence was circumstantial. His residents already had an eye on him for reasons of their own, but you knew that, Nell?'

'I was aware. It was all their own doing, though I did comply with Monica Mason's last requests to inform her solicitor of her death, and of course information about legacies to Dr Block was public knowledge.'

Julian smiled. 'Of course.'

Nell had a half a bottle of port in the cupboard, from Christmas. She took it out, along with two glasses, saying, 'It's lunch hour. I'm off duty.'

'So am I.'

She poured. They clinked glasses.

'I'll be writing to you formally to express thanks for the cooperation of your staff and residents.'

'They'll be very glad to know that.' So was Nell. She would include the letter with her full report to T5. 'How soon might you have forensic results?'

'Very soon. Lancelot Chapin was an important man. The chief constable wants a result as much as we do. And the accusation of malpractice and ending the lives of his residents before their time has given the new coroner a lot to look into.'

Fifty-One

Fred made the call to Amanda's boss at the Royal Academy to tell them of her bereavement and that she would put her resignation in writing. When a letter of condolence came, saying Amanda's job would be kept open for as long as she wished, Amanda wrote back. She appreciated their sympathy and thoughtfulness, but she and her stepmother had much to deal with. After their period of mourning, they would be taking over her father's business interests. Amanda would not be returning to London.

It was two weeks before police released Lancelot Chapin's body for burial. The wait had seemed interminable to Amanda and Penny but, by then, it was clear that Dr Rupert Everard Block would be charged with murder.

It was as if a veil of quiet and inactivity draped itself over the village of Brackerley. Protesters against the sale of the meadows went silent. Dandelions were allowed to grow in the Thwaites' garden. When people did begin to speak of the events of that Saturday, it was often to say that they always thought there was something fishy about Dr Block. He was too good to be true. Too charming to be genuine. It would not surprise them if he were not a doctor at all but a complete fake.

The possibility that coverage of her father's tragic death might have helped in creating a sell-out tour for the Northern Knights – a tour the group were contractually obliged to continue with – was something Amanda did not like to think about.

Newspapers had acquired photographs, including a picture of Amanda, Fred and Lancelot taken on the wedding day just after the speeches. After that first picture, others followed. Two tour dates were postponed, due to the efforts of the Northern Knights' new manager, but then organisers refused to budge on any other changes to the itinerary. It was not often that a new band received such an unexpected boost, and a run on ticket sales.

Finally, a date for the funeral was set. The wait for Amanda seemed interminable.

She and Gloria had trekked back and forth to see each other every other day. Gloria had refused Amanda's offer that she should move into the manor house permanently, until one day Paul surprised his mother by bringing home his fiancée, Shirley. Gloria and Shirley hit it off. Paul and Shirley would take on the rental of the Willow Lane house.

Gloria came to tell Amanda that her Uncle Norman had been cremated, and asked if Amanda would come with her and Paul to collect the ashes.

Of course Amanda would.

Steven came to join them at the restaurant in Harrogate, where they had high tea and a glass of port. They raised their cups and glasses to Dad, to Norman. His urn was on the chair between Gloria and Paul.

Paul said to Steven, 'Why are you looking as if I've done something wrong?'

'I'm not,' said Steven.

Paul drove them back to the house.

The weather was fine. They went to sit in the garden, taking the urn.

'Auntie Gloria, where do you think Uncle Norman would like to be?'

Nobody was mentioning parentage or tricky, upsetting details in front of Steven.

'I don't know,' said Gloria. 'Not among the dandelions.'

'What about putting the urn on the mantelpiece, or the sideboard?' said Steven.

'No.' Gloria, Paul and Amanda spoke in unison.

When no one else made a suggestion, Amanda said, 'In the tree, in the dead letter box, in his urn, for now. He wouldn't like to be in an urn forever. There may be a day when he would want to leave the urn and become part of the tree.'

No one had a better idea. Amanda did not tell them that she had a mind to write her Uncle Norman a letter.

There was a further spate of interest in the Northern Knights when Fred, Bob, Tim and the unknown Paul Thwaite were pall bearers at Lancelot Chapin's funeral.

It seemed apt that precisely a week after the funeral, Dr Block was charged with the murder of Lancelot Chapin. When confronted with forensic evidence, he pleaded guilty.

Penny and Amanda still rubbed each other up the wrong way, but there was a good deal of left-over champagne. That did not lessen the pain of loss, but a glass of bubbly made the

333

task of looking at what lay ahead more bearable. The solicitor and the accountant were immensely helpful. Amanda thought that they both fell in love with Penny.

The new coroner, Mr Kempster, came to introduce himself and to offer condolences. He explained that Mr Chapin had wanted to talk to him regarding the number of deaths at the Home for the Elderly. It was not that the numbers were unusually high, but there had been a peak, and it appeared that more residents than might be expected had left legacies for Dr Block. An investigation was underway. Penny gently explained that they already knew of the investigation, from the police.

Without needing to exchange words, Penny and Amanda were of one mind when the coroner asked would they keep the Home for the Elderly and the Maternity Home open.

They did not trouble him with information regarding building projects and flats but told him that there would be no more admissions to the maternity home. When alternative accommodation was found for the last residents of the Home for the Elderly, the home would close.

The meadows would remain unmolested. As well as being good for the village, retaining the meadows was a business decision. They were an attraction. They were 'countryside'. It made more sense to convert the maternity home into flats. Water, drainage, energy and telephone lines were in place. An extension was no great difficulty. The same went for the Brackerley Home for the Elderly. After all, no one would now send even the most tiresome old relative there, while suspicion hung in the air that an ancient personage might be done in and their nearest and dearest swindled of dwindling fortunes – if, indeed, there was anything left of an old person's fortune after the deduction of charges.

Emma, Susan and Victor engaged their favourite driver and hired his London taxi to hunt for alternative accommodation. They decided on a complete change of scene, choosing a delightful town in Cumberland called Ulverston. Unlike Brackerley, which was one of those places between places, Ulverston had a long history, was surrounded by lakes where a person might row a boat or ask a younger person to row a boat for one. It also held the distinction of being the birthplace of Stan Laurel. The three friends loved Laurel and Hardy. Ulverston had a picture house.

They packed their bags with light hearts and looked fate in the eye. On their way to new lives, they stopped at the prison to say goodbye to Miss Lewis, her officers, and the charming occupants of HMP Brackerley, bringing chocolates, cigarettes, and good wishes.

They urged Nell to visit them. Susan hoped that it would not be necessary for them to appear as witnesses at Dr Block's trial for murder. Emma had every intention of appearing if required, and if not required would want to know why.

Victor would certainly be excluded from court proceedings. His Whitehall minders made the decision to change his name again, for his continued protection. This time, Victor refused. He had grown used to his name, and to telling the story of how his parents named him in honour of Queen Victoria.

Nell was summoned to London headquarters to report in person on events in Brackerley, and to receive a commendation. She did not mind in the least that Londoners preferred not to come north.

Nell had telephoned Roxana. 'Which evening would suit you for a meal at Veeraswamy?'

Author Note

Like many writers, I'm often asked, "Where do you get your ideas?"

After I had happily written another Kate Shackleton novel, a different question was put to me, by my editor. She asked did I have ideas for anything else I might like to write.

I could have said no. Kate Shackleton has more adventures to come. I said yes because I did have an idea, perhaps more a thought than an idea, a thought that had stayed with me for years.

On a long-ago holiday with my mother in Lanzarote, we met up with mam's old friend and neighbour. They had worked together as dinner ladies at Cowper Street School. The friend's son, also on holiday, was a prison officer, working in one of those forbidding Victorian prisons. I wondered what it was like to go to work each day through high gates that would be locked behind you. I didn't ask. The son was on holiday. Let him be. The unasked question stayed with me.

Crime novels often end at what might be a beginning. A person is found guilty of a crime. The punishment is loss of freedom.

Years ago, I read a book that hooked me: *The Story of a House,*

Askham Grange Women's Open Prison, produced by Yorkshire Art Association in collaboration with Askham Grange. This is the prison where, in 1979, two women expanded the Christmas show and went on to set up Clean Break, a theatre company with charitable status that 'exists to tell the stories of women with experience of the criminal justice system and to transform women's lives through theatre.' They do that brilliantly. I have read some of their work and was impressed by their performance of *Favour*, by Ambreem Razia, a co-production with the Bush Theatre. www.cleanbreak.org.uk

My editor and I agreed that I would write about an open prison for women, and my central character would be Nell Lewis, prison governor. For that first prison governor book, I started to read. I started to talk to people. I talked to Judy Gibbons, who had served in HM Forces and joined the prison service after the Second World War. She retired in the late sixties, around the time *A Murder Inside*, and now *Six Motives for Murder,* are set.

I met Veronica Bird OBE, retired prison governor. Veronica began her working life in prisons as Judy Gibbons retired. Together they provided a long look at the prison service. Veronica had recently published her book *Veronica's Bird* – do read it! Veronica was the first woman governor of HM Prison Armley, a male prison. She was appointed because of the high suicide rate and did much good work, including bringing the Samaritans into the prison.

Economist Vicky Price went to prison after a conviction for taking her husband's speeding points on her driving licence. She kept a diary. After release, she wrote *Prisonomics*, an excoriating account of the economic and social cost to Britain of the failing penal system, though she had good words for the open prison East Sutton Park, where she spent the final weeks of her sentence.

In *Bad Girls, The Rebels and Renegades of Holloway Prison*, Caitlin Davies writes that very few women in prison have ever posed a threat to society.

'Eighty-four per cent of women have committed a non-violent offence, often theft in order to support their families.' Davies quotes Frances Crook from the Howard League for Penal Reform who believes that if other agencies offered sufficient help with debt, mental health, drug and alcohol abuse, there would be twenty to fifty women left in England and Wales who require a custodial sentence.

Home secretaries visit prisons and ask all the right questions because they are well-informed, yet nothing changes. To speak the truth would be politically inexpedient.

Prisoners must become used to this sort of important visit, which may provide a break in routine. In preparation for one such visit, Veronica told me how prisoners planted bulbs that were meant to spell out a welcome when in bloom.

As the day drew close, and the floral buds of welcome peeped above the soil, prisoners watched carefully. At the right moment, they alerted the press, told them when to come, and to bring cameras. The press obliged. The photographs showed not words of welcome but an invitation to 'F off.'

By then the gardeners had gone from the prison. Their timing was perfect, just as one would expect of those who for whom the word TIME looms large.

I asked Veronica to tell me a few things about prison that I might not know Veronica said.

You never hear the positives. Prisoners from a men's prison designed garden schemes for Chelsea Flower Show.

A prisoner was transferred to an open prison from a closed prison.

She looked at the lawn and said, "Is the grass real?" She bobbed down to kiss the grass.

Many women are inside because of a boyfriend or husband.

There is training in painting and decorating, plumbing, gardening, and accountancy. It might be the first opportunity a person has to gain qualifications. Prisoners can do exams to a high level.

They are paid for the work they do, earn real wages, save money, have money to go out with, and leave prison equipped for a fresh start.

There is a lot of humour. One of the jobs was packaging exclusive chocolates and completing the "best before" date. One prisoner added "best before sex", and when challenged claimed it said, "best before six."

In the days when cushions were made for Woolworths, the labels placed on the back said "stuffed".

HM Prison Leyhill is where MPs or doctors are sent. On the prison's hundredth anniversary, the Queen visited.

I had a letter from the mother of a young woman saying that her daughter had been "sentenced to a better life." The daughter had been on drugs, never had a routine, couldn't hold down a job. In prison, she learned skills, and to be organised. It was her new beginning. On release and off drugs, she held down a good job.

At HM Prison Askham Grange, there is a café, staffed by prisoners. The plants on sale have been grown by prisoners. Every year there is a pantomime or Christmas show for residents, staff and invited members of the public.

Veronica told me about the work of the **Shannon Trust**: "Over 50% of people in prison can't read, or they struggle to read." Shannon Trust helps people to learn to read and improve basic skills.

www.shannontrust.org.uk

Acknowledgements

Once again, thanks to Veronica Bird OBE for her patience in answering my questions and for her friendship and continued encouragement. There is nothing Veronica does not know about prisons and the prison service. Thank you to Viv Cutbill and Michelle Hughes for sharing their knowledge of police procedures, and to freelance copyeditor and proofreader Karyn Burnham.

Many thanks to the team at Piatkus, especially Hannah Wann and Tanisha Ali for editorial support. Thanks to agents Judith Murdoch and Rebecca Winfield, and to Lynne Strutt for her unwavering support. Roger Cornwell and Jean Rogers of Cornwell Internet maintain my website with meticulous care.

My sister Patricia McNeil keeps me supplied with commonsense and cups of tea.